PRAISE FOR THE LAS

Basile's debut novel is impressive and consuming. I had hesitations about reading this novel but did so at the request of a dear friend. I was pleasantly surprised. It was shocking and thoughtful. Honestly difficult to put down. I would highly recommend this book to anyone who is interested in alternate timelines, fantastic tales of cyberpunk like science and a plot twist that demands your attention. Normally I would expound on the storyline but honestly that would spoil a great read. Give this book a chance. You won't regret it!

– R.D. Perry, Publisher Black Ink, Cedar Grove

*

Typically, I don't tend to write reviews. However, I was asked to give an honest review for an advance reading copy. For his first novel I was impressed. The characters come alive and jump off the pages.

The plot is shocking, and I am honestly looking forward to the sequel. Set in a dystopian alternate future, the reader is invited to explore a desolate future that has one desperate hope left. This book has much to offer – time travel, action, science fiction with a historical twist that must be read to be believed. If you enjoy fantastic stories that will keep you on the edge of your seat, this is it.

– Larry Evans, novelist, scientist and historian

*

What an impressive Tour de Force this book is. Knowing Joe personally, I must admit, I never expected his foray into writing to be so engrossing and difficult to put down. I've heard him speak on many occasions and experienced his ability to weave a story together. But this blew me away. It's a difficult to describe book.

The reader will be pulled into a timeline twisting, history altering, mind bending journey into the fantastic.

Do you like stories with great action? Check. Mind bending cyber science? Check. Demons? Check. A plot twist that will make you reread pages more than once because you are in disbelief and wondering how things can be pulled together? Check.

It's my great pleasure to invite you to read this story. Keep an open mind and expect to be impressed and a story that is thought provoking and will stay with you long after you put the book down. Strap in. You are in for a wild ride!

– Jim Callahan, author of *The Blood of Angels Trilogy, Power Lines: Mastering your Imagination volumes 1-10* and the forthcoming *A Crooked Path: Finding Grace*

*

Impressive. Action packed and hits you with one of the coolest twists I've seen. Read this.

– T. Johnson, author of *Tribe*

THE LAST QUMRANIAN

INFINITY CHRONICLES, BOOK 1

JOE BASILE

ODYSSEY
BOOKS

Published by Odyssey Books in 2019

www.odysseybooks.com.au

A Cataloguing-in-Publication entry is available from the National Library of Australia

ISBN: 978-1-925652-67-3 (pbk)

ISBN: 978-1-925652-88-8 (hbk)

ISBN: 978-1-925652-66-6 (ebook)

This book is dedicated to God.
With Jesus, All Things Are Possible.

1

Present Day – Israel – 1000 Feet Beneath the Dead Sea – The Qumranian Compound

Lukas opened his hand. As he slowly rolled back his fingers, he saw he was holding a tiny cosmos. Planets rotated, stars burned, asteroids drifted from one side to the other, all in the palm of his hand. Catching a glimpse of what he intuitively knew was Earth, he reached his right hand into the cosmos and gently grabbed his planet with two fingers, pulling it out of its orbit and setting it on its new axis. A sense of curiosity and wonder caused him to let go of the cosmos and focus all his attention on Earth. Putting his right index finger alongside Earth, he pressed down until it stopped spinning. Once it had completely stopped, clocks appeared all around the planet, and all around Lukas. Looking at each of them, he saw they had stopped working at different times. Still more interested in Earth than the clocks, he started to push the planet in the opposite direction. Slowly at first, and then quickly, and that is when he noticed the clocks spinning backward in sync with the Earth's rotation. Smiling and amazed that both planet and clocks obeyed his commands, he stopped the spinning abruptly to test a theory. Rotating the Earth forward, Lukas laughed as the clocks also moved forward in time. Stopping again, but this time not by his own volition.

"What?" Lukas said out loud.

Black strings, dripping with soot, were attached to each of his fingers, controlling their movement. With his other hand, he reached to pull the strings off, but that hand was yanked back by the slimy, ashy strings attached to it. Feeling powerless to move either of his hands, Lukas followed the strings upward, hoping to find its source, only to be terrified by an enormous figure in front of him. He could have easily mistaken the figure for a black hole had it not had continuously shifting edges, grotesquely large horns shaped into a pagan-like crown, and a laugh that sounded like a thousand children trapped in a roaring inferno. He was the master and Lukas his puppet. As though he were having an out of body experience, Lukas helplessly watched as this creature pulled his strings with speed and expert precision, causing Lukas to spin and spin and spin the Earth backward until the clocks became sundials. With a final tug, he made Lukas stop the tiny planet.

Turning Lukas's open hand to a fist, the puppet master pulled it far back into a deadly offensive position only a Hedge Master like Lukas would be familiar with, then drove it forward with deadly force into the miniature Earth.

"No!" Lukas yelled as he felt his powerful fist sink deep into what felt like the soft flesh of a child.

The strings were gone. The creature disappeared. Lukas, as slowly and gently as he could, removed his deadly hand from the severely damaged planet. The moment he had fully removed his hand, the Earth spun forward as though someone had hit the reset button. Lukas would have been more captivated with the blood on his hand if not for all the changes he saw the Earth going through as it continued to spin. When it finally came to a stop, it was no longer the green and blue planet with a healthy dense cloud cover that he first saw. Now, most of the sky was scorched black, with noticeable holes in the ozone layer. The little bit of water that remained was a dark green, and the lines connoting the land formations had changed, with ninety percent of the land a dark brown with only a few visible green places.

With an overwhelming sense of guilt, Lukas quickly tried to remove the blood from his hand by wiping it on his shirt, but it wouldn't come off. He kept wiping, trying to separate himself from his actions. "It's not my fault. It's NOT MY FAULT!"

Lukas leaped forward in his cot, breathing heavily, sweating, whispering to himself, "It's not my fault."

The dreams were always bad, but he never expected them to get this bad. They were normally some variation of the same; he saw the entire world—the world above as it had been, though he could only guess—open sky, glistening oceans, cracked deserts, lush forests. When he thought the beauty of it would tear him apart, the dreams shifted to give him a glimpse of his own reality, his world below, no less perfect for what it was, until the whole of it was consumed by darkness and fire. And he always woke with the screams of the dying echoing in his head. But this was different.

Lukas steadied his breathing and rubbed his hands over his face, removing some of his perspiration. Trying to reassure himself, he thought, *Today will be like any other day... except, if I'm not successful.* Shaking his head as if he didn't recognize himself, he shifted to his normal determined disposition that had brought him to this point. "Well, that's not an option."

Slowly, he slipped his bare feet onto the tiled floor and went to the window. He preferred to keep the blind down while he slept. It kept out the constant low glow of the simulated moon and stars so he could spend the nighttime hours in complete darkness, and it made his morning view that much more incredible when he opened the blind. He did this now, blinking against the yellow glare outside, and gave himself a few moments to stare out at the vast expanse of his home, his people's hidden paradise on Earth.

The luminescent ceiling panels had already brightened, the light and heat and ultraviolet measurements meticulously calibrated to mimic the true sun, complete with the timing and rhythm of the Earth's rotational cycles. Even this far underground, the timeline followed the natural order of things to near perfection, and when he did not think about it too hard, Lukas found himself able to forget sometimes where he was.

For miles upon miles, the ceiling panels stretched before him in this vast underground cavern, shining down upon the Agricultural Sector. Directly below him at the base of the cavern wall in which his quarters had been built, thick, lush grass grew right up against the rise of the gray stone. Then it gave way to an apple orchard, spanning some twenty acres, the tops of the trees a mere blur of green from where he stood so far above them. The plots of farmland spread seemingly without end—acres of rich soil sprouting corn, wheat, beans, potatoes, fruit in all varieties, and greens in thousands of documented strains.

Lukas took all of it in as if he were seeing it for the first time, then turned from the window and padded across the small room toward the cabinet built into the far wall. The overhead lights blinked on as he moved, softly adding to the manufactured and no less stunning daylight streaming in through his window. He opened the cabinet to remove what served as his daily uniform— slate-gray pants, thin and breathable yet durable, and a long-sleeved shirt of the same color that stretched when he pulled it over his head.

On the low table beside the cabinet, a crystalline box no bigger than his hand pulsed to life, emitting a soft blue glow with each syllable of the steadfastly optimistic female voice coming from it.

"Lukas. It is First Dimming. Your presence is required in the Sector One Main Laboratory in thirty minutes."

With a pair of socks in hand, Lukas closed the cabinet doors and walked across the room. "Thanks. What's the status of the power grid and energy lattices this morning?" He stopped at the small desk by the wall and leaned against it to pull on his socks. He glanced at the only two items there—a framed certificate with *Hedge Master* printed at the top in large, dark letters, his name slightly smaller beneath it; and the black, loose-fitting sparring uniform, pants and shirt both folded neatly, the frog-closure buttons of the shirt centered perfectly beneath the collar.

"Both are fully operational," the box replied.

"Good. We need everything and everyone at their best," Lukas muttered, slipping his feet into his boots and lifting a leg onto the chair to tie the laces.

"The Circle of Elders and the Teachers of Law all send their best wishes for today's final test run and—"

"Appreciated." Lukas gave an obligatory thumbs up as if the disembodied voice could see him, then finished lacing up his boots. "Give me a rundown of the energy fields."

"Solar flare activity is within normal limits. Electromagnetic field activity is within normal limits. There are no reports of geological anomalies. You have prepared contingencies for all eventualities. There is no reason for concern."

Lukas puffed out a sigh. "I wish I had your confidence."

"You now have twenty-eight minutes until your presence is required in the Sector One Main Laboratory."

"Yep. Got it." Finished with his boots, Lukas turned toward the plain door to his quarters. A bowl of apples rested on the short, low counter beside the door—the only color in the entire room—and he grabbed one. He couldn't start the day with an empty stomach, but this was about as much as he could handle.

Stepping out into the hallway, Lukas closed the door behind him and headed toward Sector One.

The entire Qumranian compound had been cut into the very stone of these caverns, the endless maze of passages a blend of roughhewn walls and smooth, tiled floors lined by metal paneling, track lighting illuminating the wide spaces with a soft glow. When he finally reached Sector One after navigating turn after countless turn through the corridors—all of which he could make successfully in his sleep at this point—the hallways were wider and lit with an intense white fluorescence. Lukas walked quickly, his footsteps echoing around him. Then he heard another set of swift footsteps matching his until a man in the same uniform with short brown hair turned into the hallway from the opposite end.

The men smiled at each other and met in front of the next passageway to Lukas's left. "Good to know I'm not the only one running late this morning," Lukas said.

"You're the only one who seems happy about it," his cousin said, his jaw set tightly as he offered a wan smile.

Lukas clapped Ben on the shoulder. "I would say expectant more than happy. After five years of work, we finally get to test it. We've been over every equation and simulation hundreds of times. The data tells me to expect success. Deborah will tell you the same thing."

Ben frowned and took a deep breath. "I know."

"After this successful run today—and it *will* be successful— we'll prove to the Elders that we have nothing to fear from those Above. This technology puts us a hundred years ahead of them. Maybe even a thousand. There's nothing we won't be able to do, and *nowhere* we can't go." Lukas nudged his cousin down the hallway toward the Main Laboratory.

"I know," Ben repeated and rubbed the back of his head. "I just can't help wondering about the unknown variables—"

"Well, we can't account for those, can we?" Lukas said with a chuckle. He didn't understand how his cousin could harbor so much doubt on a day like today. They had done everything right, never skipping a step, they would not fail.

They reached the end of the corridor and paused at the steel double doors of the Main Laboratory. Grinning, Lukas pushed open the doors and gently nudged Ben inside. Like the living quarters, the underground stone walls in the Sector One laboratory complex had been completely covered. One might even forget the thousands of tons of pressure resting above them this far underground. The walls were a smooth, sterile white, the tile floors polished enough to see their own reflections. In the center of the Main Laboratory sat a wide, circular platform raised six inches from the ground. Around it, a dozen computer consoles were spread in concentric rows, each with its own monitor and set of command keys.

Deborah stood at one of these, and the rest of their staff milled about checking the last-minute details. When Lukas and Ben entered, Deborah glanced up and smiled. Her long brown hair was pulled back into a ponytail above the same slate-gray uniform her brother Ben wore, but slightly different to her cousin Lukas's, as he was distinguished as a Hedge Master.

"I'm still amazed by the fact that you two are always late."

"We allowed for a thirty-minute gap in our schedule," Lukas said. "I'd say we're right on time." He turned and elbowed Ben in the ribs, who then stepped toward Deborah.

"Right on time to get started on initial preparations." Ben rubbed his hands together and peered over his sister's shoulder at the numbers scrolling across the monitor.

"Everything's already been done," she said, leaning forward a little to wink at Lukas. "We're all ready to go."

Lukas raised his eyebrows in mock surprise and took his

place beside his cousins while Deborah leaned back and called out to the rest of their team.

"Okay, everyone. Get to your stations. We're about to begin." As their team of eleven scientists took up their positions at the consoles around the central platform, Ben and Lukas stood on either side of Deborah, glancing together at the display on her monitor. "Just think," she said, her voice low enough for just the three of them. "If this works, it changes everything. Lukas, you and I could go Above."

Lukas, without missing a beat, said, "All of Qumran could go Above—"

"Stop," Ben interrupted. No one in the team seemed to have heard her, and he forced a smile onto his face before continuing. "The law is the law. Even suggesting something like that could bring this whole thing crumbling down around us. Not just our jobs." He glanced at his sister quickly, but she only stared straight ahead at the center platform, her expression unreadable, but her tone familiar, "We have an incredible opportunity here. Resources and possibilities no one Above could even dream of—"

Ben cleared his throat. "The law is the law," he muttered, his voice strained with tension. "You could both be executed for treason. Please don't talk about this here. Not now. I'd also suggest not ever."

"I'm not trying to fight the law," Lukas said. "I understand its meaning and the purposes behind it, and I support it fully. All I'm saying is we may be opening new avenues with our success today."

"We have been developing this technology for a reason, Ben," Deborah said. "Do you really think the plan is for us to remain down here?"

"That's heresy," Ben hissed through gritted teeth. "We follow the law, Deborah. In everything we do. Two thousand years we've been down here waiting, provided with everything we need until *he* arrives, and we've been given a purpose. The fruits of that provision are all around us. And that purpose"—he gestured to the center platform and the low steel table resting upon it—"*this* is that purpose fulfilled. If this is successful, we can ensure our safety until the *Messiah* comes. If we are meant to leave this place, he will take us."

"*When* this is successful," Lukas corrected. They would not fail in this today; he felt it in his bones. What they accomplished would go down in the records for all posterity—how this team brought knowledge that would change both worlds, Below *and* Above.

"Every Qumranian scientist knows the Above world has changed," Deborah added. "Even you can't disagree, Ben. And we've changed. What if we could live in peace with those Above? What if we could go to Jerusalem? The chosen city. We are so close to her, Ben! She is just above us, and the temple is there! And what if—"

"That's enough," Lukas interrupted, tired of the debate they have had so many times before. "Conjecture doesn't produce results, does it? Until we perform this last test, nothing is certain. So let's get to work, huh?"

This was what they were meant to do, not sit around and argue law and philosophy. Ben and Deborah turned to look at him, and despite the strain in Ben's brow and the flush rising in Deborah's cheeks, they both nodded. Ben left the station and headed toward the nearest console.

Lukas stepped toward the center platform. "You made all the final adjustments?" he asked Mark, another of the top-rated scientists on their team.

Mark nodded. "We set your new parameters and adjusted the internal web fields. We're good to go."

Lukas gave a curt nod and continued his path toward the platform. "Ben, set the codes for five minutes into the future. Return time at thirty seconds from now. Deborah, I want maximum data on this. Everything the web fields affect. The whole region, not just the lab."

"Got it," she said.

With a deep breath of anticipation, Lukas climbed the steps onto the platform and approached the steel table. He gazed down at the quantum sphere in the center of the table—their final test, the product of so much hard work and dedication. About a foot in diameter, the translucent sphere swirled within the outer membrane, its contents constantly shifting like cream stirred into a cup of coffee. Tendrils of circuitry lay beneath the sphere's surface, coiling around each other, floating in stasis as if they were only waiting for Lukas to bring them to life. And that was exactly what he intended to do.

Raising his right hand, held as steady as his certainty, Lukas eyed the sphere and plunged his hand slowly and carefully into the swirling mass, passing through the exterior membrane as if it were water. The circuitry inside blinked to life, unfurling like snakes entwining around his outstretched fingers with just enough pressure to assure him they'd made the connection.

"All right," he called, unable to look away from the sphere, feeling the power humming around his hand. "Give me a countdown."

"Five. Four. Three. Two. One."

The circuitry glowed a bright white, like metal coils heating over a flame, then the glow burst out from his hand, through the sphere, and past Lukas's body to encompass him, the table, and the center platform. He glanced up at the glowing fluid dome curving above him, then turned his head to meet Deborah's wide-eyed gaze. He only caught a glimpse of Ben before a blue wave of light followed the first, growing and then bursting around him. An icy cold blast rippled through his fingers, up his arm, and into each follicle of his scalp before another blinding flash erupted through the Main Laboratory. And then Lukas couldn't see anything at all.

2

Deborah blinked against the glaring blue flash on the center platform, taking a moment to remind herself that this was supposed to happen. Lukas, the steel table, and the quantum orb were gone. She punched in the new timing sequence to count down five minutes. Licking her lips, she turned to her brother at the next console over, and Ben met her wide-eyed gaze, looking as pale with anticipation as she felt.

He cleared his throat. "Watch the monitors," he instructed the team. "Look for any anomalies in the web field, even if it seems insignificant. Deborah, everything looking good on your end?"

She glanced back down at her screen, the numbers working in her mind almost as quickly as they sorted themselves out in front of her. "Yes. All the readings are consistent and still within the viable range." And still, even the hard proof before her wasn't enough to combat her racing heart or the fact that her sweaty fingers had nearly slipped on the control keys. If they'd made even one mistake—one tiny miscalculation—they could have just sent Lukas anywhere in space and time... or nowhere at all. That thought was agonizingly unbearable, so she forced herself to focus instead on the timer she'd started again at zero.

The lab had never been so quiet, the unspoken tension quivering in the air like a web spun between each one of them, caught in a soft breeze. When the timer reached twenty-eight seconds, Deborah opened her mouth to announce it, but Ben beat her to it.

"It should be right—"

The huge globe of blue light burst into existence around the central platform, blinding Deborah again with another twinge of heart-shocking cold that gave her goosebumps beneath her long-sleeved top. Just as quickly, the blue faded into a warmer amber, shrinking in on itself until the light disappeared completely and revealed their results.

Lukas looked over his shoulder at them with a grin. "How'd we do?"

Mark let out a whoop of triumph, nearly making Deborah leap out of her own skin. Ben gave a surprised chuckle, and then Lukas erupted into his own burst of laughter.

"All right. First part's over. We're not done yet, people. Someone help me clear the table and the machine off the platform. Gotta be ready for the next stage."

"I got it." Ben left his station at the console, nearly skipping toward the platform in his excitement.

Lukas slowly slid his hand out of the quantum orb, giving the circuitry time to uncoil from his fingers. Their lights dimmed and faded, but the orb maintained its swirling effect. Together, the men lifted the table from the platform and eased it off. The quantum orb trembled in its cradle bolted to the table, but it held even when Ben's back foot didn't take the full step off the platform and his heel bounced against the edge of it.

Deborah took in a sharp breath, feeling lightheaded and nauseous. But her cousin and brother safely delivered the steel table to the lab's tiled floors, and everyone fixed their eyes once more on the platform.

Lukas offered her a ridiculously overconfident wink. Then he clapped a hand on Ben's shoulder, shook him just a little, and waited. When the timer reached the five-minute mark, the blue glow erupted a third time to engulf the platform. Deborah turned her head against the glare; the next time they used this machine, she better remember to bring a heavier jacket against the instant drop in temperature. This time, the web field remained around the platform, though the light dimmed slightly to reveal what was inside. There stood Lukas, his hand in the quantum orb upon the table. She glanced quickly from the newly arrived version of him—the Lukas from five minutes ago, looking a bit shocked and yet still entirely certain—to the Lukas of the present with his hand on Ben's shoulder. The two identical figures grinned at each other and waved like children catching sight of their best friend, and then the entire web field vanished, leaving nothing behind but the cleared, empty platform.

The silence in the lab was deafening. Lukas turned around to address the team, opening his arms in mock insult. "What, you can't handle two of me in the same place at the same time? C'mon, people. There's your proof. We warped time." He paused, then shook his arms again and shouted, "We can control *time!*"

The team burst into cheers all around them, and Deborah found herself laughing hysterically, burying her face in her hands. She vaguely heard her brother mutter, "Maybe we should have had you step out of the lab. I don't know if we calculated all the risks of two of you in the same place—"

"It was only thirty seconds, Ben," Lukas replied. Deborah lowered her hands from her face to watch the exchange. Lukas had his hand on Ben's shoulder again, leaning in until their foreheads almost touched. "Thirty seconds of success. Life-changing success."

Ben seemed to finally catch the contagious excitement churning through the lab and his frown of concern melted into a goofy grin. "We did it."

Seeing her brother relax made Deborah feel even better; what they'd just done was nothing short of a miracle, and despite all the work they still had ahead of them, this changed everything. Taking a deep breath, she lifted her gaze in a silent prayer of thanks, then froze. Something shimmered in the air between Lukas and the platform—a wavering, slightly skewed, humanoid form. She blinked and looked again, but it was gone. Maybe they should wear protective eyewear next time against the glare of the web field.

The only other woman on their team appeared beside Deborah and nudged her with a shoulder. "They'll be getting drunk tonight and raving about this for the next twenty-four hours."

Deborah turned to her with a wry smile and folded her arms. "That doesn't sound too bad. I think they deserve it." Laughing, the woman walked around the console to shake hands with the rest of the team.

"The next thing we do," Lukas started, speaking to them all, "is to send the data to the Circle of Elders. We still have to collect it all. Sort it out into analyzed evidence. I would have invited them to join us today, but I didn't want to ruin the surprise." That brought a round of relieved laughter from the team.

Deborah watched her cousin in his element, directing and congratulating, encouraging everyone on the enormous breakthrough they'd just witnessed. She couldn't believe this day had finally come, and she couldn't wait to get started on their next steps for securing the safety of the future—everyone's future. The prospect of what that might mean brought her earlier conversation with Ben and Lukas to mind. With the manipulation of time at their fingertips came so many other possibilities for technological advancements—for real defenses to be built, greatly superior medical capabilities, boosting agricultural production. Why would they have to use it against so many people Above when they could put it to use for the greater good of every living soul on this Earth?

She blinked, seeing the wavering outline of a human form oscillating in the air again just above her cousin, only this time, it was larger. Lukas seemed oblivious, as did everyone else, so caught up in their excitement. But it had been too much time since the glare of the web field for this to be a retinal afterimage. And it was *moving*.

Trying to both listen to Lukas's speech and watch this strange new image at the same time, Deborah found herself wondering if this was one of those risks Ben had seemed so concerned about. She glanced down at her monitor again, scanning the data, flipping through what they'd already captured. Their system had caught absolutely nothing outside the normal ranges.

"This is the single greatest invention in the history of mankind," Lukas said, then lowered his head and looked each of his team members in the eye. "I am so proud of all of you and the years of work you've put into this—" He stopped, as though someone had pressed pause on the entire moment. The victorious scientists all looked at him with eager anticipation, smiles widening at what had to be another of their team leader's many gags. But it went on just a second too long and it looked like Lukas had stopped breathing.

"Lukas?" Ben asked, leaning forward to catch his cousin's gaze. Lukas let out a thin sigh and lowered his hands by his side, but he stared blankly ahead. "What's going on?"

Lukas brushed past him and walked stiffly through the ring of scientists who had just been listening so intently to his celebratory speech. He moved around Deborah's control console and stopped beside her to open one of the drawers at hip level. His fingers wrapped around the red globe of the energy phaser kept for security, sliding it effortlessly into one of the side pockets of his gray pants.

"What are you going to do with that?" Deborah tried to whisper, feeling herself tremble when she wondered if he'd changed his mind about the protocol with the Circle of Elders. Had he seen something when he jumped through time? But this wasn't Lukas; she leaned forward to try to get him to look at her, but his gaze slid across her face as if she didn't exist at all. This close, the sight of his eyes horrified her—glazed over without the natural shine of alertness; darkened as if covered by a thin black veil.

When he stepped in front of her, focused intently on her command console, Deborah was too stunned to resist the force of his body nudging her aside. "Lukas?" she said again, then jerked her head up to find her brother. "Ben, something's wrong—"

A whirring tap came from the command console. Lukas's fingers moved with inhuman speed across the keys, his hands blurring in her vision. Deborah's stomach dropped as if she'd just fallen down into a great cavern and she could only stare.

"What's going on?" Ben called, but Deborah couldn't answer. She could barely even breathe. "Deb? *Lukas?*"

Lukas turned and headed back around the console, completely oblivious to his cousins' concern. The other scientists watched him in confusion, and then he approached the steel table and the quantum orb resting there. He plunged his hand through the membrane, bringing the circuitry to life again.

"Hey," Ben called. "We haven't—"

The circuitry lights pulsed around Lukas's hand in the startup sequence. Ben ran toward his own console and vaulted over it, sliding on the floor and catching himself with a hand on the console's edge. He typed furiously at the keys, though to

Deborah he seemed impossibly slow now after what she had just witnessed.

That thought sparked her into action, her terror momentarily forgotten when she realized what was about to happen. "Get away from the table!" Most of the team had already backed away by this point, but Mark had been too focused on Lukas's odd behavior. With a low hum, the first-stage web field blossomed from the center of the quantum orb. It enveloped Lukas and washed over Mark's rigid form, which blistered out of existence, leaving a metallic stench mixed with burnt hair and charged flesh.

A woman shrieked, and Ben shouted from his console, "Deb, he's set it for 4 B.C. and the sequence is locked. I can't get in. I don't know—"

"Lukas!" Deborah's throat burned with the force of her scream, but even that did nothing to get his attention. He didn't turn back to look at any of them before the freezing blue explosion of the web field seemed to take all the air out of the room, and then he was gone.

3

4 B.C. – The Province of Judea

Against the brilliant glow of the eastern sunrise, a shadowed form blurred across the dazzling desert sand. Clouds of dust billowed in its wake, leaving the scent of burnt earth and charred metal behind the thing that moved too quickly to be of this Earth. Over rolling dunes and past rising peaks of harsh, unrelenting stone, baked by the sun into a merciless wilderness, the figure sped. Its shadow shortened behind it as the sun rose to its zenith, and still the dark thing did not stop the straight, terrible line of its singular purpose in the suffocating heat.

When the sun glowed fiery red in the west and winked over the Sea of Salt, the otherworldly being ceased its unnatural pursuit and stopped beneath the curving arch of white and brown stone. The gust of wind behind it brought a surprised squawk from the chickens pecking at the fine sand, and they spread their wings and hopped away from the man standing now in their midst.

The peddlers stared in animosity toward such a stranger,

coupled with fear of the man dressed so strangely and in such dark colors beneath the desert sun. None of them interfered, choosing instead to watch and wait, whispering to neighbors when he passed and hoping he would not stop to ask of them what they knew not one of them could answer. The man continued toward the other end of the small, dry settlement until he reached the wide, dusty square home of baked clay and the stable fashioned against the back wall. A donkey brayed inside, and the man's figure cast a long shadow across the dirt and the straw and the thin, tired family huddled within.

"May I help you?" From where he lay atop a pile of straw, the man with a long brown beard and exhausted eyes looked up at the strange visitor.

The oddly dressed stranger slowly removed from his pocket a red orb, which shot a thin stream of blazing light into the man's chest and filling the stable with the nauseating odor of singed flesh. The bearded man slumped sideways into the straw, smoke curling from the gaping hole in his chest. A scream erupted from the woman reclining beside him, and she threw her body across the babe, swaddled in rags, who had been lying between his parents.

With another hiss and whir, the orb in the stranger's hand turned its fury upon the woman as well, her selfless act of defending her innocent child unnoticed—ineffective. The babe did not once cry out as it stared up at the blank void of the stranger's eyes within an expressionless face, nearly crushed beneath the dead weight of his mother's lifeless arm. For a moment, the whole of existence flashed behind the infant's calm brown gaze—worlds upon worlds, time unending, love and light and what any other man might only call rapture. Then another red flash of light erupted, and the infant silently joined its parents.

The donkey brayed again, its eyes rolling as it jerked its head up and down against the thin wooden rails of its pen. Outside, the chickens screeched and flapped about the yard, scratching and pecking at each other in terror.

Without a word, the stranger turned away from the bodies inside the stable, took one step forward, then burst across the dirt to resume its unearthly speed. The pillar of stacked stones supporting the town's welcoming archway rumbled and cracked when the dark thing streaked past. The force of the stranger's departure upturned the peddlers' tables and sent crates and thin tents flying against the sunbaked walls of the buildings. The foundation of the town itself seemed to shudder in the ensuing stillness, left to endure the coming darkness of night.

4

Present Day – Inside the Qumranian Lab – Altered Timeline

The world reeled around him, and Lukas barely registered the blasting cold of the web field before it dissipated and left him standing once more beside the steel table. His arm thrummed with the power of the quantum orb's circuitry coiled around his fingers, then they released him, and his hand slumped out of the orb's external membrane and down against his side. He had no idea how he'd ended up here; he'd just been giving his team a congratulatory speech, and then... Lukas blinked when an image burst unwelcome across his vision—two calm, shining brown eyes, studying him with an intensity he'd never felt from any other living thing. Peace, infinite wisdom, ceaseless and undying love. The wonder in those eyes filled Lukas with a weakness he seldom experienced, and then they were gone in a flash of red light.

Something toppled to the floor by his feet, and in a daze, he briefly glanced down to see the red energy phaser rolling across the Main Lab's pristine tiles. How did that get there? His knees buckled, and in an attempt to remain standing, Lukas took a trembling step away from the table.

"In the eyes..."

It took him a moment to recognize it as his own voice, and the next thing he knew, he'd fallen to his knees. He blinked again, and Deborah's wide eyes, her brow creased with concern and fear, now hovered inches from his own. She opened her mouth, but no sound came out, drowned by the ringing Lukas suddenly heard in his ears. His palms smacked against the tile floor beside the red energy phaser, and he willed himself not to fall flat on his face right there.

"Lukas, can you hear me?" Her voice was muffled, but he heard it now and he raised his head.

"What happened?" Ben knelt beside his sister, reaching out to lift Lukas's arm up and over his shoulders before helping him to stand.

Lukas swallowed, his throat dry and oddly sandy, but he could only shake his head. "I don't..." The words croaked out of him, and he couldn't piece together the fleeting images of what felt like so much lost time before they drifted away into vague memory.

"That last jump was not approved," Ben mumbled as he and Deborah supported Lukas over to a chair against the lab's far wall.

"That wasn't Lukas," Deborah hissed, looking at the other scientists, all of whom stared at Lukas with what could only be horror. Just moments before, it had been admiration and pride. "Something else did this. Something—"

A deep, muted boom echoed from somewhere beyond Sector One, unmistakable in its impact. The white paneled ceiling above them shuddered, and Lukas looked up to see a sheet of dust sifting through the cracks in the panels. The memory of his dreams returned to him, and his stomach sank into a dark pit, thick with emptiness. His cousins almost had him sitting down in the chair, but he summoned the strength back into his legs and stood.

"I'm fine," he muttered, and when they wouldn't let him up, he jerked his arms up off their shoulders. "I said I'm fine."

They released him, eyeing him with wary concern, and he put a hand against the wall for a moment to steady himself. "Something's wrong," he said. "Something's different."

Another boom, this time closer and louder, rocked the foundations of the Qumranian compound and set the test trays rattling on their shelves. Deborah stumbled beside him but didn't cry out. Ben whirled around and stared at the trembling ceiling, as if he'd find the answer there. The next wave of explosions sounded even closer now, followed by the distinctive rapid fire of automatic weaponry. The soft, humming whir of Qumranian energy phasers echoed the pounding retort of machinegun fire, a few shouts of alarm interspersed among the sound of what could only be an attack. Lukas glanced first at Ben, then at Deborah, who both stared at him in mute horror, neither of them able to voice what had always seemed so impossible. And deep below the surface of his consciousness, he could not ignore the burning certainty that whatever headed down the corridors toward the Sector One Main Laboratory was here now, in their home, where they were working to change both worlds, because of something he had done and could not remember.

"What's going on?" a woman shouted.

This seemed to tear Deborah out of her own inability to act, and she whirled away from Ben and Lukas to head toward the lab's steel double doors.

"Deb, you don't know what's out there," Ben shouted, but it could very well have been lost in the nearly deafening chaos of the fighting outside.

Before she could even reach the entrance to peer through the reinforced windows, both doors burst open on their hinges, one of them nearly ripped free and left to hang there like a dislocated shoulder. The screams and gunfire in the hallway intensified, followed by two ominous figures who stalked into the lab and looked around as if they owned the place and had come to reclaim it.

A man and a woman, their facial features almost identical copies of each other, most notably, their almond shaped eyes and high cheekbones, stopped after a few steps through the doorway. A fearsome assemblage of armor decorated them both from head to toe—deep-purple, black, and blood-red leather stitched to thousands of metal plates across their chest pieces. The man's helmet boasted intricate, square detailing beneath the burst of black and red feathers along the crest, the half-face armor crafted to resemble the sharp, wicked hook of some bird or raptor's beak. His female counterpart's armor seemed a mirror image in color and geometric design, varying only when necessary to fit her feminine form. Curved, sharpened spikes curled up from the massive pauldrons, lending the warriors an image of a stature far larger than Lukas thought either of them could truly claim. Every inch of their arms and legs had been wrapped in the same flexible sheets of linked metal, leaving them both completely protected and highly maneuverable. As he studied them, Lukas realized how difficult it would be to pierce armor like this, and he could not say whether Qumranian energy phasers would have had any effect, even if he hadn't left the one weapon in this lab on the floor by the table.

All this he noted in a mere instant before a contingent of less-armored but no less formidable troops swarmed into the lab behind their commanders. Lukas tried to get a good look at the red star tattoo that each of them bore on the backs of their hands, but his focus was disrupted by another scream from his female team member, followed by the pleas of the rest of his team as they begged for mercy from the intruders aiming automatic rifles at their heads.

Without a given command, the soldiers unloaded their

weapons into the best of the Qumranian scientists—on their knees with hands raised, scrambling uselessly away in an attempt to find cover, calling out and reaching for each other. Lukas dove away from his cousins and the open fire, rolling under one of the smaller control consoles and inching his way toward the opposite end of the lab.

The man dressed as fiercely as the woman beside him raised his fist in a sharp, swift motion and the firing ceased, though the soldiers had wiped out more than half of Lukas's team. The remaining few whimpered and covered their heads, but not Ben. Lukas watched in surprise as Ben lurched toward the invaders. His cousin wasn't an Enforcer class soldier, but he had completed the combat training required of every Qumranian. Before Ben could swing his fists wildly at the man in ornate armor, the woman stepped in front of her counterpart and intercepted Ben's wrist with one simple upward motion of her hand. Her fingers clamped down around his flesh, then she jerked sharply downward. Even from where he lay under the console, Lukas heard the bones in his cousin's arm snap, followed by Ben's shriek of agony.

"Take this one. I assume by his pathetic attack that his skills lie elsewhere," the woman ordered, her voice low and syrupy. "And that woman." She nodded briefly to where Deborah cowered just beside the open lab doors. "Then find the third main scientist on this team. We need them all." One of her soldiers beside her trained his weapon on a frazzled female scientist who'd managed to crawl across the floor toward Deborah. The fierce female commander, her grip still tight on Ben's limp wrist, in one fluid motion grabbed her own soldier by the throat. The underling choked and dropped his weapon. "If you kill any more of these scientists we were told to bring in alive, you will be joining them shortly thereafter." The soldier could not respond, but gave a barely audible gasp when his commander released her grip. "Do it."

The insurgents set about securing the lab and rounding up the other scientists. Ben cradled his broken arm, his face frozen in a rictus of pain and shock. Lukas watched the black-spiked boots of the male commander stepping toward the steel table where the quantum orb rested untouched in its cradle. He could not see the man's face, but he heard the low hum of greed and excitement coming from the man's throat. The ruthless female leader walked out of Lukas's view from beneath the console to join her co-commander, and Lukas wanted nothing more than to leap out and protect the product of so much labor, attention, focus, and prayer. But he knew it would do none of them any good.

"This is for you, my Lord," the armored man said, his voice oozing like spilt oil over sand.

"And for us," the woman added.

The man's armored boots turned swiftly, and Lukas heard him call to the troops, "Take this machine and the prisoners out of the compound and back to the city. Unharmed. Or your lives are forfeit."

Amid the scuffle of invading soldiers herding petrified scientists toward the Main Laboratory's doors and his cousins' terrified cries as they reached for each other, Lukas took the opportunity to make his move. He crawled on his belly to the other side of the lab where the instrument panel rested against the far wall. It took only a little force to pull free. Between the scientists' shouted protests, the brusque grunts of the foreign soldiers, and the rapid gunfire and steady screams splitting through the echo of explosions, no one heard the instrument panel fall away before Lukas climbed into the ventilation shaft and made his escape.

5

The ventilation shaft only took him as far as Sector Two. Lukas couldn't stay in there forever; the acrid scent of burning chemicals and toxic smoke had followed him all the way from the Main Laboratory where their attackers had most likely set fire to every lab in Sector One. Even if that weren't the case, Lukas was not the type of man to sit in a dark, confined space and leave his team—and his cousins—to their fate. He'd rather wield his fists and his strength built over many years of Hedge Training to face whatever onslaught this new enemy threw at him than cower away in hiding.

It took only two swift kicks with his booted heel before the mesh panel at the end of the ventilation shaft gave way and clattered to the floor. Another massive explosion rocked the foundations of the compound, and he nearly tumbled to the ground before he steadied himself against the wall and emerged into one of Sector Two's narrow hallways. Above him, the track lighting shuddered where the rows of long bulbs were bolted to the stone walls, flickering once with a warning hum. To his right, the sounds of more rapid gunfire and hundreds of booted footsteps rose amid screams of terror and shouted commands.

To his left, Lukas knew he would find the other main rooms of Sector Two—the Qumranian compound's maintenance division. He figured this had been situated so close to the labs of Sector One for ease of access to control panels and new technology configuring the layout of their databases and many of their systems' mainframes. Lukas had spent a few years working on improvements to their system, mainly in automating some of the newer machinery for the Agricultural Sector, but that was almost a decade before he'd reached the pinnacle of his scientific achievement. Now, he was grateful for the experience he'd thought had only been a stepping stone in his career.

He took off running down the hall, away from the screams and fighting. His boots echoed along the hallway, and when he rounded the third corner, the traction they provided had never been more appreciated. Lukas skidded to a halt, faced with a new, smaller contingent of the invading soldiers who had yet to notice his presence behind them. As he approached, Lukas counted nineteen, and those few seconds were all he needed before he seized the opportunity provided by taking them by surprise.

Just before he reached the closest man, the soldier turned, his eyes widening beneath a dark, thick brow. He had only enough time to lower his weapon a few inches toward Lukas before the Hedge Master was upon him. Lukas grabbed the butt of the automatic firearm and used the soldier's own momentum to swing the weapon up into the man's jaw. A sickening crack rang out in the hallway, the soldier slumped to the floor, and Lukas kept moving.

The soldiers were well aware of him now; the odds would have been stacked wholly against him if he had not spent his entire life training for a moment just like this. He ducked beneath another soldier's wild swing with his firearm and sent the weapon smashing into the face of his closest neighbor. Lukas disarmed his opponent, thrust the butt of the firearm into the man's gut, and when the soldier doubled over, the Hedge Master brought his elbow cracking against the back of the soldier's skull.

Fighting so many opponents in such a narrow hallway didn't hinder Lukas's ability to make his way through the contingent; in fact, it might have aided him. When two more soldiers in black approached him from both sides, Lukas spun and kicked the first in the chest, sending the enemy reeling back into his own comrades. Then he crouched and brought the same foot sweeping under the legs of the other soldier who had nearly trained his weapon on the Hedge Master. The man went down with a crash, firing a volley of automatic gunfire into two more of his own men before the rounds collided into the stone wall of the hallway and up into the ceiling. Shards of cracked stone and dust and shattered glass rained down on all of them, the echoing shots all but deafening in such an enclosed space.

Someone grabbed the back of Lukas's gray uniform shirt, and he spun around to rip the grasp free with an open block before bringing his left palm up against the underside of his attacker's chin. He whirled again and brought his fist into another man's face, then grabbed him only long enough to knee the man's midsection with enough force to render the soldier breathless and inert. His enemy had enough sense not to fire their weapons again in such close quarters, but they used these now as clubs instead, lunging and stabbing at Lukas as he moved. He spun away from all of them, ducking and twisting and countering with fists and elbows, open palms and jabbing fingers, the jarring force of a thrust shoulder.

The last enemy insurgent standing had far more space to maneuver than the rest of his team, and he raised his weapon to bring it down toward Lukas's head just as the Hedge Master turned to face him. Lukas caught the firearm with both hands, struggling with the man's vice-like grip on it. The soldier pushed him back against the wall, bearing down on Lukas until the length of the automatic rifle nearly pushed down on Lukas's throat. Putrid breath blasted into the Hedge Master's face as the soldier grunted through a vicious sneer. Lukas managed enough of a push away from the wall to throw his head back and then forward into the soldier's forehead. His attacker reeled back, and Lukas shoved the weapon up, released it, and crouched to bring his shoulder into the man's groin before lifting the enemy up and tossing him over his shoulder. He did not stop to see whether the soldier had hit the wall head-first as he planned; Lukas kept running.

Another explosion wracked the hallways of Sector Two, much closer and much louder. He stumbled into the wall but pushed himself forward. When he rounded another corner, he spotted the plain gray door to his right where he'd find one of the main control rooms. Lunging toward the door, he punched in the access code on the wall panel, waited for the click, and shoved the door inward. He found no sign of the enemy having entered, and he stared up at the dozens of huge monitors mounted to the walls all around him. The hellish vision caught by every surveillance camera greeted him from each of the screens.

The hallways of the living quarters had been completely destroyed and now lay in ruins, lights flickering to illuminate the bodies of those who could not escape. Plumes of thick black smoke rose from the fields and orchards in the Agricultural Sector, where furious and insatiable tongues of thick flame ate away at the tended crops beneath the huge lighting panels. These flickered and dimmed, casting an eerily unnatural, fading glow across the scorched earth. The spacious training rooms in Sector Four were filled with bodies, the acolytes training under Hedge Masters scattered in piles of black sparring uniforms, all motionless, all riddled with bullets. The empty and destroyed Main Laboratory had indeed been ransacked and set to burn.

Through the haze of smoke almost filling the entire room on the monitor, Lukas caught a glimpse of the steel table by the lab's double doors, the quantum orb's metal cradle somehow severed from where it had been bolted to the table's surface. And the orb, of course, was gone.

Lukas's mind churned with these images. He'd thought at first he might find where this strange army had infiltrated the compound, that he might seal off their escape route or quarantine some of the sectors for at least a chance of survival here. But now, he knew in his bones there was nothing he could do for his people or the precious world in which they'd labored and trained and thrived for so long.

Another explosion rattled the walls around him. One of the monitors on the wall slipped from its mount and crashed onto the control panel beneath it. Glass and sparks erupted from both, the monitor sizzling and smoking where live wires had been severed. Lukas stepped away from the damage and turned to the far end of the room where a ladder of bare and dusty rebar jutted from the stone wall and rose to the control room's ceiling. He ran to this and hoisted himself up the ladder; his only option now was to escape the compound or risk his certain end when everything came crashing down around him.

He'd almost reached the vaulted hatch at the top of the ladder when he heard the synchronized pounding of so many running soldiers and a shout of command. "Check in there, then join us at the central breach. We move out in ten minutes."

Lukas reached a hand up to the circular lever in the center of the hatch. He jerked on it with all his strength, balancing precariously on the rebar ladder when he used both hands now to try to force the crank to turn. It wouldn't budge.

A low hum gave him a split second of warning before the red streak of a Qumranian energy phaser cracked against the steel hatch almost at his fingertips. Dust and fragments of the stone ceiling rained down on him, and he gripped the ladder again to steady himself before looking down. One of the soldiers in black aimed a seized energy phaser at him, scowling as he tried to position the red orb correctly for a better shot. Lukas clutched the

hatch's wheeled lever again, but before he could pull it open, the
soldier had let off two more shots of the phaser right into the
stone ceiling beside the hatch.

The ceiling crumbled above him, and Lukas had just enough
time to release one hand and foot from the ladder and swing
wildly aside before the steel hatch fell. It clanged against the
rebar on which his other foot still supported him, sending a
shuddering jolt through his leg, then crashed into another
control console and nearly ripped the thing in two. Not both-
ering to see if the enemy soldier had discovered how to improve
his aim with the energy phaser, Lukas climbed the last three
rungs of the ladder and hoisted himself into the cavernous
opening above him.

When he stood, the tunnel before him was dark and damp,
water trickling in slow rivulets down the nearly black walls of
stone. He thought there had been lights in these tunnels, which
led to the intricate matrix of catwalks above the huge expanse of
solar panels in the Agricultural Sector. Either the destroyed
controls in the maintenance room below him or some other
explosion in the compound had knocked out the energy grid,
leaving him now in almost complete darkness.

Lukas moved swiftly down the tunnel, his sight adjusting
marginally with each passing second. The floors were not nearly
as smooth as the main thoroughfare of the commonly used hallways below, and he tripped a few times on mounds of rough,
jagged stone sticking up in his path. In less than two minutes, a
muted light appeared ahead, and he quickened his pace into a
jog. Something whirred in the distance—a thick, heavy, mechanical chop he did not recognize. Then the tunnel curved slightly,
and the light intensified enough to make him pull up and shield
his eyes against the glare.

Blinking, Lukas gave his vision a moment to adjust, then
took two steps back from the gaping edge of a sheer drop right in
front of him. He peered down into the cavernous hole clearly

blasted into being by the intruding army and could not see the bottom of it for the blaze of bright light coming from all directions. When he looked up, he found the ceiling of bedrock no longer existed, but the lights made it impossible to know whether this hole driven into the compound extended all the way to the surface.

A shout of alarm came from somewhere below him, followed by a blast of both automatic gunfire and the humming drone of energy phasers. The tunnel wall beside him sparked and cracked, lit up with enemy fire, and then a thick pane of rock crumbled away from the tunnel wall and toppled down into cavernous hole below. Lukas darted backward, then found another opening had revealed itself in the wall of the tunnel.

He leaped to this new hole in the wall and squeezed himself into it, knowing it for his last chance at escape. On his hands and knees, he crawled through this small fissure in the earth, his back scraping against the rough stone above him when he didn't crouch low enough. Cool water dripped onto his head and splashed beneath his moving hands. Another rumble shook the earth around him, and he paused beneath a sifting cascade of damp dirt and pebbles. But his escape route held, and he continued.

Fortunately, the tight passageway did not deviate from its upward slant, and with some luck, Lukas thought, he'd make it eventually to the surface. The water on solid stone beneath his palms gave way to earth slightly more stable than mud, then he found himself moving along a fine, soft dust. A reddish glow appeared up ahead, bringing with it a cloying blast of warm air. The rhythmic, mechanical chop he had not recognized in the tunnels below now returned, echoing a little around him. Before he realized it, Lukas had climbed out of the cleft that had been his fortunate escape and into the open air of the Above.

Never had he dared to imagine what such an emergence might actually feel like. Even if he'd given in to the heresy of

such impossible daydreams—much like he knew Deborah had—
he would have been entirely wrong.

Turning on the warm red sand beneath him, Lukas looked
out over a world vastly and horrifyingly different to anything the
Qumranian records had maintained over the last two thousand
years. The Dead Sea under which he'd lived and worked his
entire life stretched before him as he'd expected. But its waters
were thick and murky, reflecting the ghastly, haze-infused glow
of a blood-red sunset. The sky churned with dark clouds, not
thick and bursting with life-giving rain but charred-looking,
roiling in erratic bursts like static moving through a smear of
soot. He could not see the sun behind them, only an echo of its
dying light, and he thought he saw a blazing fire across the sky
until he recognized his own memory of the scorched Agricultural Sector below and pushed it aside. Then he noticed the
attacking army filing out of his home, and he could not look
away.

Droves of black-clad soldiers marched up a ramp fashioned
against the side of the gaping crater of the Qumranian
compound. They moved in swift, tight formations toward two
massive contraptions perched on the edge of the fractured earth.
Lukas surmised these hulking vessels of black metal were some
type of aircraft, far more technologically advanced than
anything his people had ever designed. Through the ringing in
his ears, he caught again the thick chop of machinery and found
against the blackened backdrop of the marred skyline two more
of these same crafts hovering over the chasm in the compound.
Airborne, they resembled huge, formidable beetles, the smooth
black exterior of their hulls reflecting the sickened hue of sunset.
From the center of these extended a number of thick metal
cables, at the bottom of which hung crates, machinery, mainframe components, and any manner of other spoils this invading
force deemed worthy of pilfering. Lukas realized, when he
watched the cables retracting into the bellies of these hovering

vessels, that everything he'd dedicated his life to building—centuries of data and technology—was now in the hands of an enemy he never even knew existed.

A hot clench of protective rage turned his gut, but then the loud whine of another aircraft cut out even the sound of his own thoughts. The thing moved quickly a few meters above him, headed toward the rest of its small fleet, and Lukas scrambled in the sand toward a jutting rise of red baked stone behind him. He pressed himself into the nearest crevice, hoping not to be discovered, and watched from there as the fifth aircraft slowed above the smoking remains of the Qumranian compound. The two insect-like crafts finished hauling up their plunder before the central doors in their bellies slid shut. The last of the soldiers filed into the vessels on the ground, and when the exterior doors also closed, these aircraft lifted neatly into the air without so much as disturbing the sand in which they'd rested. Together in tight formation, the five black aircraft turned away from the sea and the sunset and headed east over the dry expanse of desert, staying relatively low.

After a few breaths, Lukas thought it safe enough to step out of his hiding place in the outcropping of rocks around him and stare after the vile force that had so succinctly laid everything he'd ever known to waste. He did not expect to see the vast metropolis on the eastern horizon, rising like a metal splinter from the desert sand. This, too, looked nothing like the images of Above civilization stored in the Qumranian records; even from a distance, the sprawling urban complex looked mechanical, soiled, vapid even, with the blinking of its thousands of multicolored lights below the blackened skyline.

A cracking groan and a ferocious hiss made Lukas turn away from the unexpected sight and he trained his eyes once more upon the gaping hole in the ground leading into the underground paradise that was. The earth trembled, something shifted beneath him, and despite himself and the meters between him and the wreckage, he took a few steps back. One end of the chasm tilted in on itself and collapsed, bringing the rest of the huge network of caverns and tunnels tumbling down on themselves. It sank lower and lower, rumbling as if some unseen hand were pulling it into the fiery bowels of the earth. The rush of spilling water added to the terrifying discord rising all around him, and the edge of the Dead Sea tipped into the ruptured earth to fill the wreckage of Lukas's whole world in seconds. Huge gusts of steam and black smoke erupted from below, salt water spraying in fine mists miles up into the noxious sky. Centuries spent below ground, and it took so few seconds to bury it all beneath the murky, churning waters and the unrelenting pressure of silent nonexistence.

The Qumranian compound was gone. Lukas allowed himself only a brief moment to scan the Dead Sea's new shoreline, just in case an unsuspected survivor showed himself. But he knew even daring to hope for such a miracle now was pointless. Lukas was alone.

He had not realized he'd fallen to his knees until his fingers clenched huge fistfuls of red sand; even this sifted through his fingers and he was as powerless to hold every grain of it in his grasp as he'd been to stop this destruction. But he was still alive, and he was not entirely without options.

Lukas pushed himself to his feet, feeling the weight of his failure and his singular escape as one blended defeat. But when he put the Dead Sea and the barren waste of his home behind him, gazing at the foreboding monolith of steel towers and flashing lights and any number of doubtlessly trying obstacles rising to meet the charred sky, his mind returned to his purpose. If he could no longer do his work from within the underground walls of His design, he would do his work here, in the unknown world, Above.

As he trudged east across the stretch of sand, the words left Lukas's lips in little more than a whisper. "Yea, though I walk through the valley of the shadow of death, I will fear no evil: for thou *art* with me; thy rod and thy staff they comfort me." With everything else stripped so violently from him, he now had to be both rod and staff. "Below I am a scientist who can be a weapon. Above, I am a weapon, and if I do this right, I can be a scientist again."

6

Present Day – Altered Timeline – The City (Jerusalem)

By the time he reached the city, the deadly glow of the setting sun had completely disappeared, and night had fallen. Lukas had never seen the true stars in the world Above, but even if they had been visible through the blackened grime of the roiling clouds stretching in every direction—which he highly doubted— the blinding glare of the city lights now would have drowned out those twinkling gems in the sky anyway.

Even before he'd passed through the wide, glistening arc of a glass walkway that might have been a formal entrance to the metropolis, the sound of the place had overwhelmed him entirely. The air split around him with the bustle of traffic, the whine and buzz of vehicles both bound to the roads by gravity and hovering through the air. Bells chimed, whistles shrieked, people shouted, screamed, laughed. A blaring cacophony of slightly skewed, warbling human voices, impossibly loud and deceptively pleasant-sounding, had risen above all of it. All the words jumbled together as they vied against each other to draw the unsuspecting gawker's attention. Lukas heard this first, but it could not have prepared him for the sight of this place when he entered.

The towers rose to impossible heights, hulking shards of metal and glass thrusting bright colors up into the sooty sky. Over half of them boasted the striking, elongated forms of ancient pyramids, though Lukas had never seen them built like this. These towers were built with such explicit detail and made mostly of glass. Holographic images flashed across their glittering surfaces, making it impossible to know if he saw a reflected image or what truly lay behind the glass walls. Glyphic letters in a language he'd never seen scrolled top to bottom and right to left, superimposed over the images screaming at him from nearly every direction.

He did not see more of the military aircraft like those of the army that had desecrated his home, but he'd never seen the type of vehicles now shooting across open highways and down alleyways and up into the sky between the buildings either. These were smaller, perhaps with far less deadly purpose, but they too resembled insects in their design—rounded cabs and hulls that glistened in the artificial light like carapaces; some boasted what even looked like wings as they lifted off from the ground and went about their business.

While the design and layout of this place was far more technologically advanced than anything he'd ever dreamed the people Above capable of producing, the streets of the lower level itself held up to his expectations completely. It was filthy, packed, reeking of chemical smoke and cloying perfumes that did little to mask the underlying stench of so many bodies packed so closely together. The holographic images still moved over every surface here, but even then, they were smudged and grimy, their canvases in need of a good washing, yet Lukas anticipated that would do very little to improve the place. As he walked through the loud, suffocating, dissonant streets, he stared up at the tops of the rising pyramidal structures and thin, piercing towers in awe and confusion mixed with no little disgust. How had the Qumranian records failed entirely to capture an accurate portrayal of life on the Above? This was not what he'd spent his life studying—not the proof around which he'd built his scientific career and his preparatory training as a Hedge Master.

A fight broke out at the far end of the packed street far too narrow for this many people. Lukas took in the faces, realizing with another bout of unexpected confusion that this urban sprawl boasted all nationalities known to him from every part of the world—and some he had not had the opportunity to recognize. He drifted with the bustling of loiterers and determined individuals alike, the press of bodies moving him along like a bit of drifting seaweed in an ocean current. A huge man almost half again taller than Lukas—bare-chested and every inch of his skin covered in tattoos depicting bloody, violent scenes—passed Lukas and bumped him aside as if he were swatting away an irritating fly. Lukas stumbled into a squat man with thick lips blistered and cracked, who shouted something unintelligible at him before shoving him away.

A shriek of surprise or maybe delight came from beside him, and then he felt hands on his arms and back, clutching at his slate-gray uniform, now soiled with gray dust and dried red clay from his escape through the compound. He turned to see three women with gaudily painted faces leering at him, their faces and body language directed at him implied their intimate attentions. One of them bared her breasts and winked. Frowning, Lukas shrugged the grasping hands aside and pressed through the throng of bodies, readily ignoring these advances.

The more he moved through the streets, the more he discovered of a place so entirely unimaginable. Between the densely packed shops open to the night air below so many vertical miles of what might have been apartments or living quarters, Lukas spied bodies in the dark alleyways. At first he thought them corpses, until the closest rasped out a rattling cough and extended a supplicating hand to anyone who might take pity on him. Eventually, the thick crowds thinned, then trickled into much more manageable numbers as he continued down the dirty streets, finding himself unable to stomach even the idea of glancing at his feet to discern what new slick, squelching substance he'd stepped into next.

When he came to the first large intersection, he looked around the corner to see a tightly organized group of soldiers marching in perfect formation. They moved away from him down a much wider, slightly cleaner-looking street. He could not tell whether these were the same soldiers of the army that had infiltrated his destroyed compound, but they were trailed by a trio of small, hovering machines a little larger than a man's head. These too resembled mechanical insects, each complete with a sextet of curved appendages protruding from the undersides of their metal bellies. Wobbling beneath them, the spindly attachments looked like legs but could have been anything. The street these soldiers patrolled, however, was almost entirely empty.

In the opposite direction, this wider avenue intersected with the street he'd followed into the city. It was much less densely packed as well, and most of those moving about were dressed in rags, maybe once of the same design as the odd robes and flowing attire he'd seen other people wearing but no longer distinguishable as such. They were thin, malnourished, bending slowly with heavy, hopeless gazes to scrub at the very street itself, their fingers raw and blistered. A few of them dashed across the avenue from one building to the next, carrying bulging canvas sacks. One man stumbled over his own bare feet, and the much healthier, straight-backed man in a clean gray robe behind him prodded the poor soul with a long metal rod, much as one would nudge a distracted sheep back toward its fellows in the pen.

Across this intersecting avenue, the throng of people seemed to grow again, as if no one here wished to cross the junction of the narrow, gritty thoroughfare and the clean, empty avenue at the wrong time. Lukas did not cross the street either, instead stopping at the corner and leaning against the slick metal wall of the nearest building to watch some hurried movement across the way. The milling citizens out after dark shuffled and stirred, then the mass of bodies filling the street split in two. They gave the man walking toward the intersection a wide berth, bowing low as he passed, some even falling to their knees and pressing their foreheads to the filthy street.

The man wore a long, sleek robe of brown leather, the dual tassels at the top swaying with each step. His head was covered beneath a huge, wide leather hood that draped across his shoulders. He walked fully erect, his chin lifted with self-importance. The hush on the other side of the street seemed to echo to where Lukas stood, and he turned briefly when a woman beside him let out a muffled gasp and sank to one knee. The hooded figure stepped into the wide avenue, then headed directly toward them through the middle of the packed street.

"Phar-asai," the woman muttered, lowering her gaze before the hooded figure was upon them.

This pulled Lukas from his focus on the stranger of importance, and he leaned down a little toward the woman. "What was that?"

She blinked and glanced up at him, her cheeks stained with tracks of dirt, her hair matted and greasy. But her eyes were clear. "Teacher of the Law," she said in a harsh whisper, nodding at the approaching figure as if Lukas should have known better than to talk now while they could be noticed. Then she bowed her head again and mumbled something Lukas thought was not meant for him to hear.

The Phar-asai neared them, stepping slowly and almost silently over the ground. Lukas thought he saw the man's nostrils flare, but he kept moving and did not notice the stranger among them brazenly staring. When the robed figure had passed, Lukas made the call; if this man was indeed a teacher of the Law, he would most likely be able to clear up at least a few of Lukas's most confusing concerns.

"Excuse me," he called out, pushing himself up from against the wall to follow the man. The woman kneeling beside him gasped again but did not look up. "Excuse me." He jogged into the street where it had thankfully cleared down the center to allow the teacher's passage. "I heard you're a teacher of the Law. Do you know the Manual of Discipline?"

The man stiffened and turned slowly, as if touched on the back of the neck by a clammy hand. With a raised brow, he took in the sight of Lukas standing there, filthy-looking and with no bearing of importance, and the Phar-asai's eyes widened.

"How dare you?" he said in a low, slow growl. "Your kind is forbidden to speak to me."

Lukas spread his arms to show he meant no harm. "Sir, I only have a few questions—"

The man moved quicker than the apparent thickness of his apparel would suggest. Lukas only had a glimpse of the silver rod produced from the Phar-asai's robes before the man pressed the tip of it just below Lukas's collarbone. Searing pain burst through his chest and into his extremities. Losing consciousness, he could not do a thing to stop himself from slumping to the ground before his cheek hit the vile street below him.

7

"Hurry up, Deb. You won't *believe* what I found!" Lukas ran through the field, his nine-year-old legs pumping fiercely in his excitement. He gazed up at the beautiful blue sky; his father told him once that it looked just as the sky above Above, but Lukas always knew theirs was better, brighter, more beautiful.

"You're going to get us in trouble," Deborah called back, lifting her skirts to keep after her cousin. "My father told us not to wander off."

"He won't even know we were gone," Lukas said, turning to grin at her when they crested a small rise. "Not if we hurry." He pointed down the other side of the hill where the grass ran all the way up to the very edge of the vast, cavernous rock wall stretching endlessly in both directions. Deborah frowned, but she took off after him anyway when Lukas raced down the hill toward the cavern wall.

A few overlooked shrubs had grown up against the cavern, and with a mischievous smile, Lukas brushed aside the wayward branches to reveal a fissure in the stone just large enough for a child. He wiggled his eyebrows at his cousin, pulled a flashlight from his back pocket, and clicked it on. The light only went so far into the darkness, but he knew the way. And he knew Deborah would follow him.

They crawled through this new tunnel beneath the earth, moving slowly at a shallow descent. But the channel went on for minutes that felt like hours, and Lukas knew they'd be there soon.

"Are you sure you know what you're doing?" Deborah finally asked, her voice muted by the damp earth all around them. "I've heard people talk about the caves. That anyone could just fall in and no one would ever be able to find them." She took a deep breath, and Lukas heard her stop behind him. "How do you know there won't be a rockslide, or some hole—"

"Just wait till you see this," Lukas said with a smirk. "Then you'll stop complaining." He moved the flashlight across the narrow tunnel. The temperature dropped drastically, and he knew they were almost there when the light curved around an open cavern up ahead.

Deborah scoffed. "I'm not complaining, you goat-face."

Lukas snorted and would have turned around to make a face at her if he'd had room for it in the tunnel. "What did you just call me?" He heard Deborah pick up her crawling pace behind him again.

"I called you a goat-face, *Mister* Goat-face."

"Say that again, and I'll just leave you here all by yourself." Finally, the tunnel opened into a wider cavern, and he stepped aside to wait for Deborah to crawl through.

"I could find my way back out of here no problem," she replied, swinging her legs in front of her to slide out of the tunnel and into the wider opening of the small cavern before them. "*You're* the one who always gets lost. Like at the bazaar that time, when you couldn't find my father's tent and you—" A low, deep rumble echoed around them, perhaps sounding larger than it was within the spanning cavern. "What was that?" she asked, turning quickly to meet Lukas's gaze.

He swallowed, then looked away from her and shrugged. "I don't know. But we're almost there. Come on." He moved along the cavern wall until it veered off to his left, and when they turned the corner, Lukas no longer needed his flashlight. A large crack about two fingers wide split from the floor of the cavern to the lowered ceiling, spilling a harsh white light onto them. Lukas grinned. "Look in there," he said, nodding to the crack in the wall.

Slowly, Deborah steadied herself with both hands against the wall and brought her eye up to the crack. After a few seconds, she leaned back again and stared at Lukas. "Wow."

"I know."

When she pressed her face back to the wall for another look, Lukas crouched next to her and did the same, leaning against the wall below Deborah and taking in every inch of the sight on the other side.

Two standing work lights burned brightly at the bottom of a new cavern below, though a recent rockslide had knocked them both over onto their sides. Lukas thought they must have had incredibly strong power sources to still be on after he'd found this place two days before, but what had amazed him the most was the bodies strewn beneath the rubble and the scattered, crushed equipment surrounding them.

Pressed so intently against the wall, neither child had a chance to steady themselves when another rumble rolled through the cavern and the already fractured wall gave way. Deborah tumbled forward just a fraction of a second before Lukas, her shout cut off by the echo of crumbling, sliding rocks, and tumbling debris. He scrambled for a hold as he tumbling head over heels, but everything around him fell too. Then he stopped, a particularly large rock wedged between his shoulder blades. With a groan, he pushed himself up and searched for Deborah.

He heard her gasp just a few feet away. "You okay?" he asked.

She moaned and slowly inched herself up to sit on the rubble. Blinking heavily against the light, Deborah reached a hand up to the side of her head, then brought it down to see a smear of blood across her fingers. "I don't know."

Lukas crawled across the shifting rubble toward her, thankful for the still-functioning work lights as he studied the gash on her temple. "It doesn't look that bad," he said.

Deborah glared at him. "I *told* you there were rockslides."

Lukas rolled his eyes and turned away from her to take advantage of where they now were. Judging by the amount of equipment here, he thought there might have been more people buried beneath the rubble, but three of them were visible amid the debris —two men and a woman. He couldn't tell how long they'd been down here; maybe the cave-in only happened a few hours before he'd discovered the tunnel. Through the haze of dust sifting up from the rockslide that had brought Lukas and Deborah this far down into the cavern, he could still smell the sweet, unpleasant odor of death and what he guessed were the bodies' beginning phases of decomposition. But even that smell didn't turn him away.

Deborah, though, pulled the outer layer of her skirt up to cover her mouth and nose and gagged a little; Lukas wrote that off as particularly dramatic.

"Look at them," he said, crawling toward the closest body of a man who had been crushed by two large fallen boulders. All his short life, he'd been told about the world Above, how different these people were from Qumranians, God's chosen Below. Though he knew they were forbidden from traveling to the surface, Lukas had still daydreamed of what those Above might look like, how they might act and speak. The whole doctrine had seemed nothing more than legend until now. Their clothes were strange, their skin in different shades than most he'd seen. What other details of the teachings and the law were so accurate and true when he'd thought them to be only stories? Lukas reached out toward the tan lapel of the dead man's jacket.

"Lukas, don't," Deborah shouted. "They're unclean." He jerked back his hand, more startled by the terror in her voice than the idea of dirtying himself. "We shouldn't have come here," she added, keeping well away from the bodies on the cavern floor. "Let's go back. Please."

Slowly, Lukas turned away from one final view of the strangers from Above. Then he helped Deborah climb back up the precarious slope of boulders and crumbling rocks that had sent them sliding down here in the first place.

When they reached the top of the embankment and headed into the darkness of the cavern and the tunnel beyond, Deborah whispered, "I can't believe you wanted to touch them. Why would you do that?"

Lukas switched on the flashlight, handed it to her, and waited for her to climb back into the ascending tunnel first. "I don't know," he said, lifting himself into the crevice after her. He thought he'd leave it at that, but then he found himself wanting to share it all with her. "I feel like... like I'm supposed to help them."

"They're dead, Lukas."

"No, not them." His voice fell flat in the enclosed space as they crawled upward on hands and knees. "I mean all the people Above."

Deborah slowed in her crawling only for a moment before she sped up again. "You can't say stuff like that. The Circle of Elders would try you for heresy. Probably kill you. Maybe worse. We can't tell anyone we were down here." She sounded just like her mother.

Lukas took a deep breath and put the most convincing remorse he could manage into his next words. "You're right. I'm sorry, Deb." She let out a little humph of frustration but didn't say anything else.

When they finally crawled out of the tunnel, pushed the shrubs aside, and stood on the soft grass of the rolling valley once more, Deborah handed Lukas his flashlight as if he'd forgotten it all along. Then she put both her hands on his shoulders and fixed him with a stern gaze much more mature than her eight years warranted. "We can't tell anyone," she said. "Don't go back there."

Eyes wide, Lukas nodded. He couldn't bring himself to say he promised; he didn't want to lie or have to break his word. Whether or not he did as she said, he didn't think he'd ever view the tales of Above or the laws they followed the same way ever again.

8

It was the chill in the air that slowly brought Lukas back to consciousness, which he immediately thought odd. Slowly, his head pounding and his shoulder feeling like it had just sustained a massive blow, he peeled his face off the slick, grimy street and realized why he'd started to shiver.

His clothes were gone. Whatever desperate urchin—or group of them—had removed his outerwear while he was unconscious had been either gracious enough or in such a hurry that they'd left him some semblance of dignity. Namely his underwear and socks. But his boots were gone, as were his uniform shirt and pants, his ID badge, and whatever other trinket he'd had in his pockets.

He had no idea how long he'd been out of it, though he assumed by the pain in his shoulder and the clearing of the previously crowded street that the teacher's weapon had left him lying there for quite some time. Even if he could read the strange language still scrolling across the holographic surfaces despite the emptiness of the street, knowing the time would have been of little help. Lukas had no idea where he was or where to go from here, and all he had now were the three items of underclothes left on his person.

Now, it seemed he belonged among the homeless beggars, the sick and poor he'd seen in the alleyways when he'd first arrived. Lukas pushed himself off the ground and stumbled down the street, still unable to fully comprehend the extent of his sudden destitution. But he didn't make it far before his aching exhaustion overwhelmed him. He hadn't had anything to eat in the last twenty-four hours or more except for the apple he'd taken with him from his room that morning. Even then, that seemed like a lifetime ago, in a different world entirely—which perhaps it was. That morning, he'd been a top Qumranian scientist, leading his team of experts toward a breakthrough that would change the course of history. And now, his people were all but vanished, destroyed by a strange military force from a world far different than Lukas had truly realized. None of it made sense.

All the determination and resilience that had fueled him before he'd set out from the ruins of the compound toward this city had seeped out of him. If he had not been as entirely depleted as he was, freezing and hungry, he would have spent more time considering his fate. But all he could do was limp a bit farther before lowering himself onto the stone curb of a walkway and bowing his head.

A few of the strange, insect-like vehicles whizzed past him, their shining exteriors reflecting the neon glow of the images scrolling and flashing, scrolling and flashing from all directions. Amid the chaotic din of all these moving signs, despite the fact that the streets were now nearly empty, one sound rose above all the others.

The voice was incredibly beautiful, heartbreaking in its sadness. Lukas felt the emotion behind it even though he had no knowledge of the language in which the woman sang and couldn't pick out a single word. Lifting his head from where he'd hung it over his exhausted limbs, he found a giant screen lit up on the side of a building across the street. On it was the singing woman, her almost-black hair falling loosely about her shoulders as the melody flowed from her lips. She looked just as sad as her song. Her large, dark eyes softened with wordless emotion, and for a moment, Lukas imagined she could see him and sang now as the only balm she could offer for his misfortune.

He pulled his bare knees up to his chest, wrapped his arms around them, and just watched her. Maybe, if he watched her long enough, he'd wake up in his cot, ready to look out over the Agricultural Sector and start his day with a fresh wash of optimism and confidence. That hope seemed all he had left.

The woman on the screen raised a dead branch in her hand, though he could not discern its purpose when he did not understand her language. Then her song took on a different tone, something hinting of hope and a new beginning. The branch in her hand shuddered, twisted of its own accord, then burst into life. Leaves sprouted and grew fully along the once-barren twigs, flowering buds appearing among them to then open and bloom with color more vibrant and real than any of the neon lights flashing around him. Captured by the image and the woman's voice, Lukas let himself drift in this new dream until he realized three pairs of feet stood just beside him on the walkway, and a warm, heavy hand came down upon his bare shoulder.

"Friend," a low, gentle voice said. "You can't sit here right now. They'll arrest you if you don't get up."

Lukas turned a heavy head to eye a huge man with a thick black beard. His two companions looked upon Lukas with the same measure of concern, their common features clearly marking them as family, perhaps even brothers. They shared a silent glance, then the big man lifted the flap of the leather satchel slung over his shoulder and pulled out some type of bar wrapped in thin, glistening packaging.

"Here," he said, peeling back the wrapper and offering the food to Lukas. "Eat this."

Lukas accepted the gift, feeling lightheaded and hungry enough that he might have eaten dirt if the men had offered it and called it a meal. The bar was thick, chewy, and nearly tasteless, leaving a faint trace of chemical processing on his tongue. His jaw ached as he chewed, but it was better than nothing.

"Come with us," the man said. "We know a safer place than this."

When the companions stooped to help Lukas to his feet, he did nothing to protest their sudden, unexpected kindness. They led him down two, maybe three different side streets—he could not focus enough to discern any of it—then came to a wide, metal staircase recessed between two storefronts that had closed for the night, their front doors and windows covered in double sets of steel bars. The large man descended the stairs, and Lukas was guided down behind him by the two companions, one on either side of him.

The underground room they'd entered expanded in all directions, the massive, domed ceiling rising farther above them than Lukas had thought possible underground. The entirety of this ceiling was one giant screen, where the characters of this city's language flashed, scrolled, and danced in flickering alerts. The place seemed to be an open marketplace, full and busy even at this hour but far cleaner, more relaxed, less pestilent than the streets above. Various groups of people gathered in front of vendor carts or at hastily flashing screens on the far wall. These projected some kind of game, judging by the cheers and congratulatory pats on the back one man received when he pressed something on the screen. Lukas bit off another piece of the food bar and took it all in, only briefly aware in the back of his mind that he was, in fact, the only man here missing his clothes.

His three guides moved silently toward one of these gathered groups a few yards down the marketplace from the bottom of the staircase. Several dozen people sat on the ground in various stages of repose, sharing meals and drinks, talking in low tones, laughing good-naturedly. But they all seemed to be waiting for something, Lukas realized. Then he noticed every person among them turned slightly toward a figure sitting in the middle of this haphazard semi-circle. This man did not engage in much conversation, though he seemed to be participating in every individual discussion with a kind glance and a smile, a nod here and there. He sat cross-legged, relaxed and confident, occasionally running a hand across his short beard when he smiled.

Lukas let himself be led toward this group, wondering what this small crowd was waiting for. His new companions sat at the outer circle of those gathered, and Lukas steadily lowered himself to the ground once more, grateful that no one seemed to notice him at all. Just as the man in the center of the gathering opened his mouth to speak, an explosion of angry voices echoed down the staircase toward the market. Seconds later, half a dozen men trudged into the underground meeting room, two of them ushering a wide-eyed woman before them who stumbled down the stairs and gazed about for anyone she recognized or who might help her.

This assembly made their loud, bickering way toward the crowd where Lukas and his new friends sat. He noticed a few of the others whisper to each other, looking concerned and frightened until they turned to the peaceful man sitting in their midst. He merely eyed the newcomers with an open patience, waiting to see what they would do or say when they reached him. The man's gracious presence itself seemed enough to put his gathered friends at ease, and then the men and the frightened woman were upon them.

"Jesse," said the man leading the chaotic procession. It came out as more of a shout despite how close he stood to the man seated almost at his feet. "This woman is an adulteress. I've seen it with my own eyes." His neighbor yanked the frightened woman forward by the wrist, glaring at her as she lurched forward and lowered her gaze. "The Law and the Phar-asai demand that we hand her over to the Janiss-arai for execution. I want to know what you say we should do with her."

Silently, the man called Jesse leaned down over his crossed legs and with delicate fingers began to draw unseen shapes on the floor before him. There was a bright flash overhead, and then colored characters and symbols Lukas still did not understand appeared on the holographic ceiling. They shone first huge and bright, apparently as the man drew them upon the floor, then faded into some semblance of written word. Lukas found himself wishing now more than ever that he'd seen this language before. Some of the gathered people around him looked up to read what appeared on the ceiling, but most of them watched the man who put the words there himself.

"Well?" the angry man prompted, far more irritated than Lukas thought the situation warranted.

Jesse stood slowly and turned to the scowling newcomers and the woman in their grasp. Her head remained bowed, but even from where he sat, Lukas saw the tears streaking down her face beneath the curtain of dark hair.

"Which of you here hasn't broken the Law in some form, whether in your heart or silent thoughts?" Jesse's brows flickered slightly inward, but he remained entirely calm, gazing at the gathered crowd before turning toward the half-dozen men surrounding the silently crying woman. "The man who's never done that is the man who should take this woman to the Janiss-arai."

The angry men stared at Jesse, then the leader finally caught sight of the glowing glyphs shining upon the domed ceiling and took a step back, as if what he read there surprised him, and his eyes grew wide. Then he turned and stalked away. A few others opened their mouths as if to speak, but when they read the words, they too deflated in their purpose and left. The man holding the woman by the wrist looked back and forth from her to the characters on the ceiling, then released her as though he'd just realized she was someone else. He blinked, eyed Jesse with something between fear and gratitude, then lowered his gaze and walked away behind his fellows.

With a shaking sigh, the woman closed her eyes and sank to her knees. Jesse approached her and lifted her chin with a gentle hand so that she gazed up at him with teary eyes.

"Is no one going to turn you in?" he asked, no hint of either amusement or disgust upon his features. If Lukas had not watched this whole scene unfold, he would have thought these two knew each other very well indeed.

"No one, Teacher," the woman whispered. Her rigid demeanor shifted and softened, as if she'd just sunk into a padded chair before a full meal and a fire.

"I won't either." Jesse bent and placed his hands on the woman's arms, helping her to stand again. "Go," he said. "Walk in a Way that honors God and honors yourself."

The woman took a deep breath, gazing into the man's eyes with wonder and devotion and gratitude from the unexpected mercy, then nodded. The corners of her mouth turned up in a shy smile, as if she'd never expected to smile again, and her entire face brightened. Jesse lowered his hands, and the woman walked off into the moving bodies within the underground marketplace, turning back once for another glance before she disappeared.

A few of the gathered onlookers whispered new conversations, not in any way critical toward either the dispersed group of angry men, nor the adulterous woman freed from her otherwise certain fate. Instead, Lukas caught the hushed tones of awe and recognition, of agreement and admiration. He wanted to hear what they said more clearly and he leaned forward, his gaze absently flickering around the group sitting in front of him.

Jesse sat again among his friends, and Lukas found himself

unexpectedly trapped in the man's piercing gaze. He froze, and for a moment, time seemed to stop completely. It felt as though Lukas were the only man in the room, perhaps the only man in all of existence; such was the intensity of compassion and pure presence glistening behind Jesse's eyes. Lukas's heartbeat pounded in his ears, overwhelming him just enough to make him forget his recent torment and the destruction he'd witnessed hours before. But then a shame bloomed in the back of his mind, some otherworldly wrongness he couldn't quite pinpoint, like a deep, persistent itch below so many layers of muscle. Captured in Jesse's stare, he felt as if he were drowning in a forgiveness he did not deserve—that he himself, out of all the souls on this Earth, was the least worthy to receive such a gift of being *known* by this man, inside and out. There was something about the man's eyes...

The large bearded man beside Lukas cleared his throat and laid a hand once more on Lukas's shoulder. At the same instant, Jesse looked away from Lukas, his attention redirected to one of his friends. Lukas, though, found himself longing to gaze upon this kind stranger for just a few moments longer.

"It's getting late," the bearded man said beside him. "Time for a real meal and a clean bed, hmm?"

Lukas turned in the direction of his new guide, but his eyes remained on Jesse. "Who is he?" he asked, his voice hoarse with exhaustion and wonder.

"Jesse?" Lukas nodded.

"He's a teacher. Not a teacher of the Law, but he's come to show us a new Way." The man said it quite simply, as if that were all the explanation anyone would ever need, but his words danced with humbled admiration. "Come." He stood, and the other two men who had supported Lukas into this meeting room helped him once again to his feet.

Finally, Lukas managed to turn toward his generous companions and glanced at each of them in turn. "You don't know me at all," he said, and his brows knitted together against his will in shame of his hardship and confused appreciation. "Why are you helping me?"

The bearded man placed a hand over his heart and briefly dipped his head. "I am Cephas. This is Yaakov." He gestured to the man who had given Lukas the small bit of food from his satchel. "And his brother Yohanan." Each of them nodded at their introductions. Cephas smiled. "Now you know us. We are fortunate enough to be able to give what we can to aid others." He briefly glanced down at Lukas's near nakedness, the bruises covering his body, the dirt of his escape from the compound, and the gritty, stinging scrapes on his neck and cheek from when he'd fallen at the Phar-asai's electric rod. "You are clearly a man in need, and this is our Way." Lukas swallowed and tried to return the smile, though it felt forced and wary still. "Come," Cephas repeated. "We can discuss everything after a bit of food and rest."

With a meek nod, Lukas allowed these men to lead him further down a corridor branching off from the main meeting room beneath the huge domed ceiling. He glanced back once more to look at Jesse; the man still sat in the crowd, his head bent slightly as he listened with a faint smile to the words spoken to him by friends.

———

At the far end of the domed marketplace, Nehmiah clasped his hands together beneath the wide folds of his robe's leather sleeves. No one had paid him much attention in the last half hour he'd stood here, away from the crowds. They had most assuredly noticed his presence but kept a respectful distance. As one of the Phar-asai, he made his presence known when he wished and remained in the shadows when he desired at least a semblance of anonymity.

Beside him, Hylas grunted from within the dark hood of his own Phar-asai robes. "You knew he would be here?"

Nehmiah lifted his head but remained silent another moment, letting his peer guess a few more seconds as to the purpose of their visit. It had been a long time since he'd been required to wield the power of his silver rod in punishment, and having sent some vile, brain-addled stranger in foreign garb crashing to the ground in the middle of Camar Street had left him in a fouler mood than usual.

Finally, he spoke. "Jesse has been coming down here for weeks now. Mostly at this time of night, but recently, these desperate fools have flocked to him during the day, too."

Hylas hissed out a sigh beside him. "The man is a heretic and a fraud. He blasphemes the Law with his prattle of forgiveness and love while ignoring justice and holiness—" The man fell silent when Nehmiah turned to fix him with a disgusted glare.

"You think I need a lecture on the Law?"

The other Phar-asai glanced quickly away with a small shake of his head. "Forgive me."

Slowly, reveling just a bit in his companion's masked fear, Nehmiah returned his attention to the guileless charlatan. Jesse was still surrounded by the hopeless men so bent on licking up the crumbs of blasphemy the false priest fed them.

"I do not wish to see our people more agitated or our city more disturbed than they already are. Something must be done."

"You know what that is," Hylas said. Though the man clearly tried to mask it as a statement, Nehmiah felt and heard the hopeful question behind the other Phar-asai's words.

His lips curled up in a sour, devious smirk. "I have an idea, yes."

9

Lukas could not fully comprehend the graciousness of his new host, leaving him skeptical and a little wary of the man. His three guides had led him into Cephas's home—a small apartment half underground with low ceilings and gray, stuccoed walls riddled with cracks. The inside of the man's dwelling boasted very little of the flashing, scrolling holographic surfaces found in the city streets and Lukas found his mind finally able to settle into a semblance of peace.

Yaakov and Yohanan apparently knew their way around Cephas's home intimately; while Cephas heated some food Lukas did not recognize over the small, two-burner stove placed against the far wall of the main room, the brothers stepped off together into a side room and returned with a small metal box and a metal bowl of slightly warm water. The metal box was dented, the latches on the sides bent so completely that it did not lock. Yaakov placed this on the low table in the center of the main room and opened the lid on squeaky hinges. Then he set to laying out an array of items Lukas had never seen as well as what looked like linen bandages and some type of salve or ointment. Yohanan placed the bowl in front of Lukas, eyed him with a nod, then went to sit beside his brother on the mound of drab-colored pillows surrounding the low table.

Lukas eyed the bowl of water, wondering why it was on the ground and not the table. He bent to dip his hands in it, quickly warming to the idea of washing his face despite the strangeness of doing so in the company of three other men and in Cephas's living room. But when Yaakov clicked his tongue, Lukas stopped, looked up, and noted the man's pointed and unmistakable nod toward Lukas's bare feet caked with dirt and grime and God only knew what else.

Some shock of recognition went through Lukas then—some feeling of having been here before. With it came a new wave of shame burning up the sides of his neck until he was sure he was blushing; he berated himself for not having automatically known the water was for washing his own feet until he remembered he could not possibly have anticipated the ritual practices of a people he had only just discovered.

Tentatively, he peeled the noxious, now clearly useless sock from one foot to find it had done almost nothing in keeping the filth of the city streets from reaching his skin. Some black substance lined his foot and glistened a little in the dim lighting of Cephas's home. He lifted his leg and aimed a pointed toe at the water. When he glanced up at Yaakov again, the man eyed him sideways, nodded almost imperceptibly, and returned to laying out the items from within the gray box. It seemed counterintuitive to attempt uncaking so many layers of filth from the soles of his feet despite having only lost his boots a few hours before, but the water was surprisingly effective in doing so, and it made him wonder if some form of cleanser had been added.

When he'd done this with both feet, Yaakov handed Lukas a thin, rough towel. The brothers watched him silently, looking both entirely at ease and yet still expectant of something Lukas could not begin to guess. He dried his feet, then Yaakov took the towel and placed it in his lap. Then, apparently satisfied with this first step, the man focused his attention on the items arranged before him on the table. There were a number of flesh-colored strips Lukas thought were bandages, designed in various widths and lengths. Beside them rested what resembled a thick pen with a two-inch plastic box attached to the end. Orange symbols flashed across this box, and Yaakov slid a cartridge into place within it before turning to Lukas with another nod.

He gestured to his guest's face, and Lukas was made aware again of the constantly stinging scrape upon his cheek. He brought his fingers to it briefly, felt what he hoped was only crusted blood and nothing else, and nodded back at Yaakov. The man raised the pen-like instrument, pressed the end of it to Lukas's cheek, and there came a small click followed by a sharp burn spreading across his face, making his eye water.

"What is that?" he asked, noting how quickly the pain receded.

"Antiseptic," Yaakov replied with a small smile. Then he lifted the smallest of the flesh-colored bandages and without having to peel away a backing or secure it in any way, he pressed this over the cut on Lukas's cheek, where it stayed.

Lukas wondered how long he'd have to walk around looking a little foolish with a bandage plastered to his face until he watched Yaakov administer the same care to the rest of the lacerations and raw burns he'd sustained from his escape into the world Above and during his disrobing in the street. The sting of the antiseptic pen became a familiar, pleasant buzz, and the bandages, while he felt their weight and saw them shimmer, seemed to melt into him until they had either camouflaged against his flesh convincingly or had become his flesh itself. It surprised him to find he could not tell the difference. He watched Yaakov closely, and though he could not read the symbols flashing on the box attached to the antiseptic pen, the result was not lost on him; with every use, the symbols became one less, until only two remained. With all the sick, dirty, destitute people Lukas had seen in the streets and alleyways of this strange new city, he imagined supplies like these were difficult to come by and perhaps expensive. The guilt of having so much of it used on him mixed with his gratitude, and he had no choice but to focus on the kindness these strangers had freely given him.

Yohanan, silent, rose once more to take the metal bowl of now blackened water out of the room. He returned with a set of thin, faded tan pants and a long, wide tunic. He offered these to Lukas, who thanked him and dressed himself with more ease than his exhaustion warranted. The clothing was simply made and loose-fitting, reminding him of his black sparring uniform with a pang of loss. That uniform itself did not make him a Hedge Master, but he'd grown fond of it over the years.

Somewhat cleaner, thoroughly bandaged, and fully dressed, Lukas was less surprised than he'd expected to feel his stomach knotting in hunger and his mouth watering at the mere sight of Cephas finally coming to join them at the low table. He carried a thin, gray plastic tray with four plastic bowls on it. From these uncurled rivulets of steam, bringing with them a scent not unlike freshly baked bread with a sour, astringent tang. The more the odor reached his senses, though, the more that unsettling undertone strengthened. Cephas set the bowls on the table, each of them containing a thick, plastic spoon, and then brought out four plastic cups and a canteen. The bottle hissed when he cracked the seal, then he placed it in the center of the table. Yohanan took it upon himself to pour what looked like water, but was undoubtedly not pure water, from the canteen into each of their cups. Lukas took a long draft of his drink before choking on the acridly chemical liquid, a tinge of something perhaps meant to be strawberry lingering in the back of his throat.

Cephas gave him an apologetic smile and lifted his own cup to his lips. Then he nodded at the bowl in front of Lukas containing a gray, gruel-like substance with flecks of black mixed throughout. "What it lacks in flavor," he said, "it makes up for in nutrition. And it will keep you full."

Lukas watched the brothers lifting sticky spoonfuls of the stuff to their own lips, so he followed their lead. Cephas's attempt to warn him of the taste could not have been more of an understatement; the stuff tasted like millet flavored with dish soap. Lukas quickly swallowed the first bite and, for lack of a better option, washed it down with the burnt-strawberry water. He tried as much as he could not to make a face and wanted to apologize for such an ungracious reaction until he noticed the stifled smiles on the brothers' faces and the acknowledging smirk from Cephas as he chewed the awful mash himself.

But the man had been right in that it filled Lukas's belly with a warm, surprisingly satisfying weight, and he felt his strength returning. Sitting there on the pillows, the foursome ate together in silence, and Lukas took it upon himself to refill the empty cups from the canteen halfway through; it was the least he could do to show his gratitude during the silent, painstaking meal and it gave him some semblance of autonomy over his own person, so lacking since he'd entered this strange new world just after sunset.

Finally, when they had finished every morsel of the gruel with a solemn acknowledgment of necessity, Yohanan stood, collected the plastic dishes, and took them to what was either a sink or a low basin for washing beside Cephas's tiny stove. Just like with the medical supplies, Lukas guessed these men went to great lengths to afford and procure even food and drink such as this; though they obviously did not find any of it pleasing to the senses, they'd grown accustomed to it and looked far healthier and with more vitality than those dozens of coughing, dirty, sore-riddled, homeless people Lukas had seen in the streets. And his new benefactors gave everything of what they had to him, nothing more than a stranger in need, as if they were kings with plenty to spare.

Sucking the last of the bitter, sticky morsels from between his teeth, he nodded at the brothers, then at Cephas. "I can't thank you enough," he said, sounding even to himself far more like the man he'd been when this nightmare of a day had started. "And I'm not quite sure how I can repay you for all this."

Cephas smiled and wiped at his thick beard and mustache. "You can start by telling us a bit about yourself, if you like."

Lukas dipped his head, feeling quite embarrassed for the fact that he had offered so little of himself; they had seen him hungry, beaten, and nearly stripped naked, and he hadn't even told them his name.

"My name is Lukas," he said, then swallowed thickly as he tried to decide how next to approach his odd introduction. "I'm sure you've realized by now that I'm not from here." Yohanan's smothered chuckle was not unkind, making Lukas grateful for a little levity under the circumstances. "I'm from a place... well, by the sea." He caught the quick glance shared between the brothers but forged ahead. "A military force I've never heard of attacked my home, and they... they destroyed everything. Almost everything. They took my cousins as prisoners. They also stole our research and... important developments."

He pressed his lips together and stared at the smooth, worn surface of the table. "I can't explain what it is or why it's so important, but I have to get it back. Free my cousins. There's nothing left for me to return to, so I came here. But I realize I can't go to your authorities." Yaakov shook his head, as if disgusted by the simple fact that what passed for authority in this place did little to aid the citizens of the city. "I don't know my way around, and I don't know the laws here. If you can show me, help me how to navigate the city to find what I'm looking for, I will do anything I can to repay you for your troubles. I'm sorry to ask for more after everything you've already done for me." It felt like an abrupt end and such a condensed summary of Lukas's recent horrors, though describing them even like this seemed to make it all the more real. He finally looked up at Cephas, who smiled and nodded.

"You've been through a lot," the man said. "And we recognize hard times when they fall upon any man. Knowing we've helped you is thanks enough."

"We'll do whatever is in our means to help you get where you need to be," Yaakov added.

Yohanan merely smiled and nodded his silent support.

"Thank you," Lukas said softly, overwhelmed again by the inexplicable kindness of these men. "I—"

A light double knock came at Cephas's low, slightly skewed front door. Without waiting for an invitation, whoever it was on the other side pushed the door inward. The grate on the bottom of the door sticking upon the rough, cracked floor seemed particularly jarring in the moment. All four men turned to see a woman step into Cephas's tiny apartment; she stopped briefly when she noticed the stranger sitting among them.

Though she dressed far more plainly now, it would have been impossible for anyone not to recognize her as the same woman Lukas had seen singing on the massive projection while he sat on the curb a few hours before. She wore a simple, undyed shift that fell just above her ankles, the sleeves long enough for only her hands to show, and the loose cut of her garb nearly swallowed the whole of her figure that had been so apparent in that moving image of her with the dead branch bursting to life. Her hair, though, remained loose and spilled over her shoulders in dark, glistening waves. She turned her wide, dazzling brown eyes upon Lukas, then addressed Cephas.

"Am I interrupting something?"

"No, Marya. No," he replied and waved her to the table to join them. "This is Lukas. Marya," he told his guest, "comes with us sometimes to listen to Jesse's teachings. She also follows his new Way."

"Have you seen him yet?" she asked Lukas as she knelt on the pillow between Cephas and Yaakov.

For a moment, Lukas found himself without words, recognizing the fact that these people had so quickly and easily accepted his presence without question. "I have."

Marya nodded in greeting to the brothers, who returned the gesture in silence. "Lukas was just telling us a little of himself," Cephas told her, "and asked if we might show him around the city so he may more easily seek what he came here to find."

The woman took a deep breath. "I know the city very well," she told Lukas, her voice as gentle and lilting in speech as it had been in song. "Perhaps better than most. Before I found Jesse and started listening to his teachings, I had... many different experiences." She blinked and quickly glanced down at the table in front of them. Lukas thought he saw her cheeks coloring, but the low lighting overhead made it hard to tell. "In nearly every level of the streets."

Some unnamed tension filled the small space among them, and then Cephas brought his hands together with a soft clap. "That settles it, then. Marya will help you through the city, Lukas. But that can wait for tomorrow. It's late, and after the trials that brought you here, I imagine you'd like to rest."

With a wary smile, Lukas nodded.

"Good. Yaakov, will you show Lukas to the spare room upstairs?" Yaakov stood, and Cephas turned to Lukas again. "You'll be safe here tonight, my friend. Sleep well."

"Thank you." Lukas slowly pulled himself up to stand. He did, admittedly, feel immediately better for the medical attention and the food. For the first time since the lab was destroyed, he found in the moment a deep sense of peace. He followed Yaakov to the opposite end of the main living area. In the corner was a steep, narrow staircase, and he followed the man up the short flight of steps to the upper floor.

With so many people crowded into the city streets and the

lower levels, Lukas was surprised that Cephas's apartment had a second story at all, though the ceilings here were perhaps a little lower than those downstairs. Only three doors existed in the short, unadorned hallway, and Yaakov opened the middle door at the far end and nodded for Lukas to enter.

"Good night," he said quietly and headed back down the hall.

The room was small and simple, lit softly by a glowing circle in the center of the ceiling, which only gave off as much light as a candle flame. A thin pallet with one pillow and two thin blankets rested on the floor against the far wall. Beside this were strewn a few more pillows for sitting, and just above these was a small, squat window covered by two thin shutters. He pulled them open, curious to see what view might greet him through the window. The shutters were an important necessity; neon-green light flooded the small room, glaring violently from the holographic screen lit up on the closest building. Lukas assumed this was another complex of crowded apartments; he could have touched the next building with his fingertips if he leaned far enough out the window. Peeking his head out the window so he could look upward, he thought that even the morning light would not improve the foreboding dreariness of the black-stained skyline filled with roiling clouds, and he had a feeling even those would remain right where they were.

Pulling his head back into the room, he closed the shutters and was struck by how fortunate he'd been to spend his entire life within the Qumranian compound where his view of the Agricultural Sector had greeted him every day with such hope and inspiration. Feeling a jolt of motivation just thinking about Qumran, Lukas instinctively went into his morning Hedge Master calisthenics, and in a flash, he was doing a one arm hand-stand. His body was completely still, with no tremble or shake. Lukas could hear his father's voice in his head as he lowered his face to the floor and then back up. "It's not about strength. It's about mastering leverage and physics; strength is the result." Continuing on, he pumped out twenty more up-downs from his one-armed handstand position. Now that he was warmed up, he raised up to his fingertips. His body never moved, only his elbow like a piston... up, down, up, down. With his final push-up he pushed his entire body completely off the ground and high enough into the air to allow him the space needed to rotate his feet downward and alight on the ground, bending his knees perfectly to absorb his weight and keep him from making any detectable sound.

Taking a few cleansing breaths, Lukas put his focus back into his current circumstance. Tucking his thoughts of Qumran away, as they were only a distraction to him right now. He didn't need them for motivation, and he didn't need them to help him grasp what was at stake as he completely understood that if he failed, all that would remain of Qumran, would be his memories.

With a sigh, he lowered himself onto the pallet, left his new clothes on, and slipped under the blankets. The pillow offered him just the right amount of softness beneath his head, and he fell asleep quickly and with almost no reluctance.

When Cephas finished recounting the brief, vague description Lukas had provided earlier, Marya took a deep breath and studied her clasped hands in her lap. Yaakov had returned to his seat at the table, and the four of them sat in ponderous silence for a few moments.

"Do you think..." She knew she had no reason here to feel foolish for the question, but she couldn't quite bring herself to fully acknowledge her own suspicions. "Do you think he's from Qumran?" When she looked up at Cephas, he only raised his brows in response. "Is he the one we were..." She cleared her throat. "Jesse said we should watch for—"

"Lukas is that man," Cephas said, sparing her the discomfort of searching for the words she wanted. He reached out to gently pat the tops of her clasped hands. "Let him tell you in his own time, hmm?"

Marya nodded. When she looked up at Yaakov and Yohanan, she found the same bubbling excitement glistening behind their eyes. They felt it too—the change brewing all around them. She'd do anything she could to help this new impossible stranger, if Lukas was in fact the man Jesse thought him to be. So much awaited all of them, and though she tried to remind herself that these things took time and nothing yet was certain, she found herself thrilled by the prospect this future promised.

10

Lukas tossed upon the thin pallet, so disturbed by the dream, it moved him even in sleep.

It filled him with such joy and painful longing to see he stood within the lush, rolling fields of his home, beyond the Agricultural Sector where the land was open and tended only for the sake of the animals that grazed there and for people to walk under the clean, brilliant sky. The darkness of night brushed across his home as well, but in place of the gently luminescent ceiling panels under which he'd spent his entire life, the sky was open, pitch-black, and studded with stars. The round globe of the true moon, though Lukas still had not yet seen it with his own eyes, filled this dark sky above him, casting an otherworldly glow upon the hills within the underground caverns.

Just over the rise of the closest hillside stood Marya. She wore a dark, flowing gown studded with gems, as though the night sky had drifted down to dress her in itself. And she sang.

The haunting tune echoed in this place, coming at Lukas from the thick, expansive walls of the compound he'd called home. And then, almost as if the moon itself were joy and happiness and peace, the stronger Marya's song raced through the caverns, the faster the moon above them dimmed.

Lukas wanted to go to her, to ask her to be careful. He felt as if her song, whether or not he understood the words, endangered her more than helped her—that if she kept singing, the moon's darkening would be joined by her own disappearance. He thought she might sing herself out of existence.

Down from the night sky and up from the lightless crevices of the hills and stretching stone, darkness stirred. At first, it was just a slithering coil, a flutter of dark wings, but these took only seconds to grow into something more. Shrouded figures rose out of nothingness and shadow, swooping across the rolling hills, filling what remained of the fading moonlight spilled across the meadow. They made no sound, had no true form, but they were undeniably there.

Still, Marya sang. As if she moved through water, she turned her head ever so slowly, and when her gaze fell upon Lukas and locked with his own, he saw her as if she stood mere inches away instead of across the field. She seemed completely oblivious to the menacing figures moving toward her, reaching for her, stretching impossibly long to cover the distance. Only when they were upon her did she seem to recognize the danger. As a final act of defense, she brandished the dead branch in her hand, raising it before her face like a shield.

An uncurling, smoky limb without features jerked from the mass of blackness, reaching toward her like the head of a snake before it struck the branch. Marya's insufficient weapon snapped in two, one half tumbling into darkness. But her song did not waver, even when the remaining half of the branch in her hand burst into life. Budding flowers and green shoots sprouted from the dead wood, illuminating the space around her with golden light, a brief echo of birdsong, a wave of fresh air and hope. It was strong enough to drive the roiling black forces away from her, but only for a few seconds. Then, as if the absence of more defenses renewed their deadly intent, the shadows fell upon her from all directions.

The last thing Lukas saw was a flash of green leaves beside one wide, despairing eye still staring at him. Then Marya was consumed by the wave of darkness, and her song was cut abruptly and left to ring out, unfinished, through the emptiness.

11

He thought he'd awakened before dawn, though even if he'd opened the shutters over the single window to peer outside, Lukas doubted he would have recognized the time of day beneath the soot-stained sky. Now, he felt fully awake and a little disturbed by the remnants of his new dream. It differed so drastically from the repeating nightmares he'd had of the compound's destruction before his life had been upended. He hadn't taken the time to think of his dreams before this; they seemed so inconsequential compared to what he'd endured and what he now faced. But he realized with a sick, twisted guilt that all the nights he'd spent in his own living quarters, dreaming of death and destruction and failure, had in fact been more premonition than anxious expectation of his team's success. The horrors that had wracked the Qumranian compound were so very much like what had filtered into his cyclical dreams that he could not help thinking he should have paid more attention to them. And he worried this new dream might herald something truly awful for Marya.

Shifting slowly out of the blankets and the low pallet on the floor, Lukas stood and tentatively stretched his limbs. The deep ache of his weariness had faded with food and care and a night of sleep, though his shoulder was still a little tender and the dryness in the air stung his nose and eyes. But he was ready to face whatever the day had in store, hoping it would be as fruitful in discovery and assistance as the night before.

He straightened the blankets on the pallet and stepped out of his room in Cephas's apartment. The door swung silently open, and he moved down the short hallway to descend the stairs, not knowing what he'd find when he stepped into the main living room. Nothing was out of place or particularly surprising, but the scent filling the room made him wonder if he was still dreaming.

Cephas turned from the small stove beside the front door just as Lukas stepped away from the staircase in the corner. The man's beard twitched beneath his smile, and he headed toward the low center table with his tray, this time laden with a small plastic pitcher between the two cups.

"How did you sleep?" he asked, laying the tray on the table before he knelt on the pillows and gestured for Lukas to join him.

"I feel much better," Lukas replied, hesitant to fully embrace where he was for fear Cephas would somehow change his mind about having him in his home. But he joined his host at the table, eyeing the pitcher. "Is that... coffee?"

Cephas let out a low chuckle, then poured the thick black liquid into the two plastic cups. "It is indeed," he said, then glanced up at his guest. "I hear they use cream and sugar in the upper levels, but I don't quite understand how anyone can justify wasting such things on sludge like this." He finished pouring and handed Lukas a plastic cup warmed by its piping contents. "If I lost my sense of taste, this drink would not improve. But it does what it was meant to do."

Lukas nodded, then raised the cup to his lips and took a slow sip. Cephas had not understated the flavor; what passed for coffee here was thick and syrupy without any of the sweetness, almost as if the beans that had been ground to make this—if they even were coffee beans here—had been filled with mud as well. But it brought him energy and warmth and comfortable familiarity, and he kept drinking.

"Marya will be here soon," Cephas said, blowing on the surface of his own drink before slowly sipping it. "I thought you'd want to get started as soon as possible."

"Thank you." Lukas didn't quite know how it would make him feel to see the woman with the memory of his dream still so fresh, but he didn't want to talk about that now, either.

"Are you hungry?"

Lukas blinked at his host, momentarily stunned by how odd the question seemed. Then he realized he was not hungry at all; he felt as full as if he'd eaten the bowl of acrid gruel only an hour ago instead of the night before. "No, actually."

Cephas nodded. "Good. Sometimes, a bowl of what we had last night keeps me going for almost an entire day. But if you find yourself needing something else, ask Marya. She knows where to find passable food at a reasonable price. Some of the stuff they try to pass off as edible in the streets..." The man wrinkled his nose and shook his head.

He couldn't say why, but Lukas found himself amused by this, at least as far as he thought he could be amused by anything, given the circumstances. Before he could thank his host for the advice and ask just what it was they'd eaten the night before that could sustain a man for so long, the single knock came again at Cephas's front door. Again, Marya pushed it open and stepped into the small apartment without a response or invitation.

"Good morning," she said, closing the door behind her and taking a few steps into the main room.

"Coffee, Marya?" Cephas asked, nodding at the pitcher.

The woman clenched her eyes shut and shook her head. "No, thank you. That's..." She swallowed. "That's not coffee."

Cephas barked out a hearty laugh, nodding as if she'd just delivered a clever punchline. "I imagine you know what is," he said, then pulled on his beard.

Marya offered a subdued smile in return, not in embarrassment, Lukas noted, but as if she acknowledged the separate joke in Cephas's words—good-natured banter between two friends. "Are you ready?" she asked Lukas.

"Yes." He forced himself to down the rest of the coffee. It was still just a little too hot and made him cough afterward, but he didn't want to seem ungrateful in any way for wasting what had been so freely offered. Judging by the size and state of Cephas's apartment and the strange quality of the food shared, Lukas had a feeling his host had provided the very best of what little he had, and that this was not done very often, though Cephas had neither said nor done anything to hint at a sense of lacking or resentment.

"Perhaps I'll see you two later today in the lower marketplace," Cephas added, lifting his plastic cup toward them.

"I'm counting on it," Marya said. Then she opened the door again and stepped out of the apartment to wait. Lukas turned to give his host one final nod of gratitude, then closed the door behind him.

The narrow hallway of the apartment complex was wide enough for them to walk single-file. The doors to other homes pressed so closely together that Lukas was amazed at how so many people could actually exist in so small a space, though this apparent overpopulation more than accounted for the filthiness of the main streets, the noise, the homelessness, and the prevalent disease. Lukas hadn't thought to ask, but he wondered now what Cephas did for a living to afford even this much.

Once Marya led him out of the cramped hall and into the street, Lukas felt a little better for the comparative spaciousness around them. Even still, the streets were busy in the morning, full of people scurrying about to get where they needed to be.

The hovering, insect-like vehicles whizzed by overhead, the roar of some mechanical highway a constant background to the jingles, beeps, music, and shouted ads projecting at them from the holographic surfaces. Somehow, this made the city feel even dirtier, more desperate than it had under the darkness of the night before. Lukas glanced up briefly to find only a sliver of visible sky amid the rising towers and the buzzing crafts and the glare of neon screens. The morning light was just as bloody as the previous sunset, the haze stretching across the sky making him feel even more oppressed than he ever had during a lifetime underground.

Whether or not Marya picked up on his discomfort, she gave him a few moments longer to acclimate himself to the new sights of the day and the clamor of this unknown metropolis. She walked slowly but with purpose, keeping her eyes trained on some vague target in the distance. Only when a shout of surprise or a mourning wail rose over the din did she turn her head, and even then, it was brief and—Lukas guessed—just so she could make sure none of it was directed at them.

She'd said the night before that she would be the best person to show him around the city, so Lukas decided to wait for her guidance. Even if he'd wanted to ask questions, he had no idea where to begin; so many of them battled for dominance in his mind that he could not settle on any one enough to voice it aloud. And something told him he'd be discovering a little more than he bargained for, even under Marya's direction.

Finally, she broke the expectant silence between them. "I thought I'd show you the closest markets first." She turned her head only a little to eye him sideways as she walked. "The places that are safe to enter. Those that are not. The fastest routes back to Cephas's should you find yourself needing to lie low again."

"That's smart." His voice was low and a little scratchy, and while he meant it as a compliment and a kind of thank you, he noticed the corner of her mouth twitch up in a short-lived smirk.

"Last night, Cephas told me a bit of your story." She clasped her hands in front of her loose shift. "Did you come to the city from very far away? Somewhere on the outskirts?"

Lukas cleared his throat, not quite ready to reveal everything. He had no idea where that might land him, and he had a feeling that opening up to anyone here would change more than just their knowledge of him. "Something like that."

Marya nodded. "Had you heard much of this place before you decided to come?"

"Almost nothing." That was the truth. He knew of the Above, but only from the records and only as it existed before the orb was stolen.

Apparently, his dishonesty went unnoticed. "In ancient times, this place was called Jerusalem. Now, it is only 'the city'. It was conquered and destroyed in the Fourth World War and rebuilt as the Consortium's capital—"

"The Consortium?" It sounded ominous, but he'd never heard such a name.

"The governing body of the most powerful international corporations in the world. If you're not a member of the Consortium, you might as well not even exist. Most people here spend their lives toiling in hard labor, used and manipulated like tools that can be thrown away and easily replaced when they break. And so many of them do. There's a strict hierarchy matched with the different street levels of the city. In some ways, it's quite complicated to understand. In others, it's very simple. We follow the law, we don't attract attention to ourselves, and we're left mostly to our own devices."

"And the men in the leather robes. The Phar-asai," Lukas added. The word felt strange on his tongue as he spoke it aloud for the first time. "They're part of this governing hierarchy?"

"Yes. They are judges and teachers of the Law. At least, that's what they say of themselves and what they pretend to be. The Consortium pays them more than you could imagine to keep the peace on the lower street levels, and they have the explicit authority to do so by any means they choose. That tends to be through violence and fear, and they particularly enjoy reporting anyone who does not cower before them." Marya fought back a shudder, remembering her own experiences with the Phar-asai, then took a deep breath and continued. "It's almost impossible not to see them coming. It's the only time the streets fall silent. If you see them, keep your eyes down and wait until they pass. More often than not, they're just waiting for an excuse to kill someone."

"I met one of them yesterday," Lukas muttered, rubbing his shoulder and chest where the Phar-asai's electric rod had prodded him the night before.

She stopped so abruptly, Lukas took a few steps past her before he realized it. Then he stopped as well and turned to see what was wrong. A tiny frown flickered across her face. "You're lucky to be alive. Especially as a stranger here."

"I know." He'd escaped the worst of fates when he'd crawled through the fissure in the earth and away from his home's destruction, and he'd now apparently escaped being murdered by a lawless man simply for daring to address him.

Marya took a few deep breaths while continuing their path, appearing to try and regain herself after such an unexpected surprise. "I worry about Jesse in all this." Lukas listened intently at what now sounded very much like a confession. "It's a miracle he hasn't been arrested and carted off for sentencing, though he tells me constantly there is no reason to fear. It's easy to believe him entirely in the moment when he says these things. But when I'm alone... I find it harder to have faith."

"It sounds like you two are close."

She raised her eyebrows. "As close as anyone can be with Jesse, maybe. Before I met him, even before I heard him speak for the first time, I already believed nothing good existed in this life anymore. There were so many things that I—" Blinking, she glanced up at the sky and offered a wry smile. "Well, I thought nothing could change my mind. But the first time I listened to him, this strangely calm man who seemed immune to the things we face every day, I found myself thinking maybe there is a God. Maybe there's a better way, a different way to live our lives that brings hope and joy even to the darkest places of the world. To people who have never felt those things before. The first time I spoke to him myself... I felt I'd been given a second chance. No one down here ever gets a second chance."

The smile lighting up her face seemed to come from nowhere and everywhere at once, and Lukas couldn't help but wonder what that first conversation must have been like. He briefly imagined confronting Jesse to experience it himself, but what could he possibly have to say to the man who already seemed to know everything there was to know when he'd held Lukas's gaze? The memory of the man's dark, encompassing eyes brought a tingle up his spine that wasn't entirely unpleasant but made Lukas feel like he'd forgotten something crucial.

Up ahead, between two imposing buildings, the crowd seemed to ripple and swell, then broke away into hundreds of scattered fragments. People hurried away in every direction, their heads bowed low and their eyes trained on the filthy ground. As a path opened up amid the quickly retreating throng, Lukas saw four men huddled around something on the ground just within the alleyway. They wore the same long, thick leather robes as the Phar-asai, but these were all black. Nothing of their faces could be seen beneath the wide, draping hoods, but Lukas realized he didn't actually want to know what these men looked like. Then he realized the wrongness of what he saw; the figures carried a veil of darkness with them as they moved, as if they blocked what distorted sunlight there was with their very presence. The light around them, brilliant in comparison and fractured by the thousands of holographic displays in bright colors, stopped abruptly in an unearthly ring around them, and not even when they stepped out of the alleyway did their forms cast individual shadows upon the ground.

The black-robed men moved slowly away from where they'd gathered, and Lukas forgot about their lacking shadows when he saw what they'd left behind. A woman lay on the ground in the mouth of the alley, her simple shift stretched taut between her awkwardly sprawled legs and her arms lying beside her head as if she'd tried to protect herself. The dark, glistening wetness surrounding her was unmistakable; the blood already drenched most of her shift in a growing stain.

Lukas tensed, glancing quickly between the murdered woman and the four hooded men walking toward them. "What—"

The strength of Marya's hand clutching his wrist took him completely by surprise, and he whipped his head toward her, thinking something else had happened.

"Don't look at them," she whispered fiercely, her wide eyes locked onto his in terror mixed with desperate courage. "Don't turn your head. Don't say anything. Look at me."

He felt the heat of her hand through the long sleeves of his tunic, and thought he blinked maybe once during the stretching, agonizing seconds. She obviously tried to steady herself, but her breath came in short little bursts, as if even breathing too loudly would be the end of them both.

12

Lukas itched to turn around, to face head-on the attack he knew was coming. But Marya's gaze held him with a strength he never thought possible, and then she let out a long, trembling sigh. Her eyes flickered away from his and over his shoulder toward the woman lying in the alley in her own blood. Then she tentatively searched a wider vector of the street before finally releasing her grip on his wrist and taking a step back.

"They're gone," she said, blinking rapidly as if she'd embarrassed herself with her own fear. Lukas studied her, wanting to assuage her discomfort but having no idea what had just happened. "Let's keep moving." Marya resumed her steady pace down the sidewalk, and Lukas stepped into line beside her.

"What *was* that?" he asked, watching Marya intently, though she didn't look up at him again as they moved.

"Those are the Janiss-arai." She cleared her throat, and a small frown creased her brow. "Executioners. The Phar-asai deliver the sentence for breaking the law, and the Janiss-arai carry it out. They hide their faces so none may judge them, so they can protect their own honor while they destroy others'. They will never admit it, but I think it's to hide their shame.

Only a coward would hide behind a mask to justify such awful things." She'd clenched her fists at her sides, but lifted her head, regaining some control over herself and her emotions.

Lukas thought it might have been to compensate for the terror she hadn't been able to hide, though she hadn't cried out or collapsed or shed a tear. "What happens to the woman now?" he asked. "To... her body?"

"The guilty are left in the street." Marya shook her head. "We cannot touch them, so all will learn to fear the law and respect it."

Lukas found himself with a sudden piercing desire to help the victims of such cruel punishment; with it came a heavy guilt for the woman's death, though he knew there had been nothing he could do to stop it. "That's horrible."

"Among many other things here in the city. Yes." She nodded to a side street up ahead. "The fastest way to the best market is through there. The food is clean—as clean as it can be, anyway. For down here. But the syn-cred prices are decent."

"Syn-cred?"

"Syndicate credit." Lukas blinked, and her eyes widened. "The universal currency? You... you really must be from farther away than I thought if you've never heard of syn-creds."

Lukas tried to subdue the shrug he gave her, feeling once again put on the spot for an opportunity to tell this woman more of himself than he cared to reveal. She steered them down the narrow street when they approached it.

"Well, fortunately for you, there's a large number of people on the lower levels who have never had so much as a single credit to their name. Some of them don't even have accounts. We'll find a way to help you with that. It's possible to slip by unnoticed under the system, but if you're trying to learn the city and navigate it well enough to find your... was it your cousins you're looking for?" He nodded. "You'll have to blend in enough to not draw any more attention to yourself."

"Thank you." It was all he could think to say; he felt very much like a foreign creature in this new world, perhaps even a new species. All the knowledge he'd gained of the Above over the years had become entirely useless, and the obsoleteness overwhelming him sent a ripple of anger under his skin.

The new street down which they'd turned was far emptier than the main thoroughfare, though a few people walked quickly past them toward their own destinations. Lukas found himself on high alert for unnatural shadows and black robes; he did not wish to come directly upon any more Janiss-arai with less room to escape here than they'd had before.

A section of the building to their right flickered. The neon glyphs scrolling across its surface went completely black before being replaced by the image of a man's face. He had a short, pointed beard, oiled neatly to a thin point that curled at the end, and his eyes seemed more green than brown.

"Marya!" The voice echoed between the high walls of the buildings on either side of them, much louder than any of the previously clashing jingles and electronic chimes Lukas had already begun to ignore. Hearing her name, though, made Lukas pause. "My best girl," the voice continued, and the man on the screen seemed to be speaking directly to her. "So sweet, Marya. So pure. So sad..."

Marya closed her eyes, then reached out to nudge Lukas forward with a hand on his shoulder. "Ignore the screen," she muttered. "Let's keep going."

Lukas hurried along with her, and when he glanced back at the section of holographic screen, the sly-looking man there winked at him. Instantly, Lukas took a critical dislike to whoever this man was.

They moved at a brisk walk now, and another brightly lit ad flashed and gave way to the oiled man's face. "Marya," he said again, his syrupy voice sounding far more devious than reassuring. "You know you can't hide from me. Where have you been, hmm? Following that new man of yours? The one who spouts fantastic tales of God and the new Way?"

Marya hissed out what might have been a curse under her breath, and without another word, she broke into a run down a side street. Her thin sandals slapped against the rough, grimy stone road. The sound of it echoed around them, and Lukas was forced to jog quickly to keep up with her. Then he noticed how eerily silent the street had become, and how dark, without the constant neon flashing of the holographic images.

"Hey," he called to Marya, then moved a little faster to jog by her side again. "Hey, what's going on?"

"I don't have time to explain," she panted. "Just follow me."

Another patch of blank wall blinked on a few feet in front of them. "Don't run away from me, Marya," the slick man crooned. "How many times do I have to tell you?" They passed the projection, and another came to life ahead of them. "You're my best girl. I *own* you, Marya. You're bound to me."

Lukas almost kept running past her when she skidded to a halt in front of this projection and glared at the man's conniving smirk.

"I'm done with you," she shouted. "I follow Jesse. I listen to him, and I live by the Way."

The man delivered a sickly sweet grin. "That cult leader? He's just another pretender vying for power. Trying to be different. He'll be dead soon, Marya. The Consortium and the Pharasai will execute him just like everyone else who challenges their Law. And then what will you do? You'll have nothing. No other choice. I'm the only one who can protect you, my sweet girl. You need me. And you're very lucky I've decided not to hand you over to the Janiss-arai myself."

Marya growled in disgust and whirled away from the wall. Without looking at him, she grabbed Lukas's wrist again in her powerful grip and nearly dragged him further down the side street. She ran at full speed, releasing him to go faster, and Lukas was surprised by how much effort it took to keep up. Ahead, the street ended, forcing them to turn into the branching street on their left. Both buildings on either side lit with a dozen identical images of the man pursuing her, making it impossible not to look at him now.

"Who's that with you?" the man asked. His voice rose, slightly distorted with so many echoing versions of him, and they all stared with wide, amused eyes at the only two people now running down this backroad. "Did you find yourself a new friend, Marya?" He clicked his tongue against his teeth in mock disappointment. "I'm your only real friend. You know that, deep down. And I'm going to bring you home, little songbird. There's a big party tonight, and you're the *only* girl who can give my guests what I know they need. You have such special... gifts." He bit the tip of his tongue, raised an eyebrow, then broke into a slow chuckle.

Marya and Lukas passed all the images of the man and came to the backstreet's end. Slowing to a jog, they veered right into the branching alley, only to stop short at the sight of half a dozen large, glaring men walking toward them. Marya whirled around, maybe thinking they'd run back in the other direction, but four more men were already heading their way from that direction as well. One of them closed the small steel door at the entrance to the alley, and the loud clang of it filled the air.

The entire wall between the two groups of approaching men flashed with a much larger image of Marya's pursuer; Lukas could see the flecks of bright green in the man's hooded eyes and the dark crack splitting his front tooth. "Marya thinks she gets to decide when she sings and when she doesn't." His voice boomed around them, clearly addressing the men coming in on them from both sides as well as Marya herself—maybe even Lukas.

"Leave us alone!" she screamed, then glanced at Lukas. "And he has nothing to do with this. I paid off my debt to you, Boaz. I'm a free woman!"

Boaz tilted his head back and glanced at whatever sky or ceiling under which he stood. "*Oh*, my sweet girl," he crooned, then closed his eyes and clicked his tongue. The condescension in the shake of his head could not have been thicker. "You should know by now that I find you absolutely *invaluable*."

While Lukas realized the ten men closing in weren't here for him, he prepared himself for what he knew would come next—what he was incapable of ignoring, made for just this purpose. He swiftly stepped in front of Marya, putting her between him and the wall, eyeing the thugs stepping toward them from both sides. They formed a half-circle around their quarry, most likely to add to the feeling of being trapped. Lukas heard Marya's breath quicken behind him, but his rose and fell as steadily as if he were sleeping. And in a way, when his training kicked in and the awareness flooded through his muscles and his limbs and over every inch of his skin, others might have indeed called it a trance.

The first man to step toward him was remarkably large with a thick rope of a scar trailing from his temple down the side of his face to just beneath his chin. A number of smaller, cratered, burn-like scars marked the other cheek, and the man's lips parted in a sneer to reveal his brown, rotting teeth. A low, anticipatory chuckle rose from his barreled chest, and he bent his knees in what was either a ridiculous defensive stance or an attempt to taunt Lukas into rushing him first. With hands open at his sides, the man squeezed his fingers into fists, which set all his knuckles to popping, and wiggled them again in invitation.

Lukas took all this in without ever removing his gaze from the man's throat, where his soon-to-be attacker's pulse flared in his carotid artery beneath the bulging neck muscles. The only move he made in response was to close his stance until his feet lay directly in line with his hips, then he placed his fists behind his back against his sacrum, as though he were waiting to receive orders from a nonexistent commander. For decades, he had taken this stance in preparation for his father's instructions, and later as he waited for his own acolytes to open themselves to the knowledge he passed on to them in turn. Such a simple repositioning of his body into this exact pose was enough to trigger the automatic response in his system he'd spent his whole life conditioning.

Behind the scarred man, the other brutish predators snickered and jeered. It was quite obvious from their lax poses, folded arms, and slaps to their neighbors' backs that none of them expected to engage in a fight themselves, but they all eagerly awaited the entertainment their largest member would soon provide. This seemed to spur their champion on, who obviously had already developed a taste for his victim's blood; he grunted and chuckled again, shifting his weight from one foot to the other.

Lukas's vision further zeroed in on his opponent's neck, where the flaring artery twitched with the quickened rate of his heart and the adrenaline flooding his body. The Qumranian Hedge Master knew what this meant for other men, for his opponents, but he had not felt such a rise in himself since he'd mastered his heartbeat when he was eleven. He blinked, swept his gaze languidly across the semi-circle of thugs surrounding him, and felt his own heart slow to the steady, nearly timeless rhythm found under the calming heaviness of sleep or deep meditation. Now, he was the only man alive who had attained the perfection of control harnessed by the Hedge. He was ready.

13

"In ancient times, the teachers of the Law were so concerned our people would only strive to turn against it that they created hundreds of other covenants and decrees to mask the truth hidden behind them. An impenetrable labyrinth of precepts, with the Law at its very center."

Jebed paced across the large, empty room in Sector Four, one hand clasping the other wrist behind his back. He stopped in front of his son and positioned his feet squarely beneath his shoulders. The glint of silver thread in the frog fasteners, buttoned up his loose black Hedge Master uniform, caught the low light tracked across the ceiling. His gaze came to rest upon the wide brown eyes of the ten-year-old standing in loose white pants before him.

"They called this practice 'Building a Hedge Around the Torah'. When the Qumranians separated from Jewish society, under God's command and with His blessing, they took the Law with them underground and swore to protect and preserve this knowledge and its holy purpose. Now, this compound around us"—Jebed glanced around at the dark walls and ceiling—"has become the labyrinth. We Qumranians are the physical Hedge around the Truth at our center, and each one of us is sworn to protect it with our very lives."

He paused, waiting for his son's line of questions to begin. But the boy had taken remarkably quickly to this stage of his training. What once would have been an endless string of curiosity two months ago had settled into a silent patience in someone so young. Jebed masked the smile of pride threatening to break free and instead gave his son a single nod.

"Every Qumranian must be prepared to defend the compound at a moment's notice," he continued. "We are trained almost from birth to be perfect marksmen with our energy phasers and projectile weaponry. But more importantly, we must be masters of our own bodies. To unlock the powerful forces hidden away within every one of us. This is for hand-to-hand combat, where our enemies may even have weapons of their own and think us entirely unarmed. We are not. We have the Hedge."

From the corner of his eye, Jebed saw his son's subtle fidgeting, sliding his cloth, soft-soled shoe a little farther away from the other for a wider, more comfortable stance. When Jebed flicked his eyes toward the boy, he noticed with increased satisfaction that the wayward shoe slid quickly back into place.

"With the highly advanced study of human anatomy as the foundational training for the Hedge, we learn the best way to strike effortlessly and most efficiently where an enemy is most vulnerable. This includes an understanding of how to generate maximum force by harnessing natural momentum, most often through underhand strikes. Instead of throwing punches from an overhand position"—Jebed demonstrated by bringing a slow, swinging fist toward his son's face, pleased to see the boy didn't budge when knuckles pressed gently against his cheek—"the Hedge technique delivers blows originating from the waist and the body's core to drive through an enemy target."

The Hedge Master returned his hands to rest behind his

back, then brought an underhanded fist much more quickly toward his son's abdomen, stopping it just before he made contact with the soft flesh there. The force of even his subdued strike brought a gust of air stirring around his fist. It lifted his son's loose shirt and sent the fabric fluttering around his torso. The boy's eyes widened and he looked up at his father with a mixture of fear, relief, and admiration. Jebed nodded, then turned around and took a few steps back into the center of the room.

"A Hedge Master, like you yourself will become, Lukas, can even produce blows with a force ten times the punching power of a man three times his own size. One blow from a Hedge Master may crush bones, kill, or remove limbs and sever heads if the strike is delivered precisely and accurately in the perfect spot." He eyed the doorway, which led into the adjacent sparring room, and raised his head—the signal only his top students had been trained to recognize.

Two men in the same loose-fitting sparring uniform emerged through the doorway. More followed, and in pairs, the rest of the Hedge acolytes Jebed had asked to participate today filtered into the sparring room until twenty men and women in the same shade of gray spread out around both their Hedge Master and his young son.

Lukas eyed them each in turn, the ghost of a smile parting his lips; Jebed knew his son recognized most of these acolytes, having grown up in their company. But he also knew that small amount of amusement on Lukas's part would be quickly stripped away by the lesson his father had planned for him today. "The Hedge technique will teach you to account for all enemy targets at once. You will learn to continually reposition yourself for the statistically greatest chance of avoiding discharged weapon fire while also disarming or disabling your adversaries."

Lukas seemed to understand the hidden intent behind his

father's message. He glanced up at Jebed with wide eyes, his breath quickening only a little. Jebed knew his son was ready, that this training would push Lukas to his limits and beyond. The harsh lessons were those that left the longest-lasting impressions. And for his son, that lesson began today.

A single nod from the Hedge Master was all his acolytes needed. Slowly, with calculating assuredness, the twenty students stepped inward as one to close the ring around the boy in white who had yet to enter the fierceness of adolescence.

14

Lukas looked at the man with the scar running down his face knowing he would indeed be surprised when he realized what Lukas could do. None of the people in this alley, in the city, in the world Above had ever seen the Hedge performed and meted out. In the back of his mind, a small sliver of regret sliced through Lukas's awareness; it was a shame he had to use it now, Above, when his home and the Hedge Masters who had trained beside him were now all vanished. But he remained, and he would use the gifts and the training that had passed down through generations of Lukas's people.

Finally, his opponent made the first move. The giant man stepped forward swiftly, with more agility and grace than his size implied, and delivered a surprisingly perfect right hook that would certainly destroy its target and most assuredly always had. But for Lukas, in his heightened state of awareness, the man was still too slow.

Before his attacker had swung halfway through his vicious right hook, Lukas released his right fist from its place at the small of his back, as if his entire arm were a loaded gun set with a hair-trigger. His knees bent only slightly—this man was indeed large enough not to have to crouch—and Lukas's fist drove up into the man's chest in that sweet spot just below the center of his sternum.

He watched it all as if the world moved through syrup—his knuckles landing the upper-cut with terrible precision; the give of his opponent's breastbone as it cracked beneath the instant blaze of contact; the rippling of the man's skin and tunic, as if Lukas had tossed a pebble into a man-shaped pond. The force of his single maneuver, ten times as strong as the blow his opponent had intended to deliver, lifted the scarred man off his feet and sent him flying across the alley toward his group of sneering cohorts. The hulking form slammed against the grime-stained ground and slid roughly back until stopping with a thud against the wall of the opposite building, like a cardboard box kicked across a room.

By the time the man stopped moving, entirely disabled, Lukas had already returned his hand to rest beside the other at the small of his back. He took a slow, deep breath and eyed the other thugs who'd gathered around them. Their reactions were delayed, of course; most of them still boasted foolishly confident grins. But then they realized their champion fighter no longer stood in front of his prey, and they whirled around to confirm with their own eyes what they'd never had cause to believe was remotely possible.

Now, they clenched their own fists in newly determined rage. The smart call would have been to stand down and remove themselves from the alley as quickly as possible. Lukas would have even allowed them to drag the unconscious, severely injured man away with them unhindered. But none of these men were particularly smart, and Lukas supposed that was why they'd been recruited by Boaz.

Lukas heard their breaths quickening, saw each man's chest rising and falling with fear and outrage, and he understood each of the nine remaining men were brazen and stupid enough to want to show him a lesson. He didn't want to wait for them to throw themselves at his fists, so he charged.

In a flash of undyed cloth, Lukas was upon the closest man. The idiot opened his arms as if to embrace his attacker, and Lukas dropped to one knee beside him and shot his fist out into the man's kneecap. The knee cracked and buckled before the force of Lukas's strike sent the man flipping forward in the air to land on his back. He screamed enough in those first few seconds to go hoarse, his leg below the shattered knee now hanging at a sharply twisted angle by nothing more than sinew, torn muscle, and skin.

The distinct rustle and click of weapons being drawn ricocheted off the walls of the alley, but Lukas was already on his feet once more and moving forward. Before the next man could reach the firearm at his hip, Lukas struck his arm and shattered the humerus bone beneath the muscular bicep. Before the man had a chance to cry out at his uselessly dangling arm, the Hedge Master had him by the lapel of his thin jacket with one hand and the bunched fabric at his waist with the other. Then he lifted and swung, the immense power behind his training sending the man flying into two of his companions just as they'd trained their guns on Lukas. The snapping report of gunfire blared through the alley, but their bullets instead ended in one of their own flung toward them before they both toppled to the ground under his weight.

Lukas did not have to see the man behind him to know he was there; he heard the rapid breathing and the shuffling footsteps before the click of a finger against his firearm's trigger. The man standing in front of the Hedge Master also had the same idea, raising his own weapon to aim it at Lukas's chest. Moving swiftly over a small distance was always far easier than doing so to cover larger ground, and Lukas's entire body tensed before he shifted to the side with a single, accurate step. The man standing behind him pulled the trigger first, sending a short burst of automatic fire into what would have been Lukas but was now the other thug standing in the same line of attack. The second man's head burst open like a ripe melon hurled to the ground, red and pink and gray mist splattering against the wall behind him.

The surprise of such a deadly mistake in friendly fire stunned the gunman long enough for Lukas to spin toward him and drive his fist into the man's jaw. Teeth, blood, and bone sprayed from the man's face, leaving his lower jaw dangling at the side by nothing more than stubborn cheek muscle and sinew. The man buckled and slumped to the ground, and Lukas had already turned to charge at the other five men remaining. Immediately, their firearms clattered to the slick black street below them. Apparently, the survivors were now convinced they would join their fallen if they stayed. Together, they scrambled over the bodies of their dead comrades and stumbled down the other side of the alley, moving far quicker to escape than they had to attack.

As Lukas watched them withdraw, the words of *lex talionis* echoed in his mind, and he brought his breath—coming no faster than if he'd climbed a short flight of stairs—back under control. He would not go after these men once they'd fled; that was not the way of the Hedge or of his people. Then he turned around and took in the sight of so much carnage left at his own hands. Such violent acts brought him no pleasure at all, but he'd trained under and lived by the Law of the Talion; these men had been sent with the intention to kill him, so he'd responded in kind, nothing more. It was a pity that it had taken five lives lost in such a gruesome way for the rest to change their minds.

He flexed the fingers of his right hand, feeling only a slight ache in his knuckles that he knew would pass within minutes. Then he heard a hesitant footstep and looked up to see Marya emerge from a small doorway. With wide eyes, she took in the red smears of death along the walls and the bodies left behind, then met Lukas's gaze and slowly exhaled. As if she did it all the

time, she stepped over the splintered body in her path and
moved swiftly toward Lukas.

"We need to go now," she muttered, taking him by the wrist
again and leading him in the direction they'd been headed in the
first place. "Before anyone else comes."

Lukas had no reason or intent to argue; instead he was
surprised and more than a little impressed by Marya's response
to what she'd just seen. He'd expected to see fear behind her
eyes, a battle with her promise to help him against a newfound
disgust for a man who could do so much damage. But then he
realized that here, in the lower levels of the city, this type of
violence was common, whether it came at the foreboding hands
of the Janiss-arai or from a Qumranian Hedge Master. So he
followed her and matched her pace, unconcerned by the fact
that she hadn't yet thanked him.

They emerged from the alley, and Marya steered them into
the bustling chaos of now late morning. With her hand still on
his wrist, she waited for a motorized cart with a man steering it
from a platform at the back to cross in front of them, then
glanced quickly in both directions and tugged Lukas across the
crowded street. Bells dinged and whistles blew, holographic ads
and enticements rang out from every corner, every surface. Only
once they hustled down the other side of the street and Marya
dipped into a particularly narrow alley did the sounds fade a
little.

This space seemed abandoned by any efforts to grab
customers' attentions; no lights flashed, no displays flickered to
life, no jarring electric music blasted from unseen sources. It was
quite dark as well, made all the darker in contrast to the constant
light of the city, day or night. The passageway was wide enough
for only the two of them to walk abreast, and then Marya finally
spoke.

"What are you really doing here?" she asked, slowing her

pace. Lukas thought she must now be feeling safe enough to bring it up.

He took a deep breath. "I didn't lie to Cephas," he said. Of course the woman had cause to think this of him after what she'd just witnessed. "I came to find my cousins. To free them from wherever they've been taken and to get back... what was stolen from my people."

"Did you see who took them?"

For all he'd been through in the last two days, the memory of the compound's infiltrators was as fresh when he stirred up the memories as if it had just happened. He'd tried to reveal as little as possible of himself—it was safer for everyone that way—but if he were in Marya's position, he would want a more detailed explanation of who the newcomer was, where he came from, and what he wanted. She didn't push him, but it was the only choice he had now.

"A large army in black uniform," he began. "They followed two commanders, or whatever they call their military leaders. A man and a woman, probably related. Maybe even siblings. They had the strangest armor I'd ever seen. Spikes and feathers and plates that looked impenetrable. And there was... a red star on the back of their left hands."

Marya stopped in the alley and turned her whole body to face him. "You saw Lucia and Damian?"

Lukas couldn't help but roll his eyes as he shrugged. A coarse chuckle escaped him. "I don't know their names."

"The red star on their hands looks like this?" Marya drew the shape on the wall with her finger, mimicking the exact warped curves of the tattoo he'd seen on the cruel pair.

"Yes."

Marya took a deep breath and stared at him for a moment. "They're the leaders of the Unclean. The Consortium military's elite police force. Whatever they have of yours, if they did take your cousins... it's already too late. The last world war showed everyone what those two were capable of, the vicious acts they committed. Not to mention the rumors of the science and magic that have kept them alive for so long. There's such a small chance that—"

"That doesn't matter," Lukas interrupted, determined. "If there's even a small chance, I'll take it. I have to try. I want to see my cousins safe, and I'll do anything I can to find them. But the things these Unclean stole from my home..." With a heavy breath, he added, "Marya, it's more important than you could ever know."

She leaned her head back just a little, her dark eyes searching his with conviction and assured expectation. "I told you I'd help you," she said. "And that hasn't changed. But you need to tell me more."

"Like what?"

"You can start with where you're really from," she said calmly.

He felt rather like a chastised child who'd been caught in a lie, being given one final chance to reveal the truth.

"I really *am* from far away," he said, knowing even as the words left his lips that it sounded like a rehearsed story. "Near the Dead Sea." He waited to see how she would press him, if his vagueness would frustrate her, but she surprised him with a small, gentle smile.

"No one has called it the Dead Sea for at least a century," she said, then tilted her head. "And there isn't a sea there at all anymore. Did you know that?"

Lukas blinked, wondering if she'd mistaken the true Dead Sea for whatever dried-up body of water to which she now referred. The Dead Sea had swallowed the remnants of the Qumranian compound; he'd watched it himself. He started to shake his head, then stopped.

"You spoke in your sleep last night, Lukas. We all heard you before I left Cephas's. Names muttered through your dreams. Golden Fields and Enforcers. Circle of Elders—"

"Stop." A cold, bristling tingle crawled up Lukas's spine, followed by a hot flush rising from his collarbone to the base of his skull. He didn't want to hear this. "I... don't know..."

"It's okay," she said, a gentle, sad smile of compassion lighting up her eyes and making Lukas feel like he'd done something wrong and didn't deserve such forgiveness. "Cephas and I know. It doesn't seem possible, but we know." Her brows flickered briefly together. "In the last world war, a people revealed themselves to the world from a place they called Qumran. They were technologically advanced, living in hiding for almost two thousand years beneath and around the Dead Sea, and no one knew of their existence. They emerged, showed the world who they were and what they could do, and they were destroyed completely." She closed her eyes, as if the thought pained her. "The technology they brought with them formed the basis for the Consortium's intellectual property holdings and made the entire world what it is today. So many things have changed since those Qumranians appeared from underground and were wiped away almost as quickly." She paused, as if she expected Lukas to agree with everything she said, though none of it made any sense to him.

"How long ago was the last world war?" he asked slowly, an unexplained dread rising from the pit of his stomach.

"Over a hundred years ago."

Lukas balked, then closed his eyes and swallowed. "That's impossible," he whispered. "It was yesterday. I saw it with my own eyes yesterday..." For a moment, it occurred to him that what Marya thought she knew of the Qumranians was a story drummed up by the Consortium for some nefarious purpose and deception. But what she'd said of his people was true—technologically advanced, living underground at the Dead Sea. No one had ever known of Qumran before, and that knowledge would have only been revealed by those of the compound coming aboveground to deliver it themselves. Lukas was the only one who had made it out alive, and he'd told no one a thing.

A flashing image of the quantum orb entered his mind, sitting languidly upon its steel cradle and waiting for him to connect. He'd tried to shove it to the farthest recesses of his mind after everything he'd been through, but now it came back with a punishing certainty. He'd lost time between their first successful test with the quantum orb and the shuddering explosions that had wracked the Main Laboratory shortly thereafter. He'd been holding the round energy phaser he never remembered grabbing, had regained consciousness covered in dust and sand and feeling more exhausted than he'd ever been in his life. The truth had screamed at him then, but he had not been willing to acknowledge it, and then his world had crumbled around him. Now, Lukas could no longer deny the truth of what he'd done. Somehow, against his own will and with only slivers of memory, he'd used the orb again and gone back in time. What he'd done, he could not say, but something had changed the timeline of history, could still be changing it in ways too subtle to even imagine. And he could do nothing about it—not until he recovered the quantum orb and released Ben and Deborah.

But he could not voice any of these things to Marya. Not now. "What does any of that have to do with me?" he asked instead, still wary of what she might understand of him.

"I told you I know." Marya studied his gaze. "No one living today would know what you know, Lukas. No one could do what you did back there." She glanced down at his fists clenched by his sides and gently took them in her hands. Then she turned them over and said, "And you have blood-right marks on your palms."

Lukas froze, his hands tingling where she touched him. Then he swallowed and slowly opened his fists to reveal the old, circular scars in the center of each hand, given to him by his father and smoothed over with the passage of time.

"How?" That was all he could get out as he lifted his gaze to look at her. Her knowledge of this was impossible, and yet she was as confident in it as he was in the fact that he stood here now with her palms cradling the backs of his hands.

"Jesse is a scholar and a teacher," she said, her eyes shining with hope. "He is a mystic. And he is the Messiah."

"What?"

Marya nodded. "He and the Father are one, and the Father reveals things to Jesse known to no other man. He told us a man of Qumran would come to us, even though it was impossible. We were to help you, to give you what you needed and what you sought in your own time. To help you, Lukas, in your endeavors here and to find your own Way. We've been waiting for you for some time. And now you've come."

Lukas slowly slid his hands away from hers and back down to his sides. The Messiah, he'd always known, was meant to come to Qumran, to return to God's chosen people, to protect them and prepare them for the end of days. This was why they'd lived as they had for centuries, working to ensure they defended God's word passed down to them so the Messiah, when he did appear, would know them. Jesse could not possibly be this promised Savior—not here, amid the dregs of the city's society and sitting peacefully in underground marketplaces to write things on the ground and tell stories. But when Lukas remembered the man's eyes and the things he'd seen within him, for a moment, he was not so sure.

Marya dipped her head toward him, silently urging him to say something. Whether or not she wanted him to confirm everything she'd revealed, Lukas could no more do that than he could pinpoint exactly how the timeline of history had been altered.

"This is what I know," he said with a frown. "I am from Qumran. My home was attacked and destroyed by this force you say is the Unclean. They stole valuable and dangerous things from us. The most important is a machine we created that... well, it allows time travel." He lifted a shoulder, realizing how odd this must sound to someone who had never known the capabilities of his people, but Marya only watched him with open patience. "For me, that was yesterday. But what you've told me is..."

"Come with me," Marya said, relieving him of whatever obligation he'd felt to try to explain. "We're almost there."

"The marketplace?" Lukas asked.

When she grinned, her eyes flashed with amusement. "I don't think that's what you need anymore." She continued down the narrow alley again, the smile still lingering as she watched the ground. "I have a friend named Cyrus. He used to be with the Unclean, but he was released from duty and expelled from their ranks after he was injured. Now he follows Jesse with us. I think he might have answers to a few of your questions."

"Thank you," Lukas said, walking at her side. "I think."

Marya's short, silent laugh made him smirk despite the overwhelming chaos their conversation had unleashed inside his own head.

15

The Master had commanded them, and the *shedim* always obeyed. Their hunger to succeed was rivaled only by the Master's, and they swarmed through the worldveil, seeking their prey. Within this muted copy of what was and what was yet to be, the light was dim, all sound an echo of reality. The *shedim* moved swiftly, rage and greed and consumption and no little fear fueling them—always.

Through the streets of the city within the worldveil they flew, darkness embodied. They did not show themselves here, not now. Only the briefest gust of air or the ghostly rustle from movement unseen beyond the worldveil marked their presence. They had not been told to reveal themselves, only to stop the man their Master had marked and the woman who sought to aid him.

As fluttering, weightless shadows they moved, descending upon the stranger in this place and his woman guide. Then, from beyond the worldveil—from a place the *shedim* did not go—three streaks of blinding light pierced the shadows of their domain. Three Protectors arose, sent directly to the Master's realm because they did not wish yet to reveal themselves either.

These intruders stood their ground between the *shedim* and their unwitting prey, glittering bodies of refracted light and crystalline edges. Here, they did not shimmer at the edges, smeared with the vagueness of form like everything else in the Master's realm. Here, they were clear, crisp, each Protector frowning at the *shedim* carrying out their Master's bidding.

One of them, his lips pressed tightly together beneath a helm of brilliant white crystal, slammed the butt of his elongated staff into the ground a single time. The crack of such a weapon echoed through the worldveil like nothing ever did—unmuted, sharp, deadly.

"These souls are under our protection," he said, his voice at once like the deepest thunder and the lightest tinkle of delicate glass. "Leave them."

The *shedim*, ever cunning, withdrew from the Protectors and their wards. But they merely feigned this conceding wariness; they did not return to the Master as failures. They either succeeded, or they did not return at all.

Instead, they split from each other, racing through the worldveil to converge upon their prey as they were commanded. The first to reappear was snatched by the glistening, glowing hands of the closest Protector, who wrapped his arm around what would have been the *shedim's* head, if such things existed here. Another made it much closer to its target, reaching out with fingerlike tendrils to ensnare the guiding woman in its desperate grasp. Almost there, and yet still so far away. The second Protector lifted this dark servant by the back of its billowing shadows and hoisted it away from the woman, her hands burning white-hot light into the *shedim's* very core. It screeched and struggled, but the Protector did not release her grip.

The final *shedim* did not have time to consider outsmarting the Protectors. That could never be; it had to rely on its own speed driven by need and despair. And yet, that still was not enough. The *shedim* stopped suddenly mere feet from its prey, as if it struck an invisible wall here in the worldveil itself. Its figure shuddered, then bucked, lit from within by the fiery justice of the third Protector's sword—brilliant, glaring light—thrust through the dark swarm of shadow. A shrieking wail rose from every failed servant, and the glowing Protectors released them, their faces set with impassive purpose, hardened by their duty toward the One they served.

A void opened in the worldveil, spreading along the ground like a ravenous disease. Black fire raged from this unspeakable place, its agonizing flames curling up above the gaping maw of darkness to ensnare each *shedim* within its grasp. Then they were pulled through, relegated to the harsh eternal punishment reserved only for the failures of their kind. Wailing and keening against the pull, the *shedim* struggled for a moment before they were gone entirely and the void closed soundlessly once again.

The Protectors had done what they'd come here to do—their justice fierce and swift, their surety unwavering. They looked at each other, then pulsed into a brilliant white flash that could have ripped the worldveil in two, if that was what they desired. Then they were gone.

16

At the end of the final alleyway in an incomprehensible maze of turns through which she'd led him, Marya stopped briefly beside a curved black door. She tilted her head, frowned, then looked briefly over her shoulder down the narrow, empty passage.

"What's wrong?" Lukas asked.

"Nothing..." Marya turned around again and shook her head at him with a dismissive smile. "I thought I felt something." With apparently nothing more to say, she raised a fist and pounded three times on the black door.

A viewing slide opened from the other side, and a pair of oddly purple eyes stared out at them from the small opening. Then the slide closed again, and the black door opened inward. A large man wearing a silver suit, his spiked hair the same deep violet as his unnatural eyes, stepped back to allow them entry.

"Hey, Marya," he said, his brows lifting above a surprised smile. "You coming back to sing later tonight?"

She lifted a shoulder at him with an apologetic wrinkle of her nose as the man pushed the door closed behind them. "No, not today, Ephus. Sorry."

Ephus raised an eyebrow and shrugged, then nodded toward

the second door at the other end of the five-foot wide corridor they'd entered.

The droning noise that had been so successfully dampened in the alley and even through the first door now spilled out from the next room. A strange, raucous blare of high metallic notes and electronic backgrounds flooded over a quick, steady bass rhythm; Lukas had never heard music like this, and he thought it would be pretty difficult to focus on anything but the noise itself if one spent more than a few minutes here.

Marya led him off the raised balcony outside the door and down a short flight of steps toward the main room below. Directly in front of them, the bar was backlit with glowing green and purple lights oscillating from bright to dim so the glass bottles on the back shelf appeared to dance. To their left sat a stage, the back draped in black cloth and the rest entirely empty. A few tables and chairs were scattered in front, but Marya led them to the right and past the bar again, where a collection of much more comfortable-looking booths curved around round tables. For this early in the morning, Lukas was surprised the place was even open, let alone catering to maybe a dozen people sitting in the rounded booths, engaged in conversation or sipping their drinks. He had a feeling the place was much busier at the end of the day.

They weaved through the mostly empty tables until Marya slowed halfway to the back wall. A man in a loose-fitting, dark-gray shirt and matching pants looked up from where he sat at the corner table, listening to two other men in conversation beside him. The man rubbed his beardless chin when he caught sight of her, gave a hint of a smile, then leaned toward his companions and muttered something short and direct. His friends nodded and stood to make their way to another table. The man raised his hand in gratitude, and Lukas saw the warped red star tattooed on the back of his hand.

"Marya," the man said, smiling kindly and spreading his arms in greeting from where he sat. "It's good to see you."

"Hi, Cyrus." She looked at him with comfortable familiarity, and Lukas was glad to know they no longer had to fight their way toward friends. "This is Lukas."

Cyrus nodded. "Well met, Lukas. Please, have a seat."

Marya glanced at Lukas and nodded toward one of the three chairs across from the booth, and Lukas pulled the closest back for himself as she did the same.

"You look busy," she said, gesturing toward the two men who had left the table to make room for the newcomers.

"Never a dull moment." Cyrus closed his eyes and swallowed, as though he found his own joke falling flat. "Even before my real day has a chance to begin. What can I do for you?"

Marya folded her hands on top of the table and leaned forward, speaking loud enough over the pounding music that Lukas was glad the place was relatively empty. "I'm looking for some information about your... former associates. What they've been up to the last few days. Whether or not there's been any major activity."

"Anything specific?" Cyrus asked, blinking quickly. Lukas thought it was the man's attempt to hide his surprise at the request, though he seemed entirely willing to help them.

"A little specific, yes. And a little sensitive."

Cyrus nodded. "Absolutely. I'll get you anything you need." He took a deep breath. "Let's go somewhere we can hear each other a little better, huh?" Sliding out of the booth, Cyrus stood and gestured toward the single door behind it. Marya and Lukas stood as well, pushing their chairs in behind them, and she gave him a reassuring nod. Cyrus led the way, moving slowly with a distinct limp in his left leg. He trailed his fingers along the back of the booth and then the wall, not so much to steady himself but perhaps as more of a mental reassurance of his own stability.

Then he pushed the black door inward and held it open for them to follow.

They entered a short hallway, but Cyrus chose the door directly opposite them, and once all three of them had stepped into the room beyond, the loud music disappeared almost entirely. A desk sat against the far wall, and a table with four chairs dominated the center of the small back room.

Cyrus pulled out a chair for Marya, then gestured for them to sit. "What can you tell me before I take a look?"

When Marya nodded at him, Lukas frowned and sat back against the hard chair. "The Unclean have taken something from me. An incredibly powerful machine that can do a lot of damage in very little time. I need to get it back."

Cyrus's eyes widened and he pulled at his beardless chin again. "You must be quite an important man for the Unclean to want something of yours."

Lukas squeezed his eyes tightly shut, then blinked rapidly and met the man's gaze. "Not in the way you might think." Yes, he'd been an important man in Qumran—a top-level Hedge Master and the leading scientist on a team paving the way for the Qumranians' most historical and world-changing break-through. Here, in the city, in this timeline, he was in fact no one. At least, when he didn't count what Jesse knew of him and had told his students, he was no more important than the rest of them. And despite that, he didn't know if the Unclean or the Consortium knew who he was or if he'd just been collateral damage the whole time. "They also took my cousins."

"Hmm." Cyrus steepled his fingers in front of his mouth for a moment and pondered the plastic cover of the table between them. "Okay." Then he tapped the red star tattoo on the back of his hand, and a subdermal touchscreen flickered to life from the backs of his fingers up to the curve of his forearm. He pressed a few buttons registered in his skin, and a stream of images and the written characters that Lukas was quite tired of not understanding scrolled across Cyrus's forearm in a constant stream. The man studied it, and as his eyes flickered back and forth across the sprawling information, he said slowly, "There was a full-scale assault ordered, to be executed yesterday on..." His eyes flickered again, then darkened under a small frown. "Odd. No reports on the target location. No follow-up reports, either." He glanced up at Lukas. "I've only seen them do this once. They've definitely got something they don't want anyone else to see."

"The commanders... leaders... I don't know," Lukas started. "The man and woman who led the attack..."

"Damian and Lucia," Marya added.

"Them. They took the machine and my cousins themselves. Can you tell me where they went?"

Cyrus tapped again at the images on his flesh, then raised his eyebrows. "I can, actually. They returned with four Hornet-class choppers to the main division headquarters." He looked up at Lukas and studied him for a moment. "That's here in the city. Huge maze of buildings. Barracks and the largest research facilities I've ever seen."

Marya took a deep breath and rolled her shoulders, but she didn't look away from Cyrus. "Can you get us inside?"

"I can. If it weren't for this leg"—he dipped his head toward his stretched out leg beside the table—"I'd go with you. But I still have friends there who should be able to get you where you need to be."

Marya smiled thinly and bowed her head. The grim mood of the entire conversation told Lukas everything he needed to know. They'd be walking into barracks and research facilities teeming with Unclean soldiers stationed at headquarters, most likely just bored enough to pounce on any opportunity to break the monotony. If Lukas and whoever agreed to come with him were caught, they'd be hand-delivering themselves straight to the Unclean.

Cyrus leaned to the side a bit, stuck his right hand into his pocket, and retrieved a slim, elongated black box small enough to palm without being seen. He pressed this to the red star on the back of his left hand, and two small green dots flashed on the box's thin edge. "This is a mimic," he told Lukas, handing the device across the table. "At the very least, this will get you physical entry into the facility. If they haven't updated the systems in the last two days—which I can't tell from here, sorry—it might also get you access to the mainframe databases. Maybe provide you with even better details."

"I can't thank you enough," Lukas said, pocketing the mimic.

"Well, I have a feeling you will. In time." Cyrus's lips twitched with a smile, and he glanced quickly at Marya; she only tilted her head but said nothing. "The most important thing is that, if you're spotted, don't try to fight them. Not there. You get out as fast as you can and come back here. We'll figure out something else."

"Okay." Lukas didn't like the idea of running from combat—not when he was capable of so much and had the Hedge at his disposal. But he'd already seen what the Unclean were capable of doing, and he'd made the right call the first time when he'd chosen retreat and survival over a useless death that would have changed nothing. He could make that decision a second time, if he had to.

"I'm going to tell you how to get inside," Cyrus continued, "and the first place you'll want to go. There's a maintenance entrance on the south side of the headquarters building you can access from the lower levels, so fortunately, you won't need to climb to any higher levels." He rolled his eyes. "Leaving the streets is probably harder than getting into the facility, at this point."

Together, Lukas and Marya leaned forward over the table to commit to memory every detail Cyrus relayed to them.

17

After their visit with Cyrus, Marya led him back to Cephas's apartment, her initial intention of showing Lukas around the city abandoned for their now more precise goal. Lukas counted this time as they moved quickly down the narrow, claustrophobic hallway of the apartment complex; Cephas's door was the thirty-seventh on the right, and the hall stretched on for at least twice that length until Lukas could no longer judge the distance. He still didn't appreciate his inability to read the written language of this new world, but resorting to counting and memorization through repetition would have to work well enough. He'd make it work.

Marya lifted her hand and pressed her three middle fingers onto a portion of the wall beside the door that didn't look any different than the rest of it. The panel blinked a light blue beneath her fingers, then she knocked once before pushing the door open. The last two times she'd entered without needing an invitation had made Lukas hope Cephas didn't just leave his home unlocked for anyone to enter, and he felt a little better knowing there was some measure of security. It wasn't as though there was anything worth breaking in for.

Cephas wasn't home, but that hardly seemed a deterrent for Marya. She slid her sandals off at the front door—Lukas did the same—then went immediately to another unmarked panel beside the door on the inside and typed a series of characters into the holographic screen that appeared. She stood there long enough that she could have been typing some kind of message or complex command. Then she smiled at Lukas, almost skipped to the cabinets built into the wall above the tiny stove, and set to rummaging through them.

"Where's Cephas?" Lukas asked, feeling a little odd being in his host's home without the man there.

"I stopped trying to guess a long time ago," Marya replied. The crack and hiss of a canteen being opened filled the small main room, and she poured the astringent almost-water into a small pot on the stove.

"He never told me what he does." Lukas hesitated, but when Marya didn't seem even remotely likely to ask for help, he went to the low table and settled himself on the pillows there.

"A little bit of everything, actually." She took two nondescript white packets from the cabinets and dumped them into the pot with the water before pressing a button to turn on the stove. "He did have Consortium employment at one point. Factory worker, I think. But they let him go after he passed the standard prime years of labor." She frowned and stirred the pot with an almost flat, black plastic spoon.

"Lucky for him, right?" He wanted to lighten the mood a bit, to bring some part of his old self back into the nightmare he'd entered. Even on the hardest days in the laboratory, after countless failed tests or inconclusive results, Lukas had always managed to maintain his optimism and confidence. It was part of his training, and it was part of what he always knew he had to be for his team. And, after a time, it had become a part of himself. But that was before, when the world was right and he knew exactly what he was doing every minute of every day. Of course, he still knew what he was doing; he would get his cousins out of the Unclean headquarters and remove the quantum orb from what was undoubtedly the worst possible hands. But he missed the ease of camaraderie, of looking past the difficult choices ahead by appreciating those he knew around him.

Marya turned from the stove and came to sit with him at the low table. "You would think leaving Consortium employment was a blessing, wouldn't you?" Her brows drew together, but the smirk beneath them made her look very much as if she worked hard to find amusement in the direst of circumstances. "The Consortium works people almost to the bone," she said. "A lot of them don't even make it to the prime years projected for their biological background. Very few are released, so in that sense, yes, Cephas was lucky. But the Consortium also pays their workers. Not what they deserve, by any means, but enough for this." She lifted a hand and gestured to Cephas's apartment. "Enough to survive. Enough to maybe catch a glimpse or two before the end of what it really means to thrive and prosper. But once a Consortium contract ends, at least in the city, there's no more work. Nothing else is offered legitimately, meaning no more recorded income, no more syn-creds in your account. Anyone who does make it through prime labor almost always meets the same end anyways, forced to give up their homes, their clothes, their food. Their families. But in the last few years, underground markets, payments exchanging hands for goods or services, have started to turn the lower levels around. There still isn't enough, and we aren't self-sustaining, but we do what we can for each other. And Cephas can do a lot. So, yes, I think. Cephas is lucky in that way."

"And you?" Lukas asked. Marya stared at him for a moment, then stood abruptly from her seat on the pillows and walked to the stove. A thick steam rose over whatever she'd put into the small pot. "I'm sorry," he said quickly. "I didn't mean to upset you." It was the first thing he'd asked her about herself, and he hoped it hadn't made her shut the doors she'd been slowly opening toward him. She'd asked plenty of questions herself, but something told him her stories were a little different.

She stood over the stove, staring into the pot and lifting the plastic spoon for a moment before a large, sticky glob smacked back into the rest of the contents. "I'm not upset," she said. "I've changed a lot in the last few months. Especially after meeting Jesse. Sometimes, I forget the things I used to do just to get by." Turning back to him, she offered a gentle smile and a reassuring nod. "I pulled something of your story out of you. It's only fair that you receive the same from me. Are you hungry?"

Oddly enough, Lukas realized he was; apparently, the gruel from the night before had finally worn off. "A little."

"Good." Marya took two bowls down from the cabinets and spooned the sticky slop into each of them. Then she brought the canteen of chemical water she'd used to also cook the food and tucked it under an arm before returning to the table. "This takes some getting used to," she said, setting the bowls and canteen on the table. "But once your body recognizes it, you can make it stretch longer and longer."

"I'll take whatever I can get," Lukas said. That was as much of a toast as this meal deserved, and he grinned at her before lifting the first bite of bitter gruel to his mouth.

"I used to be an... entertainer," Marya said after washing down her own uneventful first bite. "Performed all over the city and in all but the two highest levels." Lukas shot her a questioning gaze, and she shrugged. "Those are for the city officials, Consortium heads, and military leaders."

"Like the two who destroyed my home?" He couldn't help it; he wanted a better idea of where those two commanders might be if he didn't find them at the Unclean headquarters.

Marya nodded. "When they're not at headquarters. And others. The Consortium runs almost everything, but there are still a few other countries around the world. For how much longer, I don't think anyone knows. But any foreign dignitaries or trade delegates who come to the city are hosted in those top two levels." She took another drink and let out a little sigh. "I'm sure you realized it, but I used to... work for the man who sent those thugs after us this morning. His name is Boaz. I was young and desperate when I met him, thinking I had maybe a year left under Consortium labor before it killed me. He convinced me to step away from that job and work for him, and it felt like such a relief at the time." Her eyes closed briefly, and she gave a wry smile. "I didn't know very much at all back then. I did things for Boaz and his clients that I'm not proud of, Lukas. Things no self-respecting woman would allow herself to do. In some ways, it was much better than Consortium labor. When I sang..." She looked like she was remembering the taste of a delicious meal or the drift of a fresh, cool breeze on her face. "Being able to sing the way I wanted made the rest of it bearable."

"Do you still sing?" Lukas found the mash in the bowl filling him up quickly. He'd only eaten half of it, but he pushed himself to continue.

"Sometimes. It's difficult to find work singing on my own. Boaz was my... handler, yes, but he also made a good agent. I know I have an opening whenever I want at Cyrus's place, but most other clubs either want to work with an agent, or they want their entertainers to provide a lot more than just a performance on stage. But when I do sing now, the song is entirely different."

The curiosity blooming in Lukas surprised him, especially given the current subject and Marya having revealed these things to him. "Have you told Jesse these things?" he asked. "About what you used to do."

"Of course I have."

He'd expected that much; from the way she spoke about the man, it seemed Marya and Jesse might have been close, at the very least as friends. But she had told him just hours before that she believed Jesse was actually the Messiah, and he wondered what a man making such lofty claims would say about a woman who had lived in a way that did not follow any of the holy teachings Lukas had ever known.

"What did he say?"

Marya frowned at him, and this time she did seem a little offended. "He told me that if I accepted the Father into my heart again, if I walked a new Way that honored Him with love and humility, whatever life I lived before did not matter to God."

To Lukas, this kind of broad acceptance and forgiveness sounded much more like an excuse to justify anything one wished, not the word of God or a righteous path to His glory. He stared at Marya, uncertain as to whether he wanted to voice his opinion on it or how he'd even begin. Marya didn't seem bothered by his line of questioning, just by the way he'd asked and the apparent distrust he hadn't been able to hide.

Then he didn't have to decide anything at all; the front door to Cephas's apartment opened swiftly, and Cephas himself stepped inside and closed the door behind him. He carried two large, black canvas bags; they clanked when he set them down against the wall. Then he turned to his guests with a wide smile.

"I'm glad to see you've made yourselves at home. No, no. Don't get up," he said when Lukas moved to rise from the pillows. "Please. That's not necessary at all. I *want* you to be comfortable here, Lukas. I'll be right there." Cephas fetched himself a plastic cup and brought it with him to the table.

"There's food if you're hungry," Marya said, pulling herself from her obvious discomfort with the direction their previous conversation had been heading.

"Thank you." With a grunt, Cephas lowered himself onto the pillows and poured himself a drink from the canteen. "I'll put the rest of it aside for later. The stuff's been sticking to me a lot longer than usual the last few days." Then he took a long drink, wiped his beard with the back of a hand, and said, "I got your message."

"I assumed as much," Marya replied with a smirk, then turned slightly to eye the two black bags he'd brought home with him.

"You never said," Cephas continued, "but I think it's best to ask. Do you have plans for tonight?"

She laughed and slowly shook her head. "Not yet."

"Then tonight will work. That is, of course, if you're ready, Lukas."

Lukas glanced between his two companions, unaware of what the man inferred. "Ready for what?"

"Ah." Cephas stood, went to the two black bags, and hoisted them over his shoulders before returning to set them gently upon the low table. They obviously weighed quite a bit, but the man was large and strong and seemed unaffected by the weight. "Marya told me you went to see Cyrus. I thought it best that we find your cousins and this machine as soon as possible."

Lukas blinked. "You're coming with me?"

"Of course we are," Marya said.

"Both of you?"

Cephas took another sip of water, then bowed his head briefly. "We were told to help you in whatever way you needed."

"By Jesse," Lukas concluded. When Cephas nodded, he added, "I don't want either of you endangering yourselves because of what a man I don't even know has told you about me. This won't be easy, and it definitely isn't safe."

"We know that," Marya said, eyeing him with her head tilted, as if she wished him to say what was really on his mind.

That Lukas couldn't do. He already felt responsible for so many things—the destruction of his home, the death of his people, the apparent change in the history of the world that might or might not have come by his own hand directly but had definitely been of his design in creating the quantum orb in the first place. He didn't want to be responsible for Cephas and Marya too, if anything should happen to them while they broke into Unclean headquarters. And that seemed far too likely, judging by everything he'd heard and already knew of the Unclean and their two cruel commanders.

"This isn't a blind decision," Cephas said. "We know what we face. We know we do not wish to see our world fall completely to sin and despair. Things are hard enough as it is in the city. Most other places in the world, too. If what you've told Marya of the machine your people created is true, the chances of the Consortium and the Unclean using it to further shatter what hope remains are higher than I think any of us care to admit. Yes, Jesse told us to help you. And we *choose* to do this. Free will in its essence is something no controlling government can take from any of us. We're with you." He brought a hand firmly down on Lukas's shoulder.

"Thank you," Lukas said with a nod, recognizing just how much he owed to the kindness and strength of these people who had so quickly become friends.

Cephas returned the gesture, then removed his hand and unzipped the first black bag he'd set on the low table. "We'll be as prepared as we can be," he said, removing two large, sleek, semi-automatic rifles. He set these on the table, then pulled out a pistol whose model Lukas had never seen before; he guessed it was something like the Qumranian energy phasers in a more universally recognized shape. He acknowledged the three settings where the safety was normally positioned; the ability to stun opponents had its advantages given the right circumstances.

Lukas studied the weapons, completely surprised to see anything of this quality on the table in Cephas's tiny apartment. It seemed impossible that anyone on the lower levels of the city could ever gain access to such weaponry. And he had a feeling that, should anyone discover these in Cephas's possession, this would be grounds for an immediate execution at the hands of the Janiss-arai.

"How did you get these?" he asked, his curiosity bringing him nearly to the point of prying rudeness.

Cephas only chuckled. "A few friends owe me some favors. Big favors. It's worth it to call them in for this."

Lukas reached out to inspect the phaser pistol but froze when Marya leaned forward to grab one of the rifles in both hands. She ejected the empty magazine from the clip, opened the action to peer inside, then returned the magazine, lifted the weapon to aim it at the far wall of the apartment and fired off a dry shot. Then she gave a little shrug of what might have been approval and returned the rifle to the table. Lukas returned his hand slowly to his lap. He must have looked either terrified or remarkably impressed, and he couldn't tell himself which one of these he felt the strongest.

When she looked back up at him, Marya offered a wry smirk. "Like I said, I've done a lot of things I'm not proud of. I don't think Boaz ever intended to turn me into a soldier."

Speechless, Lukas turned to Cephas, unable to hide that he thought this was some kind of a joke. The man's brown eyes glittered in the apartment's dim lighting, and then Cephas roared with laughter. Marya's soft laughter followed to fill the room, and Lukas couldn't help but let out a few chuckles of his own.

"I look forward to seeing what else you can do," he told Marya, then finally took the energy pistol and examined the settings. "What else did your friends give you?"

"Protective gear," Cephas replied, unzipping the second bag to pull out thick black vests and a few other items that looked like they might be arm or leg guards. "These'll keep any bullets from tearing through us, though I haven't ever worn them under phaser fire. They're meant to act as a grounding element if you're hit with an energy shot, but I've heard they still don't absorb the impact entirely. We're safer with the gear than without it. Even so, I still recommend that none of us get shot at all, if we can help it."

Lukas looked up from the pistol to meet Marya's gaze. She studied him a little longer than he'd expected, then pulled her eyes away to return them to the rifle at her fingertips, almost as if he'd caught her doing something he was not meant to see. But another smile bloomed on her lips before a rise of color rushed to her cheeks.

Tonight, he would infiltrate the Unclean headquarters—the first step in righting the wrongs this vile army had committed against all of Qumran, against its people, and Lukas in particular. And he found himself more grateful than ever to have these two at his side, no matter what happened.

18

In only two days, the monsters already had them trained like abused dogs—fearful, expectant, quivering in their cages. It didn't help that they'd put Deborah and Ben in actual cages. Forced to hunker or sit, they hadn't been released to stretch their legs since they were delivered from the odd helicopter to this very room. They'd been given sips of water every few hours and a dry cake of something that tasted as if it were meant for animals, but beyond that, there was nothing. No word as to their purpose here, why they'd been spared, what had happened to Qumran—or Lukas. But Deborah was determined not to let herself dwell on the high likelihood of each of those questions being met with devastating answers. Instead, she tried to focus on her brother.

She looked over to her brother. "Ben?" She drummed her fingers on the cold black steel of her cage. "Ben, are you awake? Can you hear me?" Her brother moaned from where he sat slumped against the back of his own cage.

He hadn't said anything to her since earlier that same morning when he'd told her he couldn't handle the pain. The beasts who had stolen them from their labs and destroyed their home either had no awareness of Ben's suffering or no compassion whatsoever. They hadn't set his arm, which the woman had broken, and they'd given him nothing to ease the pain. Now, his face had gone a deathly shade of pale, sweat continuously beading at his hairline to spill down his face, past the dark circles under his eyes, and pool at the collar of his gray uniform shirt.

Something echoed toward them from down the hall, and Deborah tapped louder on her cage. "Ben, someone's coming. I need to know you can still hear me."

He cleared his throat, rolled his head to his other shoulder to face her, and his eyes fluttered open for a few seconds. His gaze was glassy, unfocused, but he licked his lips and muttered, "Yeah."

Deborah sighed in relief, and the echoing footsteps in the hall grew louder. "Listen. No matter what they do to us, Ben, we can't tell them anything. They can't know how to—"

The door to the lab in which the siblings were held burst open and the vile woman who had captured them entered. A swarm of soldiers in black garb and a gathering of men in long gray robes followed quickly behind her. Even here, the female commander of this soulless army wore the full array of armor she'd donned for the raid on Qumran—cruelly spiked pauldrons and black, purple, and blood-red leather and plates fitted seamlessly to cover nearly every inch of her person. The massive, plumed helmet was the shape of some raptor-like beast, its sharp etchings giving it an air of ancient power against the bright chrome, brushed steel, and black enamel of the laboratory. The woman took a moment to stare in apparent revelry at the stolen quantum orb resting in its steel cradle atop a secured workbench at the far end of the lab.

The startling bark of her next order made Deborah jump against the back of her cage. "Ten of you. Now." As if pulled by invisible strings, the ten black-clad soldiers standing closest to their commander stepped forward. "I want you stationed around this machine at all times. No exceptions. Do not presume to think that your lives hold more value to me than this. From now on, your fate is linked directly to how well you protect it." The soldiers did as they were told and rushed past their commander to form a semi-circle around the counter and the quantum orb cradled there, firearms loaded and at the ready. The woman turned from them without another word and strode across the room.

Before Deborah realized she was the next target of this cruel woman's attention, two spiked boots stopped in front of her cage. Then the commander lowered herself into a squat, her narrow, slanted eyes studying Deborah as if no conversation were necessary. A slow, wicked grin spread across her face and she brushed her fingers slowly against the wire of the cage. Deborah shuddered, thinking she felt a cold hand brush across her face at the same time.

"I am not without some mercy," the woman crooned. "I'm offering you a choice, and it's a fairly easy choice to make, little pet. The Consortium's top scientists have been eagerly awaiting the arrival of this"—she took in a sharp, hissing breath through her teeth and briefly closed her eyes—"brilliant technology. They're so very eager to learn how to put it to use. You can choose to share your knowledge with them. Reveal the secrets of this machine and how it works, and you will be rewarded for such generosity."

The men in gray robes all eyed Deborah with something she thought very much resembled both a pleading urgency and desperate hunger for what she knew.

"Or," the commander sneered, "you can choose to maintain your stubborn silence and suffer because of it. Use your companion as a reference point." She gestured at Ben, who was breathing slowly with his eyes closed. "That broken arm must be agonizing."

Then she stood and walked slowly over to Ben. Without so

much as a warning, her boot shot out to kick viciously at Ben's cage. The blasting rattle of it made Deborah jump and gasp, and Ben merely rolled his head to the side and let out another moan.

"I'll return shortly to hear your decision," the armored woman said, grinning at Deborah once more.

A soldier dressed in black with a red stripe running down the right side of his chest entered the lab and approached his commander. He held a thin touchscreen tablet toward her, muttering something Deborah couldn't hear as he scrolled through the view.

The woman raised her eyebrow, nodded, then smirked. "Good. Clear the halls between the access doors and the sublevels. Let them get far enough to think they have a chance. We'll meet them here." She cast a final amused glance back at Deborah, then left the lab.

The soldier with the tablet rushed out after her, as did most of the contingent who'd entered with their commander. But the ten soldiers remained stationed around the quantum orb, and the men in gray robes who were apparently the scientists of this place milled about at the other end of the lab, talking among themselves and casting their prisoners occasional glances of eager anticipation.

Deborah watched the strangers around them for a few minutes, wary of their presence. She soon realized none of them would pay her any attention until the commander returned. Finally, she crawled across the floor of the low cage in Ben's direction, pressing herself against the cold steel wiring to get as close to her brother as she possibly could.

"Ben," she whispered. Two men in gray robes walked across the room, and she glared at them, but they paid her no heed. "Ben, you have to hold on just a little longer. We'll get through this."

Her brother only let out a series of harsh coughs in reply, his sweaty brow creasing weakly with the pain and fever now wracking him. "They're not gonna let us live, Deb..."

"I know," she whispered fiercely. "I'm not telling these people anything." She checked again to make sure no one was watching. "I think... Ben, I think someone's coming for us. To help us get out of here. We just have to keep it together long enough."

"Nobody's coming," Ben groaned. "Nobody knows we're here. Everyone else is gone." He coughed again, winced, and pulled his broken arm against his chest to cradle it there.

"Not Lukas." Deborah felt the hope rising in her now after the last two days of being entirely without it. "Did you hear? They're getting ready for *someone*. What if it's him?" Ben's head rolled back and forth against the back of his cage. "They didn't catch him, Ben. They couldn't find him. I think he got out." She pressed her face tighter against the steel mesh. "It could be him coming for us."

Ben readjusted his arm and took a few minutes to steady his labored breathing. He wiped away the sweat on his temples with his good arm and swallowed thickly. "Whoever it is, Deb, you have to do whatever you can to make sure you get out of here. I don't care what it takes. You do it." The act of speaking obviously took a lot out of him; his frown darkened and whatever color remained in his face seemed to drain out entirely.

Deborah didn't at all like the direction he was taking this. "We'll do it together—"

"Look at me." Ben opened his glistening, red-rimmed eyes to meet her gaze. "I don't think I'm gonna be doing much of anything soon. These people aren't going to help me, no matter what they say. Don't let them use me against you." Another fit of coughs interrupted him. "You, Deb. *You* get out."

She pressed her forehead against the cold steel in front of her and stared at her brother as hot tears welled in her eyes and spilled down her cheeks. She wanted to say something witty—

tell him that she'd been right their entire lives, and she was right about this. She wanted to force them both into believing they'd get out of this alive, but she couldn't find the will to say any of it, because the thought occurred to her that saying it out loud would only release that small, flickering hope and she might not be able to catch it again.

In the uppermost level of the Unclean headquarters facility, Damian sat within what he'd come to consider more of his home than anywhere they'd stayed in the last few centuries. Of course, nothing had or ever would compare to the place of his birth, where he and his sister had spent their childhoods. But there was never any use in dwelling on such weakening memories; all that was ravaged and destroyed by all the wars.

Damian now reclined on a collection of soft, expensive pillows, their insides full to bursting with feathers from birds now extinct. Draperies of the finest silks and old crushed velvet fell about him, hanging from the ceiling and against the walls. These things did not exist anymore either, except for perhaps in the remotest parts of the world the Consortium had not yet touched. So very few things of physical beauty—of the old expressions of opulence and mastery—remained, and Damian had a particular weakness for beautiful things.

He breathed deeply, inhaling the old-world scents of the incense burning in the three bronze bowls beside him on the low table. The first was frankincense, so easy to preserve but so difficult now to harvest. The second was blood salt from the caves beside where the Dead Sea used to be—in this reality and all the others. And the third held the finger bones Damian and his sister kept for whatever ritual best fit the moment at hand. These gave the sweetest scent of all as they charred and burned, the black smoke rising thickly from each bowl spread before him. It was how he wished to wait—to prepare himself for what was to come.

Slowly, he sat up from where he reclined, crossed his legs beneath him, and closed his eyes. He had not received new commands since the last was given two days ago, which had sent him and his sister out to the brink of this dimension to retrieve the machine that now belonged completely to their Dark Lord. But so many things had changed in only two days, and so many things remained yet to be changed, and in this moment, he could not see any of the possible futures clearly. This fact grieved him desperately, as if he had lost a ritual source or a precious gem; Damian had grown so accustomed over the last few centuries to seeing what he wished to see that this blurring of all eventualities, indistinguishable from one another, left him feeling blind and helpless, fumbling in the dark.

With great humility—even though he resented having to employ it now—the leader of the Unclean rose to his knees and supplicated himself on the soft, time-worn animal pelt stretching the length of the floor beneath him. He spread his arms wide to the sides and bowed so far his head nearly touched the pelt, which still clung to the last vestiges of natural musk.

"My lord Ahriman," he called, nearly shouting into the darkness of his chambers. "Great Destroyer. What else would you have me do?"

For a moment, nothing happened—no change in light or sound, no direction. When Damian began to think his call had gone unheard, there was a sharp crack, like a twig snapping underfoot, and the black smoke wafting up from the three bronze incense bowls froze as if time itself had stopped. Impossible though it seemed, this was the sign Damian awaited, and he remained bowing low before the offering table until the air between the bowls and the tops of the frozen, smoking tendrils rent apart. Like a seam delicately ripped with the sharpest of blades, the very air before him split into a black smile, and a dark, featureless head protruded through the slash in this dimension to address him.

"Your only aim now is to ensure the safety of the Qumranian machine." The voice slithered through the blackness on the other side, sounding at once like hissing snakes and crumbling stone and the keening wails of a thousand widows.

A shiver of pleasure and unbridled anticipation ran down Damian's back, and it was all he could do not to grin at the one addressing him through the void.

"We will tell you what must be done when the time comes, good and loyal servant."

Damian gazed at the obsidian face that was no face at all, watching it waver precariously between dimensions. Then the figure turned what might have been the pits of its black eyes upon him, and the Unclean commander bowed his head low once more.

"Of course," he said. "In all things, I serve. And in this."

His words were met with a low rumble of approval, and then the formless figure withdrew. The grinning fragment of space between this world and the next sealed itself with the barest sound—like drops of water falling onto cold, dead flesh—and the curls of smoke moved once more. Only now a rift existed between what had once been long continuous tendrils, as if the smoke had been a solid chain severed succinctly in two by the same bladed edge that had cleaved the veil between worlds.

With a deep breath, Damian rose completely from his nearly prostrate bow and watched the smoke a moment longer. At the very least, his plea had been answered. If he and Lucia were now only meant to protect the machine and await further instructions, they would succeed in this as they had succeeded in every other endeavor set upon them by their lord Ahriman. But he did not intend to be so careless with allowing survivors. His sister preferred to toy with her enemy, to string them along until they broke. She loved to watch their hope extinguish like a dying star. Damian had always thought it best to eliminate his foes entirely with one swift hand. Why focus on destroying the spirit when one could simply snuff out such meaningless lives with far less effort? Damian would follow his orders, but he would make sure those who defied him did not live to believe their hope could blossom again.

Rising to his feet, the Unclean commander removed himself from his mound of pillows and the comfort of his worldly possessions. From the low table in the corner beside the door to his chambers, he retrieved the battle helm that had stricken hundreds of thousands of mortals with all-consuming fear and dread over the last few centuries. Before donning this once more on his person, he tucked his long, pitch-black ponytail into the back of his tunic beneath the chest armor, then slid on his helm and clenched his fists. Once more, he set out to perform the will of his Dark Lord in the only way he ever wished to do so.

19

Even under the starless black of the charred night sky, the constantly flashing images from the holographic displays on every blank surface of the city would have given them away—if there had been anyone there to see them. Whether it was the deadened hour between late night and early morning or the fact that they now stood so close to the Unclean headquarters facility, Lukas found himself grateful for their apparent solitude in this part of the city. And he couldn't help but feel a little unsettled because of it. Still, he wasn't about to turn down the opportunity to advance, no matter how skeptical he was of it. They'd gotten this far unmolested; now the worst of it lay just ahead of them.

Marya glanced up from the tiny, handheld screen clutched in her palm, met Lukas's gaze, then nodded toward the squat, black, steel side door just across the alley from where they stood. Lukas took one more glance around, of course saw no one, and crossed the alley to slip inside the doorway. Marya followed him, her dark cloak concealing the energy phaser strapped to her hip, and Cephas brought up the rear. Lukas had not wanted to arm himself with a weapon like the others; while Cephas had not yet seen what Lukas was capable of with the Hedge at his disposal, Marya had. And even then, she'd sided with their bearded host in insisting Lukas take a weapon. Eventually, he'd conceded. The fact remained that none of them had a clear idea of what they'd be up against, and every little bit of defensive—or offensive, if it came to that—power helped. The semi-automatic rifle felt cumbersome and awkward hanging across Lukas's back from the strap over his shoulder, but he forced himself to ignore the unnatural weight and keep moving according to their plan.

When all three of them had gathered inside, Lukas removed Cyrus's mimic from his pocket and pressed it against a low black panel on the wall beside the door. Green lights flashed on both the small device in his hand and the panel, then the steel door slid open into the wall to allow them entrance. Lukas waited for Marya and Cephas to step inside first, scanning the streets one more time as his training and his instincts now prompted. But there had been no one to see them stealing through the lower-level streets at this time of night, and there was no one now to see them pass illegally into a facility they had no real business entering in the first place. Lukas reminded himself that the laws of this place did not apply to him. He answered only to God first and then the training that had molded him into a Hedge Master of Qumran. Everything else was just an obstacle to overcome.

Lukas didn't know what he'd expected the Unclean headquarters to look like, but this entrance level looked very much like the Sector One hallways of the Qumranian compound— tiled floors, level lighting, clean lines and white walls. Nothing else within this city even remotely resembled the cleanliness and order he had been accustomed to his entire life, and the sight of something so similar now—despite the fact that it belonged to the enemy who had destroyed his home—brought a pang of longing to his heart. But he pressed on with the others.

The hallways were empty. Marya consulted the schematic layout on the palm-sized device Cyrus had given them, her brow creasing just so. They'd gone over these plans a dozen times before they'd set out from Cephas's home—enter from the lower level street, find the stairwell, descend three flights of stairs to the sub-levels four stories under the city to the laboratory corridor, and find the lab where Deborah, Ben, and the quantum orb were supposedly being held. They had no confirmation of this, of course. Cyrus had been unable to provide them any more detail than what his experiential knowledge serving with the Unclean had given him and his hunch about where the commanders would keep their captives and their technological prize. If they didn't find Lukas's cousins and the orb in the labs below, they'd have to start all over again, and he didn't think their infiltration of the headquarters facility would remain unnoticed long enough for them to do that. This was their only chance, and it was risky with so many unknowns, but they had no other options. Lukas had made the decision before they set out through the city at night that he would do everything in his power to ensure his cousins' safety and secure the quantum orb so it could not be used again by those for whom it had never been intended. The rest was up to God.

So he followed Marya and Cephas across the entrance hall, down empty corridors, and through swinging doors leading to the stairwells. Once on the landing to the second sub-level, they heard rhythmic footsteps and a sharp bark of laughter from soldiers patrolling the hallways. Marya stood on her tiptoes to peer through the window in the stairwell door, then gestured for them to follow her and led them down two more flights of dimly lit stairs.

Finally, they reached the fourth sub-level; from the stairwell, it looked exactly the same as the previous three. Marya consulted her handheld device again, then nodded once. Cephas eased open the swinging door without making a sound and led the trio into the hallway beyond. The same thing met them here —tiled floors, white walls, complete emptiness. Lukas wondered why they'd only encountered one brief and seemingly unsuspecting patrol on their way here; it *was* the middle of the night, but he'd expected an army like the Unclean to have prepared themselves for all manner of disruption. They'd come to Qumran so prepared to destroy the compound and take what they wanted. Did they truly believe they'd killed everyone—that no one remained to stand against them?

They passed two sets of black double doors over which were illuminated the large, sprawling characters of the city's language in bright white tracks.

"This doesn't seem right," Cephas muttered, frowning as he glanced down the wide hallways in both directions. "Why is there no one here?"

"That's why we chose to come now instead of during the day, isn't it?" Marya glanced quickly from her handheld to the third set of laboratory doors, then passed these to march swiftly toward the fourth. "We're less likely to be spotted. This is a good thing."

Cephas glanced at Lukas; the man seemed to share Lukas's apprehension under the unnatural circumstances.

Marya waited for them to join her beside what Cyrus's layout told her was the lab most likely to hold what they sought. With a little smirk, she added, "If I didn't know better, I'd think the two of you are disappointed that you won't get the chance to fight."

The smile was swept immediately from her face when the sound of hurried footsteps and a shout, the words garbled as it echoed down the pristine hallways, rose toward them from around one of the sub-level's many corners.

"Let's do it," she whispered. Cephas and Lukas put a hand

on each of the double doors, and together, the trio burst into the designated lab. There they found that the suspicions the bearded man and the Hedge Master shared had not been unfounded.

In the center of the lab stood just over thirty Unclean soldiers in black uniforms, one of their commanders among them. Lukas recognized the harsh, striking lines of the man's bird-like helm, so subtly distinct from his counterpart's, and instantly wondered where the woman was.

Lukas's small team had undoubtedly found the right lab; beside the gathered soldiers were two low cages of black steel. In one, he saw Ben slumped against the far corner, his chest barely moving, his pale forehead and neck slick with sweat. In the other crouched Deborah. She met her cousin's gaze with wide eyes, then scrambled forward and wrapped her fingers through the mesh of the cage.

"Lukas," she whispered, and it was impossible to tell in that moment whether she'd said it in joy or terror.

The Unclean commander with the viciously adept armor lifted his chin at the intruders, the dark feathers on the plume of his helm fluttering slightly with the movement, and clasped his hands behind his back. "Did you really think you could walk in here so easily and take what is mine?"

Lukas felt Marya stir beside him as she reached for the energy pistol strapped to her waist. He slowly reached out his hand to stop her but kept his eyes on the Unclean soldiers, all of whom had their own weapons trained on the three strangers in their midst. He felt Marya stiffen—he knew she wanted to use her weapon now—but they were clearly outnumbered and taken by surprise when they'd meant to do the same. This didn't look good.

"I'd say I admire your dedication," the commander jeered, "but I'm not in the habit of commending fools." His eyes narrowed when he met Lukas's gaze, then he raised one hand from behind his back and lifted two fingers in a silent command to his troops.

As if time itself had stopped, Lukas took in the sight of over thirty fingers pulling back on over thirty triggers. The Hedge Master had a fighting chance to survive this onslaught, but his friends did not.

20

The Protectors moved within the confines of time only when they chose. Now, they bent it to their own will, fueled by the Almighty Father himself, and lowered themselves into the worldveil. The *shedim* had left this place, or they were too craven to appear when they sensed so many of the Protectors in one place together. A dozen blazing, white, winged Warriors inserted themselves into the lower levels of the place some mortals deemed an impenetrable fortress, the Unclean's headquarters. As the Father's swift, precise weapons of justice, nothing was an obstacle for them.

Most of them stood before the man they'd been sent to protect—the last of his kind—and his two companions. They spread their crystalline wings wide and raised their weapons in fearless defense. Two of them positioned themselves in front of the man's brethren held like animals in cages. They crouched in front of these mortals, wings outstretched to provide a shield no mortal weapon could pierce. The Protector knelt before the weak, nearly departed man with the broken arm and eyed him with compassion and perhaps the closest thing to pity any of the Father's warriors would ever be allowed to feel. They were here to act as shields, to stave off the worst of this attack. Without them it would have been impossible for those under their protection to escape. They could protect them, but they could do nothing to reverse what had already been done. That was not allowed, and for them, right now, from where they appeared in the worldveil, it was not possible.

Together, of one mind, the Protectors took their places and allowed time to resume its normal course. On the other side of the worldveil, the deadly mortal soldiers fired their weapons. A deafening report flared within the mortal realm, but here, the attack only elicited a low, muffled hum. Lead bullets pierced the air, their aim only as true as the hearts of those firing them from the manmade weapons. These, of course, did not stay the course.

The Protectors held their ground, unaffected by these projectiles and blasts of deadly red light, as one can imagine a thick wall of glass being unaffected by an enraged prisoner pounding against it with his fists. The weapons meant to steal the life from the Protectors' wards before their time had come, but instead their rounds rebounded from these brilliantly faceted bodies, refracted and redirected to other targets and other ends. The two beings kneeling before the caged mortals shared a slow, knowing smile. This was not the most difficult of the tasks that would be set before them, but it was essential. Without them in the worldveil, so many things would have already been undone. But, sent to fulfil the Father's will and carry out their duty, all things are possible for them in all times.

21

Lukas had never seen what he saw now, and his decades of training made him think he'd lost something of his senses and was unable to put the facts together. But the longer those few critical seconds stretched on, the more he realized something truly miraculous had happened—*was* happening—right in front of them.

The Unclean's weapons were entirely ineffective against Lukas and his companions. Lukas had braced himself for the impact of bullets and phaser blasts, thinking how foolish it was of them to not have armed their entire bodies with the protective gear Cephas had brought them; why would the enemy not aim at their heads at such close range? But the startling pressure and pain he'd expected under such an assault of firepower never came. It was as if an invisible wall had been lowered instantly in front of them; every round bounced away from them, ricocheting around the lab, shattering lights and smashing through walls that were not, in fact, made of stone like the Qumranian compound. Some of the shots found their way most conveniently back to the Unclean soldiers who had fired them, taking down almost a third of those shooting at them without the three intruders ever having to lift a finger—or even having the chance to do so.

This went on for maybe ten seconds, though it was hard to accurately pin down the timing from the shock of the impossible —that Lukas and his friends were alive, protected by some unknown force, and their mission had not ended in failure. Broken lights flickered, and the Unclean soldiers seemed to recognize they could not reach their targets and therefore ceased their fire. Low moans of agony drifted up from those lying bloodied and riddled with bullet wounds on the slick tile floors.

The Unclean commander took it all in with wide, disbelieving eyes. "What—"

But Lukas and Cephas didn't need any more of an excuse than this to take advantage of the confusion, nor did they need to confirm they had the same intent in mind. Cephas stepped forward and ducked through the strap of his rifle before bringing the butt of the weapon cracking down across the head of the closest Unclean soldier. Lukas took the fraction of a second he needed to prepare his body; he planted his feet and pressed his fists against his lower back. Just as his awareness narrowed and simultaneously expanded into the deadly force behind the Hedge Master's training, an Unclean soldier charged. Lukas swiftly ducked the wild blow with nothing more than a small, controlled step to the side, then brought his left fist shooting up into the soldier's stomach to leave him gasping for breath on the floor.

Almost two dozen men came at them at once, but after they'd seen how ineffective their firearms had been, not a single soldier tried that tactic again. Cephas was apparently a veteran in hand-to-hand combat, but Lukas did not have the time to let the realization surprise him. He landed a swift upper-cut to the next soldier's jaw, spun and kicked the legs of the next out from underneath the man, struck his elbow into a sternum and brought the back of his fist cracking up to splinter another's nose.

Cephas fought well for a man without Qumran combat training, though he put far more effort than was necessary into defensive guards and striking his opponents. Together, the two men left little room for any of the Unclean to make it past them and get to Marya, who stood behind them with her phaser pistol now in both hands. She wouldn't be able to get off a clean shot with her companions swiftly disabling every soldier who threw themselves at the two fighters, but at least she was armed.

And then the last enemy soldier fell, and Lukas squared off again to face the Unclean commander in the wickedly spiked armor, the one known as Damian. He heard Cephas's heavy, rapid breath beside him and from the corner of his eye saw the man strike a warning, defensive pose. Behind them, Marya raised her energy pistol.

The commander gazed at them with apparent calm, the only evidence of his annoyance coming as a faint twitch in his left eye. With a deep breath, Lukas flicked his gaze from Damian to the low cages a few feet over, where Deborah had thrown herself to the floor during the useless gunfire. She now lifted her head from where she crouched, breathing heavily and quite obviously confused by the damage she had not expected to see caused by only two men. Then Lukas's eyes drifted to the far end of the lab; the sight of the quantum orb resting in its steel cradle on the counter made his heart flutter with hope, despite the fact that ten more Unclean soldiers stood around it, weapons raised. No one moved.

Damian raised a thin eyebrow, which nearly disappeared beneath the sharp curve of the raptor-like beak jutting down from the center of his helm. "You cannot possibly think me so ill-prepared, Qumranian," the commander spat. At the same moment, two paneled doors on either side of the lab slid open to allow a sickeningly large rush of more Unclean soldiers into their midst. They swarmed to fill the room like a scattered nest of cockroaches.

The hope that had blossomed within Lukas's chest still lived, but he knew their chances of surviving this had dropped even lower than they had been with thirty Unclean weapons aimed at them. He eyed Deborah one more time, who took a sharp breath, then muttered, "Marya. Cephas. Get out."

His friends didn't need any more convincing. The harsh click of the lab doors being thrust open echoed through the steadily filling space, and when Lukas realized Marya and Cephas had retreated from the lab, the Hedge Master took three steps back, eyeing the force gathering around the commander, before turning and bolting into the hallway.

Their odds weren't much better out there. Another massive contingent of Unclean soldiers ran at them from the other end of the wide corridor as Marya and Cephas headed back toward the swinging doors of the stairwell. Marya turned and leveled off an energy shot into the oncoming force. She managed to strike one soldier in the chest before a volley of returned fire nearly blasted down the wall ahead of them. Then she barreled through the swinging door, Cephas and Lukas close on her heels.

Their pounding footsteps echoed up through the stairwell, met shortly with the resounding slam of another door. More soldiers entered the stairwell from the sub-level above them, but fortunately, they were smart enough not to fire shots within such close confines. Marya paused against the wall to let Lukas pass her, then he and Cephas met the forces nearly sliding down the staircase toward them. Fists and open hands flew; Unclean soldiers toppled over the railing, screaming as they fell countless stories. The bodies piled up the stairs, blocking the advancing Unclean from moving swiftly downward as Cephas, Lukas, and Marya scrambled over the black-clad bodies to fight their way up. The last soldier lifted his rifle to use as a club, and Lukas ducked, locked his forearm into the groove behind the man's shoulder, and shoved the soldier's head against the wall with an echoing crack. The body crumpled, and the trio climbed three more stories to the entrance level.

Lukas and Cephas grabbed the energy weapons from the closest fallen soldiers, their own rifles having been dropped in the fray, and Marya led them out of the stairwell. It seemed the way was clear to them until Marya, halfway down the hall before the corridor turned, was nearly taken down by a thick line of red energy pulses that missed her by a fraction of an inch. Cephas turned instantly to fire into this next mass of black-clad soldiers coming toward them across the wide, open room of this first level, taking down five in quick succession before a soldier's blast found its mark in Cephas's arm. He whirled, letting out a choked shout of surprise, and his commandeered Unclean energy phaser clattered to the floor. Lukas nodded for Cephas to follow Marya around the corner toward the access door. Cephas gritted his teeth, pulled himself together, and took off clutching his wounded arm with his other hand.

Lukas retrieved the energy weapon Cephas had dropped and leveled it beside the one he'd taken for himself. He squeezed off shot after shot of cover fire into the mass of soldiers, who retaliated swiftly with deafening fire of their own. Then he slipped around the corner and ran as fast as he could toward the access door. Cephas and Marya had stopped like rats trapped in a maze, because the door apparently didn't open from the inside of the facility without a key pass.

Grimacing in urgent frustration, Lukas ripped the mimic from his pocket and slammed it against the panel. The green lights couldn't have flashed any slower before the locking mechanism disengaged and the access door slid open. The three of them stumbled outside into the darkness of early morning in the city's lower level streets, and the projected image of a woman with slicked-back hair exploded in a shower of cratered brick when two energy shots slipped through the access door and into the wall of the building across the alley.

Cephas turned and slumped against the outer wall of the Unclean headquarters facility, his face contorted in pain as he still clutched his wounded bicep. The access door slid closed behind them, and Lukas slipped a hand between Cephas's back and the wall to guide him once more down the dark, empty side street.

"Not here," he whispered, glancing back once to see the access door had still not opened again to release their pursuers into the night. "We have to keep moving."

22

Deborah didn't think she could be any more terrified than when she'd watched Lukas and the two strangers with him fighting for their lives, then fleeing the new swarm of Unclean soldiers that had quickly filled the lab. She was wrong.

Lukas was alive—he'd somehow survived the compound's destruction—and the fact that she'd been right to hope for such an unlikely thing brought a silent prayer of thanksgiving to her lips. But now, surrounded by so many vicious men in black uniforms, red stars on the backs of their hands, she realized just how true it was that hope only made despair that much crueler. It was impossible to tell which was more paralyzing—the fact that she'd almost seen her cousin destroyed by the army that had abducted and brutally caged her and Ben, or the fact that she didn't know if Lukas had escaped. Whether or not he was alive, unharmed.

But that dizzying fear flared anew and washed all other thoughts away when the woman commander, apparent twin and co-leader of the man in the intimidatingly foreign armor, burst through the lab's main doors and strode confidently into the center of the room. The man was bad enough as it was, but this woman… this woman was far worse. Deborah had seen it in the witch's eyes, had known it from the minute she had snatched Ben's wrist in one hand and shattered his arm with nothing more than a single precise movement. And now she was here, again, to press upon them whatever new horrors she had in store.

The black-uniformed soldiers noted her presence and jumped sharply to attention, staring straight ahead with arms stiff at their sides. Their commander entered as though everything was as it should be. Her smirk of calculating amusement made Deborah's spine tingle, but she couldn't tell if it was hot or cold. She just wanted to disappear.

A short, stocky Unclean soldier approached her with hurried steps, then snapped to attention with his hands at his sides. "The targets have returned to the lower levels of the city. We'll have them soon, mistress."

The woman tilted her head, sending the dark plumes of feathers at the crest of her sharp-edged helm into brisk flutters. From where Deborah crouched in her cage, it seemed the commander spoke to this soldier now as if he were a relative's child—a nuisance to be handled with forced patience and false sincerity.

"Let them go," she said, "but have them followed. Inform me of where they choose to lay their heads for the night. I wish to send them a gift."

"Lucia." The male commander stepped toward her from his surrounding contingent of soldiers, looking irritated beneath the sharp, wicked curve of the beak stretching over his helm. "We should eradicate them like the others."

Lucia shot her counterpart a glance, then slowly turned in a half-circle to survey the damage to the lab—the bullet-riddled walls, the spilled shelves of instruments, the Unclean bodies lying in smears of blood across the tiled floors. "That tactic does not seem to have worked in your favor, brother," she replied.

The man clenched his fists beneath the purple and black

plate and leather of his gauntlets. "They had some form of aid I did not anticipate," he said through gritted teeth.

His sister gave a noncommittal hum and lifted her chin to stare down her nose at him. "Surprise does not become you, Damian."

"I want them dead." With a hiss, he tilted his head from side to side and rolled his shoulders, making him look very much like a stiff, agitated bird ruffling its feathers to ward off potential predators.

"Did you receive some new directive that I did not?" Lucia asked, though it did not sound like she truly wished to know the answer.

Deborah rather thought Lucia was trying to teach her brother a lesson of some kind, and it seemed particularly odd that the siblings would enter such a quarrel here, amid their subordinate soldiers, without feeling any need for privacy. But she supposed that was an advantage of being the leaders of such a vile army; the soldiers' fear of their commanders was most likely far greater than any doubt in their capabilities such a rivalry might raise. While unshakable fear reminded her constantly to keep her gaze averted and not draw undue attention to herself, Deborah couldn't keep from watching the pair of commanders with horrified fascination.

"My orders were to protect the Qumranian machine," Damian growled.

"Which has been done." His sister waved a hand at the quantum orb in its cradle against the far wall, still surrounded by ten Unclean soldiers who stood with weapons drawn but lowered, as if no one else existed in the room with them. "You had your fun with them, and that is finished. Now it's time for me to have mine."

Damian glared at her beneath hooded eyes. His nostrils flared wildly, but he said nothing more. Then Deborah's heart almost stopped in her chest when the witch called Lucia turned from her brother and slowly fixed her cold black eyes on the caged captives. Another slow, predatory smile split the woman's lips as she hungrily considered first Deborah, quivering with shallow breath, then Ben, who slumped against the cage with his eyes closed, as if he'd slept through the whole ordeal.

"It's been a long time since I've enjoyed something this much."

Deborah couldn't pull her eyes away from the ungodly sight before her. The air around Lucia's head shimmered and darkened, then took on an aspect of unnatural thickness. A black halo of some monstrous figure flared behind the woman's outline, looming over her in an abomination of the human form. Then she opened her mouth, and the laughter that escaped was not hers alone; it belonged to both the evil woman and the darkness, many voices all at once, thunderous and tinkling and horrifying. Lucia stepped toward the cage where Ben lay sweaty and feverish, and the dread that had frozen Deborah burst out of her.

"What are you doing?" Her weak voice trembled, and she lurched toward the side of the cage closest to her brother. Her fingers scrambled against the steel mesh, but Lucia paid her no attention.

"Ben?" Deborah called, pressing her face against the cage. "Ben, can you hear me?" Her brother's head lolled to the side, and he let out a barely audible groan.

When Lucia squatted in front of Ben's cage, leering at him like a hungry animal about to pounce, Deborah lost it.

"Don't touch him!" Her fists pounded on her own cage, shaking the walls of it all around her. "No. Leave him alone. Ben!" She might as well have been a tool on a lab tray for all her protests did to save her brother.

23

They moved quickly through the side streets, Marya leading them away from the Unclean headquarters and navigating effortlessly through the growing busyness of the city waking for the morning. Lukas walked behind Cephas, who still clutched his arm, though Marya had ripped a strip of fabric from her skirts to use as a makeshift tourniquet. Down every sharp turn of the alleyways, Lukas heard footsteps following behind them—two men, by the sound of it, and soldiers. But every time he tried to glimpse their pursuers, he saw only shadow and the flash of neon lights projected from the holographic displays. Even still, he listened intently, prepared to fight off whoever came after them if they got too close.

Finally, they emerged from the dark, empty alleys and into one the main avenues of the city's lower levels. A huge crowd had gathered ahead, voices rising over the clanging din of business and the bright moving ads. For the most part, though, the people crowding around some unseen spectacle were silent, curious, craning their necks for a better glimpse and straining to hear what was being said. Marya turned back briefly to eye Lukas, and he nodded, encouraging her to keep moving. With a gathering this large, their chances of losing their pursuers were far greater. He didn't know if Marya or Cephas had noticed the soldiers on their trail, but he did know they both recognized the need for urgency now.

Marya stepped into the crowd, turning sideways to squeeze past the first few citizens pressing against each other. Lukas ushered Cephas ahead of him in Marya's path, and once they'd put a decent number of bodies behind them, he spared a glance back over his shoulder. He'd been right; two Unclean soldiers were now visible among the throng of people, their black uniforms contrasted starkly with the lighter tones of undyed cloth worn by most of the city's residents. No one seemed to notice their presence, but the soldiers no longer appeared intent on following Lukas and his friends. Instead, they stared with wide eyes toward the center of the crowd. One soldier's mouth dropped open, and his companion jerked his head to mumble something. Then they turned and disappeared into the shadows. If Lukas didn't know any better, he'd have thought the soldiers had seen something that frightened them. At least for now, they weren't being followed anymore.

He kept moving behind Marya and Cephas, then Marya stopped in her tracks to stare up at a huge, moving image on the building in front of them. Her eyes grew wide, and Lukas followed her gaze. There, in massive proportions, was a projection of six Phar-asai in their telltale brown leather robes surrounding a man who stood calmly with his hands clasped in front of him. While the images of the Phar-asai had been captured with perfect clarity, the tiniest detail of the tassels on their robes caught and expanded to a dizzying size, the man's visage wavered. Thinking it was perhaps a technological issue, Lukas looked overhead to search the other projections on every panel, wall, doorway, and surface of the large street around him. Dozens of recorded images were cast in vivid color and detail, all from different angles and of various sizes. But in each one, the man with his hands clasped could not be seen clearly. It was almost like a swath of thin cotton had been stuck to whatever cameras captured the scene in the center of the crowd, though Lukas knew it was impossible that every single lens would have the same defect in different places, and only where the man's face showed upon the screens.

When he heard the next words spoken over the heads of the onlookers, he realized all the projections were in real-time, lagging a fraction of a second after what was said.

"You seem to have made yourself somewhat of an agitator of the people." The Phar-asai who had spoken tucked his hands into the connecting sleeves of his robes. "And many say you are mentally unfit to wield the authority of a teacher, which you claim yourself to be. How do you refute this?"

Lukas felt a nudge against his shoulder and he turned to see Cephas standing beside him now. The man nodded toward a few women gathered at the edge of the crowd, watching him with concern etched into their weary faces.

"My friends are healers," Cephas muttered. "Hopefully they can see to this arm." He grimaced, then added, "You and Marya can return to my home any time you wish. It's still safe."

"Thank you," Lukas replied with a nod. "We'll see you there."

Cephas turned and pushed his way slowly through the back of the crowd toward the women. Lukas hoped they would be able to help him.

The voice rising now via some unseen amplifiers made Lukas jerk his head up.

"I carry the love of God in my heart. There is no room for the influences of evil." While the man with the distorted face was clearly the one who had spoken—the blurred outline of his head moved in rhythm with his words—Lukas did not have to see him at all to know who he was. The sound of his voice was unmistakable; this was Jesse, approached by the Phar-asai and put on display in this busy street for all to see. He couldn't help but wonder why such a production had been made of the man's presence when he'd so recently seen Jesse speaking among friends in the marketplace underground.

"The glory I seek is not for me but for my Father," Jesse continued. "And he seeks it with me. I'm not lying to any of you when I say that whoever listens to my word, whoever follows God in his heart and walks a different Way, will never meet death."

Lukas scanned the angled projections above him. A second Phar-asai raised his hands in exasperation and addressed the crowd. "Well, there is your proof. Mentally unstable, yes, and I say completely insane." He turned back to Jesse. "The mystics are long gone. Dead and buried. Yet you say those who keep your word will never die. Should the mystics themselves have listened to you instead?" A low rise of nervous chuckling came from the people gathered closest to the Phar-asai, but it died quickly. "Do you call these mystics false? Or perhaps you think yourself greater than all of them."

"There is only one who glorifies me," Jesse said. The single time Lukas had listened to the man, he hadn't heard a shade of irritation or frustration in the teacher's voice. Now, those were the only emotions he heard, and it unsettled Lukas entirely. "That is my Father. Not me. And I know him, truly *know* him. My father is the same you claim to be *your* God, but only one of us is lying. And it's not me."

The Phar-asai jerked beneath their leather robes, and a rustle of disbelief filtered first from them and then outward into the gathering crowd. Lukas waited for the robed men to whip out their electric rods and start beating Jesse to death right there on the spot, but they stayed their hands, and he couldn't for the life of him figure out why.

"And I keep my Father's word," Jesse continued. "I embrace it and deliver it to all of you. Yes, the mystics are dead. But when they lived, they saw what was to come—what has already happened in the last few years and the days leading up to today —and they rejoiced. If they were here, they would tell you the same."

"You are still so young," the first Phar-asai added. "Every mystic became so after the prime of his life. In his fifties, most often older. You can't yet be forty, Jesse, and you claim to have seen what the mystics saw? They were gone before you could walk."

"I don't claim anything that isn't the truth." Jesse stood his ground, but he raised his arms just a little at his sides, addressing everyone around him. "Before even the first mystic was born into this world, I was. I *am*. I will *always* be."

A roar of outrage erupted from the Phar-asai, and the crowd caught it like a contagious disease. Some of them, Lukas saw, seemed frightened for what might be done to Jesse after such a bold statement. Those who looked offended like the Phar-asai seemed hesitant even in that display, as if they wished to believe Jesse but wished even more not to associate themselves with anyone under the scrutiny of the teachers of the Law.

"Blasphemy!" the Phar-asai shouted.

"We cannot stand for this. He must be stopped."

"Others have been executed for far less than this fraudulent treason."

Lukas tried to peer over the rustling, shifting crowd, just to get a glimpse of Jesse's face in person—some reassurance that this *was* the man he'd seen and the man his new friends so loyally followed. Somewhere during the questioning, Marya had returned to his side, and she nudged him and pointed discreetly to the other side of the crowd. A large gathering of Janiss-arai had congregated on their own like a writhing black mass, just waiting to be put to use. A strike of dread pulsed through Lukas —not for himself but for Jesse—and he pushed forward in one more attempt to spot the man with his own eyes.

But when he looked back toward the Phar-asai, who argued with each other, shouting and gesticulating wildly in their fury, he found Jesse had disappeared in the chaos. Lukas scanned the crowd, fiercely hoping the Janiss-arai hadn't got to him first. Then he caught a fleeting glimpse of Jesse veering around the corner into a dark, narrow alley, the hem of his uncolored tunic waving behind him before it, too, disappeared.

Lukas couldn't help but think Jesse had not fled this gathering out of fear for his own life or any form of cowardice. Though he barely knew the man, he thought Jesse had stood so steadfastly at the center of the crowd and allowed himself to be questioned by the Phar-asai out of a sense of both irritation and amusement. Lukas thought Jesse might have been waiting patiently for just such an opportunity to shove the teachers' hypocrisy in their faces once they'd tried to discredit him in front of so many witnesses. And the man who taught a new Way had seemed surprisingly unconcerned for his own well-being but particularly satisfied by the chance to openly express to everyone what he believed and what he knew to be true. Lukas found himself admiring Jesse for this—for his steadfastness and unwillingness to be cowed when it came to his belief in God—but he also wondered if it was foolishness or something else that drove the man to the edge of flirting with his own death. He couldn't possibly think the Phar-asai wouldn't come for him after this.

Mulling this over as if it had any effect on what Lukas himself would do next, he glanced across the crowd. A man standing at the edge turned from where he too had seen Jesse depart, then his gaze fell on Lukas, and both men froze.

Lukas recognized that face, though he shouldn't have—it was impossible. He was the only soul who had escaped the destruction of Qumran; he'd been so sure of it. But the wide eyes of his father's old friend staring back at him brought that certainty crumbling down.

The man he knew to be Aaron, a veteran of the Qumranian

Enforcers, broke from his frozen shock, turned, and sprinted in the opposite direction down the street, away from the crowd and the Phar-asai and Lukas himself.

Lukas briefly gripped Marya's arm, gave it a light squeeze, and muttered, "Come with me," before he took off through the crowd, leaving the still-rising din of confusion, anger, and surprise behind him.

Quickly, he broke from the press of bodies and ran fully after the man he knew was Aaron. Marya's sandals pounded on the grimy street behind him. Then Aaron turned sharply down another alleyway ahead. Lukas almost toppled into a vendor's cart piled high with hundreds of plastic, glistening objects, but he righted himself and bolted into the narrow passage.

The alley was long and straight, and Aaron was over twice Lukas's age. The man was fit, yes, but as a thirty-year veteran the fierceness and swiftness of his physical prime had abandoned him. Lukas, however, was at his peak. He quickly caught up to the man, whose harsh breathing bounced off the close walls and the flashing holographic displays. When Lukas lurched forward to wrap his hand around the man's wrist, Aaron cried out in alarm and stumbled forward. Quickly, Lukas released him again, not wanting to alarm him further.

"Aaron, stop," he said, his breathing far closer to normal than the veteran Enforcer.

Aaron whirled around, his eyes still wide as he stepped backward down the alley. "Everyone's gone," he panted. "They're all dead. I saw it. No one survived the attack, so who in God's name *are* you?"

Lukas heard Marya slowing to a halt behind him, breathing as heavily as Aaron. He didn't turn to look back at her, but he raised a hand to signal her to wait.

"Aaron, it's me. Lukas. Just me." Slowly, he raised his palms toward the man, as if in surrender but in reality to show Aaron the blood-right scars in the center of each hand.

Aaron's gaze flickered from one hand to the other, and he glowered at Lukas. "Those could have been given to anyone, anywhere," he spat. "That's no proof."

"Then ask me," Lukas replied calmly. "Ask me something only you and I would know."

Aaron studied him, his breath finally settling into a rhythym. His gaze moved toward Marya, but she remained silent, and he ignored her. "Who was the Hedge designed to kill?"

Lukas folded his arms and tipped his head back, trying not to smile. "No one, old man. The Hedge is a shield, but not of man. It protects the Law."

Aaron's scowl melted slowly into a wary, hesitant smile, and when Lukas smirked, the veteran Enforcer barked out a laugh and let his back fall against a nearby wall. "How?" he breathed.

Lukas shook his head. "I don't know." Then he opened his arms, stepped forward, and Aaron approached his friend for a quick, rough embrace of surprise and relief.

"It's good to see you, Lukas." Aaron held Lukas back by the shoulders to take another look at him, this time unmarred by fear and skepticism. "I thought I was the only one who made it out."

"So did I."

"What happened?"

Lukas clapped the man's shoulders in response, then they released each other. "I wish I had an answer for you that would satisfy us both," he said. "We have a lot to talk about."

"I'll say."

"We should also keep moving." Lukas turned toward Marya, who watched the unexpected reunion with a calm smile. "It's not safe to stay in one place for very long, especially after what just happened with the crowd. This is Marya. She's been a... good friend to me."

Marya nodded at Aaron, who smiled and said, "Well met. I'm Aaron. I have to say, I'm glad not to be alone anymore."

24

"How did you get out?"

They moved through the alleyway and emerged into the street again. The crowd that had gathered to watch the Phar-asai and Jesse had dwindled. Lukas thought that the lingering presence of the Phar-asai and their Janiss-arai executioners had the largest part to play in that. No one wanted to spend too long around anyone in robes—brown or black—he understood this all too well.

"I was on a breach patrol," Aaron replied, casting an anxious glance back at the Phar-asai. "Completely routine. The outer tunnels near the surface are—were rougher, but they'd always held. Hadn't had a breach in my lifetime." He stopped talking to stare at the grimy street passing beneath his feet. Lukas wanted to reach out to him, to reassure him, but it seemed more befitting to let the man who had been a mentor and a friend come to the rest of his story in his own time. And that didn't take very long. "There was some kind of explosion. I haven't ever heard or seen anything like it. The tunnel collapsed, and I hit the ground. Passed out. When I came to... Well, like I said, I thought I was the only one who made it. None of my men did. But the collapse opened up a shaft to the Above. Funny, really. On a breach patrol, and the one thing we'd set out to avoid was what saved my life."

Lukas turned to look at the man, nodding in acknowledgment. "I'm glad it did," he said.

Aaron took a deep breath. "Me too. I think. None of this is anything like I expected." He waved a hand at the city around them—the rising pillars of steel and glass, the blaring images on projected holograms, the beeps and jingles and horns and whirs of modern life. It was so drastically unlike what Qumran had been and so foreign to the Qumranian image of the what the world had become.

"It's definitely... different." Lukas glanced ahead, following Marya through the streets as he still did not recognize the way to Cephas's apartment. He was grateful for her subtle courtesy in leading them and providing a little privacy for their unexpected reunion. "If you're here too," he told Aaron, "I wonder how many others survived. The compound's gone now. I... I watched them destroy it completely. But if you had a chance, maybe there are more."

"How did you manage it?"

Lukas paused briefly. This was only his second morning beneath the fiery, roiling sky Above—only his second day within the filthy, packed, constantly thrumming walls of the city. But already, he'd resigned himself to the fact that here, no one knew him. Now, it was strange to recognize how much he could share with Aaron, another Qumranian, without needing to explain or feeling like some foreign specimen under a microscope. "This city's military force is responsible for Qumran's end," he said slowly. Aaron looked at him with wide eyes. "They call themselves the Unclean. They infiltrated the compound—I'm not sure how—and found us in Sector One. Destroying Qumran was intentional on their part, I'm sure, but I think they came specifically for the quantum orb."

Aaron tugged at his beard as they walked and rubbed his fingers across chapped lips. "The machine your team was working on?"

Lukas nodded. "We finished it," he said, unable to contain a small, reminiscent smile at the memory of that blaring success and what they had achieved—what more they could have achieved if things had turned out differently. "The first test was successful."

The wry chuckle Aaron released carried his own sense of pride, dampened by the regret they both felt over such a huge loss. "Never doubted it would be," he said. "I'd say congratulations, but..."

Lukas shrugged, and the men almost laughed amid the absurdly horrid experience they shared. "We had a brief moment of it," he said. "And then the Unclean came, and they took the machine. They took so many things. Data, records, technology. They took Ben and Deborah, too."

Aaron took in a sharp breath. "That's no small miracle."

"That they're alive, yes. If I hadn't gotten out of the lab when I did, I'd be a prisoner in a cage right beside them. That's where we were just before I found you." He looked over at Marya, paused, then back to Aaron. "I saw them."

"And?"

"Deborah looks terrified but unharmed. Ben, though... . They broke his arm before they took everyone away. I don't know what else they've done to him, but he doesn't look well." Lukas gritted his teeth, feeling the guilt battling with his gratitude—guilt for having left his cousins at the hands of such a devious military force, and gratitude for his having escaped the same fate. Now, at least, there was someone who could go back for them. And he would.

"We'll do whatever it takes to get your cousins back safely," Aaron said. "At least, as safe as anyone can be in *this* place."

Lukas raised his brows in agreement, but he could not say

the one thing dominating his mind. He wanted to release his cousins from their barbaric imprisonment, yes. But if he had to make the call between rescuing Deborah and Ben and seizing the quantum orb from the hands of the Unclean, his gut told him he'd choose the latter. And his conscience told him God would forgive him for forsaking his own kin if it meant saving the rest of the world from a fate worse than it had already experienced. He knew, without a doubt, that the Unclean would not sit on the quantum orb forever without using it for their own ends, and they would never use it the way it was designed to be used—to carry out God's will and fulfil His purposes.

Finally, Lukas recognized the rise of the expansive, ugly gray apartment building where Cephas lived. Marya led them down the uncomfortably narrow hallway, then stopped in front of Cephas's door and turned to face Lukas and Aaron with a tired smile. She placed her hand on the hidden panel, the lights blinked, and she pushed open the door and ushered them inside.

Aaron glanced around him with wide-eyed curiosity, taking in the sight of the small, cramped living room, the bare kitchen, the low table and pillows. "So different," he muttered. "So very different."

"I take it you haven't yet found a place to stay in the city," Lukas said, eyeing the man's surprised awe and the navy-blue uniform worn by Qumranian Enforcers. Aaron's clothes were streaked with dirt and mud, filth from wherever he'd slept the last two nights, and a large rip in the back of his shirt left his flesh exposed.

Aaron eyed his young friend with a short chuckle. "What makes you say that?" Lukas couldn't entirely hide his subdued smile. "You've been truly blessed, Lukas. Even in this nightmare."

The words struck him, and Lukas turned to meet Marya's gaze. She'd removed her cloak and draped it over one arm.

"I know," he said.

Marya smiled, then set her cloak on the bench beside the front door. "I'm sure Cephas has a few extra clothes around here somewhere," she said.

"Cephas?"

"This is his home," Lukas explained. "He's been kind enough to let me stay here." Then he remembered Cephas's wounded arm and the fact that he had no idea when the man would return.

As she was wont to do, Marya seemed to read his mind. "I saw him go with Jeza and her healers," she said. "He's in good hands." Then she turned toward Aaron. "I'll go see about those clothes." She left the room, pausing only to lay the energy pistol she'd taken with her earlier that morning on the low table in the center of the room.

When she closed the door behind her, Aaron glanced down at the weapon on the table, then looked quickly up at Lukas and raised his brows.

Lukas nodded. "She knows how to use it."

Aaron dipped his head, apparently impressed, and took another moment to survey the apartment.

"You look tired."

Aaron jerked his head around and scoffed. "I thought you'd learned to respect your elders."

"I have," Lukas said with a smirk. "I was going to offer you my room here. It's upstairs."

He rubbed a hand down his face. "It seems impossible, but that's all I can think about right now. I haven't slept since the night before last."

"You should go rest, then," Lukas replied. "I managed a bit of shuteye in a nice alley. Rare little spot of dry ground. Minimal flashing lights. I'm sure you'd enjoy a nice pallet, then. I'll just—"

"Lukas."

His name came out short and clipped on her tongue, and he hadn't yet heard that tone in Marya's voice. He turned to face her, holding a folded set of clothes in her arms, thinking the worst and that they faced some new and unknown danger.

Her eyes were wide for just a second before they softened, and she gave him an apologetic smile. "That room was meant for you." Then she looked at Aaron. "There's another upstairs, if you'd like to lie down for a while, Aaron."

"That's fine," he replied with a shake of his head. "I don't want to put anyone out. Really. Being off the streets is kindness enough."

"You won't be putting anyone out." Marya stepped toward Aaron, holding out the undyed tunic and loose trousers just like Lukas's. "We are more than happy to share what we have. It's our Way."

Aaron took them with a smile of thanks. "A real bed sounds wonderful," he said.

Marya nodded, then turned back to eye Lukas. "I'll stay down here for a bit longer. Your friend can have the room on the left."

A sudden nostalgic wave washed over Lukas; his mother had once looked at him very much the same way when he was a child. It should have unnerved him, he thought, coming from Marya, but instead he found himself amused by it and grateful for the kindness and generosity amid the unexplained sternness.

"Thank you," Aaron told her, and Marya reached out to briefly touch his shoulder.

"You're always welcome."

"This way," Lukas said, indicating the narrow staircase at the back of the apartment. Aaron followed him with the new clothes in his arms, and together, they walked up to the low-ceilinged second story. It surprised Lukas how quickly he'd taken to his new role here in the city, whatever that might be. He appreciated more than he could say the way Marya and Cephas, Yaakov and Yohanan gave of everything they had to welcome and aid strangers among them, no matter where they came from or how little they knew of each other. And being part of the same for Aaron, though the man was an old friend and the only other Qumranian walking the lower level streets of the city, gave Lukas a sense of purpose and completion he had not fully experienced since he'd returned from their first test with the quantum orb to celebrate the success with his team that no longer existed. This was his world now, and he would do what he could to be a part of it—to make it better.

They reached the top of the staircase, and Lukas gestured to the door on the left. "Make yourself at home," he said. "That's what I've been told."

Aaron grinned, his brown eyes sparkling beneath the wrinkled lines of age around them. "God willing, we will find a way, Lukas."

"I believe that." He waited for Aaron to close the door behind him before Lukas went to his own room at the end of the short hall. It took him even less time to fall asleep than it had the first night.

25

He awoke to the sound of low conversation and easy laughter coming from the living room below. Pulling himself from beneath the covers, he straightened the pallet and briefly opened the single window's shutters to glance outside. Though he saw only the shuttered windows of the next apartment complex opposite, the light outside was still a hazy, red-gray glow, so he knew he couldn't have slept more than six or seven hours.

When he made his way down the stairs, he realized it was no longer just Aaron, Marya, and himself in Cephas's apartment. It sounded like a crowd, and he recognized with relief the rumble of Cephas's voice amid the hushed conversation. Then he stepped around the corner at the bottom of the staircase and looked upon the gathering in the living room.

The brothers Yaakov and Yohanan had returned, as well as Cephas, his wounded arm wrapped tightly in a sling of clean, undyed cloth. Aaron had already come down from his room, and Marya sat beside him on the pillows at the low table. A few steaming cups of what Lukas guessed was supposed to serve as tea rested between them on the table.

Cephas looked up to see him first. "Lukas," he said. "You look well rested."

Smiling, Lukas eyed the people filling the apartment but somehow not crowding it and joined them at the table. "You look mended."

Cephas chuckled. "God is good. So are my friends skilled at treating gunshot wounds."

Lukas sat on the pillows between Marya and Yohanan, then asked Aaron, "How long have you been awake?"

"An hour or two," the man replied. "With age comes an inability to sleep. At least, not as long as you do." His smile was warm with good-natured amusement, once again bringing a semblance of normalcy and the feeling of home into this wild displacement from their old life.

"Are you hungry?" Cephas asked. He gestured to the pot of what Lukas assumed was the tasteless but nutritious mush on the small stove.

"Not quite yet," Lukas replied.

"How 'bout the food here, though, hmm?" Aaron said, shooting Lukas a smirk. "This city may be technologically advanced, but I'll take a fresh ear of roasted corn over chemically enhanced gruel any day. Yaakov here was just telling me he's never seen an apple in person. An apple, Lukas." Lukas glanced at Yaakov, who shrugged and shook his head. "Qumran had a whole grove of apple trees," Aaron continued. "A huge orchard spanning acres and acres. Your quarters were right at the edge of it, Lukas, weren't they?"

Lukas nodded, remembering with a deep pang of loss the view he'd had every morning since he'd moved into his own quarters as an adult—the grass running healthy and green right up to the side of the Agricultural Sector's cavern; the vast stretch of treetops and fields of grain and corn below; the expanse of their paneled sky and the rolling valleys stretching ever onward; the glint of red caught through the leaves during the harvest season; the bowl of apples he kept on the counter beside what had been his own front door.

He swallowed and forced a smile. "They were," he said. "I must have eaten an apple almost every day."

"See?" Aaron jabbed an excited finger at his fellow Qumranian. "What did I tell you? And peas, carrots, potatoes. The ripest, juiciest melons you've ever cut into. I'm guessing if you've never seen an apple, you've also never tasted chicken?"

The citizens of this world shared amused glances around the low table, humoring the old man who clearly chose not to mourn the loss of his homeland and his people but instead share what glory of it he could with those who had never had the fortune of such wonderous things. He went on for at least ten minutes, if not longer, about all the things Lukas himself missed about their homeland. Qumran had been a veritable oasis, their Paradise on Earth, and while he'd always appreciated the wealth of blessings both in his own life and regarding the well-being of Qumran as a whole within the fortress of their compound, he could not help but feel as if he'd taken so much of it for granted. Especially now that his home was gone, wiped from the Earth as if it had never been; according to Marya, most of the world had already forgotten Qumran in this timeline, and it filled him with a nostalgic longing so poignantly contrasting with how little time he'd spent away from home.

Soon enough, the contagious glimmer in Aaron's eyes had spread to all their companions. They chuckled at his enthusiasm, drawn into it like bees to nectar, asking if he'd ever seen this flower, heard the call of that bird, felt the softness of a certain animal's fur. Almost every answer he gave them was yes, he had, but the natural world they'd cultivated and protected underground was only part of it. He went on to detail the bazaars, the annual celebrations, the gatherings among their people to celebrate God and life and each other— children laughing in the fields, running to their mothers' welcoming embraces; husbands and wives working together in harmony; the dedication of their warriors in combat training, though he did not mention the details of the Hedge; the brilliance of their scientists working tirelessly to improve the lives of all Qumranians and bring them that much closer to fulfilling the purpose God had set upon them two thousand years ago.

With the mention of this last item, Aaron reached around Marya to pat Lukas on the back in a distinctly familial gesture of acknowledgment and appreciation. Lukas smiled at the man—his only tie right now to the life he might never regain—then caught Marya's gaze. She lifted her plastic cup toward Lukas as the veteran Enforcer went on a bit longer, then lowered her gaze with a secret smile.

A flush of pride moved through Lukas then, and yet it was muted by the knowledge that to be so proud of his accomplishments as a Qumranian scientist was an unfounded claim now. Yes, for years, he and his team had done great work and taken massive strides toward their goals; the quantum orb and its first successful test had been the pinnacle of everything they'd worked so hard to achieve. But it had also been their downfall and the singular source of what had now become this strange, terrifying, deadened world. He would not be satisfied with himself or this new life until he'd righted the wrongs that had been committed with the use of his machine, so adulterated from its original purpose.

"Your tales are heartening, Aaron," Cephas said, grinning at their new companion. "We've all heard stories of the Old World. Green growth and natural life. Fresh food. Living things. I can only imagine what it must be like to look up at a shining sun within a blue sky. To feel like I can breathe again." The man briefly closed his eyes, and his friends hummed their approval of such a dream. "God truly did smile upon Qumran."

Aaron nodded slowly, his enthusiasm a little dampened now

by the memory of what had recently become of his people, so fresh in both his and Lukas's minds. "He did. For a long time."

The living room filled with a silence harboring gratitude, longing, and a deep measure of respect, all for things that had been and were no more. Marya stood and went to the small stove to retrieve the kettle. When she returned, she brought with her another plastic cup and set it before Lukas. He tried to protest as she poured the steaming drink for him, but she silenced him with a glance.

"You need *something*," she insisted, though her voice was soft, kind. "It's the closest thing to real tea you'll find here, and it tastes much better than anything else."

Thoroughly reprimanded with generosity, Lukas raised an eyebrow at her, then tipped his head in acknowledgment and picked up the warm plastic cup in both hands. Apparently satisfied, Marya left to return the kettle to the stove. When her back was turned, Lukas caught the looks of lighthearted amusement shared between the others at the table. Though he did not plan to ever do so, he didn't think he wanted to bring Marya's ire down on himself; the glance Yohanan threw him implied Lukas had chosen wisely in deferring to Marya as he had, at least in this.

She resumed her place between Lukas and Aaron and took a slow sip of her own tea. Lukas felt her gaze on him, then brought the plastic cup to his lips for a tentative taste. The sweet smoothness on his tongue surprised him, filling him with a warm comfort he hadn't realized he'd needed until it was upon him. He swallowed, took another sip, and while he did not tell Marya she'd been right, he felt her acknowledgment of it all the same.

"So, my friends," Cephas continued, glancing from Aaron to Lukas. "Because you are new to our city and our customs, I will tell you what we're doing here tonight. As you know, Lukas, we are honored to call ourselves students of Jesse and his new Way. Aaron, you may not have seen him yet, but we can change that tomorrow." Aaron shot Lukas a questioning glance, and the Hedge Master gave his friend a reassuring nod. "We come together when we can to share with each other and speak of what we know and what we've heard. Within the unceasing chaos of life's struggles, it is this and God's love through His word that gives us strength. Hope. A reason to endure."

Aaron hummed in acknowledgment, and Lukas leaned back just a little from the table. So much talk of God's love—and little else of His holy knowledge, His omniscient power, His promise delivered into the Law that Lukas had sworn his life to uphold and protect—unnerved him. The people of this city endured a harsh life from beginning to end, that much was true, and he understood the power and necessity of hope amid such darkness. But he could not help but feel as though the way they spoke of God and their own faith merely served as a masked disguise for their resignation to this life—their acceptance of it with no Law to fuel them further, to drive them toward bettering their world, toward changing the fate that had been dealt them. He'd heard so much mentioned of love in his brief time here Above, but it sounded to Lukas like defeat. This was not what he knew of God.

Still, he could not bring himself to say any of these things. He only watched, listened, and waited. Cephas nodded at Yaakov, who took a long drink of his sweetened tea, cleared his throat, and began.

"The Books of Phineas the mystic and Jannes the mystic speak of a Messiah that is and was and forever will be. They speak of God's original plan. That the first Messiah entered into the world as an infant, and as an infant, he was removed from it. The deceptive, treacherous hand of Ahriman, the Angel of Darkness, plucked the first Messiah from this world before the babe's day had come, and that door was closed. But only for a time. Death has no hold, no sway over the moving reach of God's hand.

"So it says in the book of Phineas, according to the Truth he received from the Spirit, when it came upon him and revealed to him these things. Within this Truth, Phineas was told of the Messiah's return, that he would come again to deliver the world from itself and the sins of its people.

"Jesse is the fulfilment of this prophecy bestowed by the power of the Spirit. He was the first Messiah, and he is the second now, made whole in our time, and he will always be. The Angels of Light are awake and walk the Earth, protecting the righteous and the blessed. A new door has opened now. It too leads us to God's side, to His unending love, and it will never be closed."

Lukas heard Yaakov's words with absolute clarity, and yet he was somewhere else entirely. As if this door, mentioned so precisely and with such unwavering conviction, had also been opened within his mind, Lukas remembered.

An unnaturally, impossibly swift trek across the red desert sands and the baked earth when the world was so much younger. A small town of dried clay, the archway overhead welcoming and yet still so distant. A stable built onto the back of a house, filled not with animals but with people—a family; father, mother, and infant child. The red hum of the energy phaser, the screams, the silent, fearless child lying between his murdered parents in the hay. And those eyes...

Lukas saw those eyes as if they were before him again in this very moment—worlds upon worlds, time unending, love and light and *God*.

Time seemed to stop for all eternity in the few seconds it took to relive the horrors of what his body had done when his mind and his soul had been tucked away, forced beneath the surface by a sharp, cold, cruel hand into the darkness of oblivion. Perhaps Yaakov's words themselves had removed the last vestiges of that awful presence; perhaps there had simply been time enough between then and now for Lukas to have released himself. Either way, he saw it all as clearly now as if he committed these acts all over again, and he raised a shaking hand to cover his face.

"As much as Jesse is and was and always will be," Yaakov continued, his words flowing seamlessly despite Lukas's horrifying revelation, "as much as God is sovereign, so exists Ahriman. We cannot see the war around us, here in this world and in the spirit realm. Yet we are secure in our knowledge of God's love and protection. We are secure in our knowledge of the Open Door and the Way that is the way beyond death into everlasting life."

"The first Messiah..." Lukas muttered, recalling the worlds and recognizing the relevance in everything he'd seen and done in the last three days. He'd known the timeline of history had changed the minute Marya revealed to him her world's version of the fate of Qumran, of the existence of things impossible for her but very much the truth of Lukas's life. The most impossible of these things was Lukas himself. And all the while, he'd thought those shifts in time leading to the creation of this world now, so vastly different than everything he'd grown to expect, were the products of one simple creation—the quantum orb, the fact that he had succeeded in that endeavor. Now, he knew without a doubt that he'd been wrong. By his own hand—unwilling, yes, but his hand nevertheless—three deaths in a time inaccessible until he'd built and perfected the machine that had changed the course of the entire world. Not for the good of his people and mankind, as he'd intended, but for so much worse— for a darker age where life and love and meaningful purpose had all but been stripped away. "What have I done?"

He must not have whispered this as quietly as he'd thought. Yohanan, sitting on the other side of Aaron, leaned forward over the table. "God is in control," he said, his voice low and gentle. "He holds the door open, Lukas. Let it be. You can do what you can do and no more."

Slowly, Lukas lowered his trembling hand from his face. It hovered uncertainly in the air before him, and he met the man's gaze. "Let it be?" he whispered, feeling as if he'd been drawn out of his own body. "How can I let this be? You have no idea what I've done." His voice broke shrilly, as if he were an adolescent again trying to navigate the agony of growing up. His head jerked wildly as he glanced at everyone gathered with him around the low table, but he saw only shapes and muted colors. "None of you know."

"Lukas," Cephas said, blinking calmly though he did not smile now. "We know."

"That's impossible. I didn't even know until..." Lukas gripped the edge of the table and leaned away from it, as if the plastic grain that was meant to mimic wood were the source of his torment and not himself. "I knew something was wrong. I *knew*, but I couldn't find it. I couldn't see—"

"Lukas," Cephas repeated, and the Qumranian finally looked up at his host, reeling within his new and sudden understanding. "We know. Jesse told us of you far before you came to the city. Of your life in Qumran, impossible though it seems to us. Of your endeavors there, your faith, your commitment. We were told to wait for you and aid you, to be your guides. And we were told of Ahriman's deception. You were used by the Angel of Darkness, Lukas. Terribly and mercilessly. No man could have withstood such a violation of the self. There was nothing you could do, and this is not your fault—"

Lukas's knees thumped against the underside of the table on his first attempt to stand. The plastic cup in front of Yohanan toppled, spilling what little remained of the man's tea. For a moment, the patter of dripping liquid upon the pillows on the floor was the only sound. Then he finally did stand on his second attempt and backed away from the table.

"You *knew*?"

Cephas nodded slowly, patiently, and the others sitting with him looked up at Lukas with nothing but kindness and understanding.

Lukas frowned. "For how long?"

"Almost a year."

"It's only been two days!" He whirled from the table and the pillows, but there was nowhere for him to go, nowhere for his energy, his disbelief, his anger. "I watched Qumran crumble before the sea swallowed it. A Qumran and a sea you say haven't existed for a hundred years. Three days ago. Just after what happened to me... what I *did*..." Lukas ran a hand roughly through his hair. "If that child was the first Messiah, what else has changed? I can't... . How can you just sit there? How can you give everything you have and risk your lives when you know who I am?" He stared down at Marya, who only looked up at him with her wide, patient brown eyes. "Why aren't you angry?"

"God's will does not make us angry, Lukas," Cephas replied.

"This is not God's will! This is a defilement of it. By *my* hand." Lukas clenched his fists, and the grinding of his teeth seemed so loud in the silence. "*I* did this to the world. All I ever wanted was to protect it. To make it better."

"He has a plan for you too," Marya said, her voice unchanged in its calm, level certainty. "You will see it."

A choked laugh escaped him. "Oh, I see it. I have to make this right. Undo what's been done. I can't just stand back and let this carry on. That army... those people have the machine *I* built. They can't be allowed to use it again. It was *my* work that made this possible. *My* hand that took the lives of—" Lukas clenched his eyes shut, realizing now how zealously he knew this to be true and how insane his companions must think him. "I have to fix this."

"There's nothing to fix," Yaakov said. "You're here, and Jesse has told us what will—"

A sharp knock came at the door, and every head turned. It did not sound like another friend coming to join their gathering;

it sounded like a warning. Slowly, Cephas stood and headed toward the front door. He stopped on the way to press a panel in the wall. It disengaged and swung downward like an opening mouth to reveal a pistol in the hidden compartment there. Then he went to the door, weapon in hand, and Lukas followed him, preparing himself for a fight. Cephas jerked open the door and paused; no one stood on the other side.

"It's okay," he called back into the room, turning his head but keeping his gaze on the hallway. "There's no one here."

"What's that?" Lukas asked, pointing to the black plastic crate on the ground. He stepped up into the doorway beside his host, aware of the four others standing to look themselves. Marya stood close behind him, and he could feel the heat of her body.

The doorway to Cephas's apartment was so small, it was difficult for everyone to view the odd delivery left in the hall. The handles on the sides of the black crate had been lifted upward from where they'd previously latched down to keep on the lid. While the others waited patiently behind Lukas and Cephas, the tense expectation thickening around them, Cephas lifted his bare foot and gently nudged the lid off the crate with his toe. The lid clattered to the floor, but what lay inside wasn't dangerous—not to them.

"What is—" Marya took in a sharp breath, and Lukas glanced at her briefly to see she'd clenched her eyes shut with a grimace, but she did not turn away.

Scowling, Lukas turned his attention back to the contents of the crate, which looked so unreal lying there inside the black plastic. But the blood-right mark in the center of the disembodied palm convinced him it was very real. He pressed his lips together, feeling the rage and sorrow building within him because he knew this too was a direct consequence of what he'd done.

"It's my cousin's," he muttered, blinking against the gruesome sight. "His arm. They cut off Ben's arm."

26

"I have to get them out of there." Lukas paced Cephas's tiny apartment, hands clasped behind his back as he glared at the floor. "They'll be dead soon if this goes on any longer." He couldn't fully comprehend the depth of his anger, whether it stemmed more from the Unclean's possession of the quantum orb or from the shame and guilt overwhelming him. He'd left his cousins in the hands of those monsters twice now—first when he'd escaped the Main Laboratory of Sector One before the compound fell, and again when he'd had no choice but to flee the Unclean headquarters facility. On both occasions, he'd acted to save his own life, but he couldn't stand idly by when he knew Deborah and Ben—the family he'd lived and learned and worked with since they were all children—had now become the objects of such indescribable torture. This was not the end of what the Unclean would do to them, he knew. He had to try again.

"They might not still be alive," Marya said. She sat cross-legged on the pillows beside the table, clutching her hands in her lap.

"They wouldn't have sent *that*"—Lukas jabbed a finger at the black crate sitting just inside Cephas's front door—"if he was already dead. It's a crude invitation. They want me to come back."

"We can't go back there," she said. There was no fear in her voice or behind her eyes, only a certainty of what they'd faced if they did return.

Lukas stopped pacing and looked at her. "You don't have to." He turned to eye everyone else in the room—Cephas sitting again at the table with Aaron; Yaakov standing in the back by the downstairs room, frowning, his arms folded; Yohanan leaning against the wall, picking at his lip and staring at the black crate beside the doorway, the lid now returned and secured again in place. "None of you have to come with me. In fact, I'm asking you not to. The things I have to do aren't worth risking your lives."

Yaakov unfolded his arms. "We were told—"

"I know what you were told, Yaakov," Lukas said. "I know Jesse asked all of you to help me. To offer everything you can and give me everything in your power to give. I'm so grateful to all of you, more than I can say. And I wouldn't have gotten even this far if it weren't for your kindness." He glanced at Marya, then at Cephas. "As far as I'm concerned, you've done exactly what he told you to do. But I don't think he'd want you to throw your lives away trying to keep a promise you've already fulfilled. I have to do this alone."

"Lukas..." Marya started, but Cephas's gentle hand on her shoulder stopped her. She turned around to look at him, and their host just shook his head.

Then he looked up at Lukas. "What do you need?"

"Can your friend at the club do anything else to get me back inside that facility?"

"Cyrus?" Marya asked. "We can ask him. I'm sure he'd meet us here if he had to."

"Thank you." Lukas took a deep breath and tried to steady himself. This much, at least, he'd accomplished.

"Reach out to him," Cephas said with a nod.

Marya stood and crossed the room to the counter beside the small stove. She picked up the tiny handheld tablet to swipe a keyed message across the screen.

"I'm going upstairs," Lukas said, the anger and the urge to take action filtering out of him now that he knew he had to wait a little longer. "I... I need a minute."

Cephas eyed him with concern, but he seemed to understand Lukas's sudden need to be alone. "That's fine."

"Will you tell me when he's here?"

"Of course."

Just as he reached the upstairs landing, he heard soft footsteps behind him. "Lukas." He turned to see Aaron moving up the staircase toward him, sliding his hand along the wall as he climbed. "Just a minute." When the veteran Enforcer reached the landing, he took a deep breath and offered a resigned smile beneath a frown of determination. "It was right to tell them to stay," he said. "But I'm coming with you."

"No." Lukas turned to head down the short hallway, but Aaron grabbed his arm. The strength of the grip surprised him, and he stopped.

"This place is their home, Lukas. Not mine. Not yours. Deborah and Ben are just names to them. Strangers. But I..." He swallowed, his eyes glistening. "I've known all three of you since the day you were born. I love them too. And there's nothing here for me." Lukas blinked, studying his old friend's gaze and what seemed to be Aaron's silent plea to reclaim a true purpose in his later years. "And if there's even the slightest chance of restoring our home, in whatever form that might take, I want to be there to help you see it done."

Lukas couldn't find it in himself to deny the man; Aaron was right. He let out a deep sigh. "Okay."

Aaron clasped his hand, then gripped Lukas's shoulder with

his other hand. "We *will* get them out of there. As long as we're alive, so is Qumran."

Lukas tightened his grip on the old man's hand and shook it once in acknowledgment. "Can you still fight like you used to?"

Aaron smirked. "God hasn't seen fit to strip me of my training just yet."

It amazed him to find that, even within the restlessness of waiting and the anticipation of what he meant to do, Lukas managed to doze off on the pallet in his room. A few hours later, a soft knock came at the bedroom door, followed by Yaakov's gentle voice.

"Cyrus is here." Then his footsteps faded from the hall and back down the stairs.

Lukas roused himself, rubbing his face, and stood to engage in yet another attempt to prepare for what was so seemingly impossible.

No one had left Cephas's apartment after Lukas had removed himself from the tension of his last decision. Only Aaron sat now on the pillows around the table, and everyone else had gathered to welcome Cyrus among them. The man looked particularly pleased to see them all, and when he caught sight of Lukas at the bottom of the staircase, he nodded in greeting, his eyes wide.

"I'm sorry to say I didn't think I'd ever see you again."

Lukas dipped his head, trying not to dwell on how prone he seemed to narrowly escaping his own death in the last few days. "Well, I'm glad you were wrong."

Cyrus smiled, and Cephas gestured for them to reconvene at the low table in the center of the room. The former Unclean soldier had a cane with him—a metal rod that, while distinctly different, made Lukas think of the Phar-asai's electric batons.

The cane thumped against the rough carpet as Cyrus limped toward the table, then he lowered himself at one of its corners to sit on the pillows with his bad leg splayed out to the side. The others came to join him, all but Yohanan, who had either resumed or never left his post against the wall beside the black plastic crate. He watched those at the table now instead of the gruesome delivery, and while Lukas wished there was a way to get the physical reminder of his cousin's enduring agony out of Cephas's apartment, he didn't think they had any viable option at the moment to dispose of it.

"Marya mentioned the main division headquarters facility," Cyrus began, his gaze drifting from Marya to Cephas to Lukas. "That you want to go back in."

"Yes," Lukas replied. "But just the two of us this time." He gestured to the veteran Qumranian Enforcer. "This is Aaron."

The men nodded in greeting, then Cyrus blinked and shook his head in disbelief. "There may be other options," he said. "It's amazing any of you made it out of there at all. Are you sure going back a second time is the best way to get what you're looking for?"

Lukas eyed him steadily, wondering why the man seemed so intent on stopping him. "It's the only way." His voice carried a warning with it; it could not be mistaken that he meant to do whatever necessary.

Cyrus swallowed. "They know who you are now. They know that you can get inside. The mimic I gave you won't work a second time. Do you still have it?" Lukas fished in the pocket of his loose trousers and pulled out the small black device. He set it in Cyrus's outstretched palm, and the man pocketed it once more. "I said I still have friends in their ranks. One of them handles the processing of supply shipments. The next one's scheduled for first thing tomorrow morning. He can get you in, but the rest is up to you. And there's no one to get you back out again."

"We can handle that," Lukas said. If it came to it, he could activate the quantum orb manually and escape into a different time, assuming it hadn't been damaged on its journey from the Qumranian laboratory or the Unclean hadn't managed to reprogram the settings of its core drive. But that was impossible; only Deborah, Ben, and himself knew how to recalibrate any facet of what they had built, and Ben's severed arm resting in the plastic box by the door was proof that neither of his cousins had given those animals what they wanted.

Cyrus opened the flap of the small, thin satchel strapped over his shoulder and produced a tablet much larger than Marya's. The foreign glyphs of Consortium writing illuminated the screen, flashing in different colors as the ex-soldier's fingers moved quickly and efficiently.

"Marya," he said, glancing up briefly from the tablet, "I've just sent you the schematics of the shipment intake dock. I know a man with a shuttling service on that side of the lower levels. He owes me a few favors. You two will meet him there before first light," he said to Lukas and Aaron. "He'll get you situated, drive you to the shipment dock, and my friend inside headquarters will make sure to load you with the other shipments. That's as many strings as I can pull."

"That's enough. Thank you." Lukas reached out his hand, and with a short sigh, Cyrus shook it firmly.

"I'm sorry I can't do more."

"This wouldn't be possible without you," Cephas added. He, Lukas, Aaron, and Cyrus then stood from around the table, the business at hand concluded as much as it could be.

"When it's done," Cyrus said as he limped toward the door with his cane, "we'll celebrate at the club. Give you an excuse to sing, Marya." He turned back halfway to shoot her a knowing smile.

She looked up from the small handheld she'd been studying. "It's the least I can do. Thank you."

The man eyed everyone in the room with a stoic steadfastness, nodded, and let himself out. When the door closed behind him, Cephas's living room was silent. Aaron folded his arms and stared down at the table.

"I'll make some more tea," Cephas said.

27

Once again, Lukas was awakened by a soft knock on his bedroom door. Then the door opened and Aaron peered inside. "It's time," he said.

Already sitting up now, Lukas was left alone for a few more minutes. He found it a little amusing that Aaron would be the one to wake him; he'd never expected to relive that kind of familiarity with the man as an adult.

After straightening the blankets on the pallet, reassuring himself this would not be the last time he did so, he made his way down the stairs just as Cephas emerged from the back room on the first level. They exchanged nods, then Marya approached with a cup of tea. She held it out for Lukas and he tilted his head, not particularly feeling in the mood for warm comfort—or anything in his stomach.

"Humor me," she said, smiling through the tension of his and Aaron's departure. "Just a little, at least. You need *something*."

With a deep breath, Lukas took the cup and sipped, yet again surprised by the sweetness in a place so rife with bitterness and finding himself quite grateful for the comfort of it. He glanced at Aaron, who now set his already empty cup of tea on the low table. Apparently satisfied, Marya returned to the small kitchen to rummage in a drawer. Yaakov and Yohanan had remained in Cephas's house as well to see them off, and the brothers approached him now with grim-set faces and nods of determination.

"Nothing lies outside God's plan," Yaakov said, placing a hand on Lukas's shoulder. "Let it be so," Yohanan added.

Despite the pressing burden of knowing he himself had changed the very fabric of God's plan for the world with his machine, Lukas accepted their words as best he could. They spoke of God's will and plan and love, but he anticipated only God's judgment. What he set out to do now might be enough to save the souls he had so imperiled through his aspirations and his achievements as a Qumranian scientist. But his own redemption, as far as he could see, lay only in his ability to restore the Law he'd spent a lifetime protecting—to return the world to what it ought to have been, if God would grant him the strength for this final righteous act. He would save his cousins, he would reclaim the quantum orb, and he would do whatever it took to repair all the damage he'd inflicted upon his homeland, his people, and the course of time itself.

Turning from the brothers, he forced the vastness of such thinking aside to focus on what he had to do in the present. That was the key—to take this one step at a time without getting lost in the possibilities. All his training as a Hedge Master pushed against this thought; he'd mastered the art of anticipating his opponents' movements long before they realized they'd decided to make them. But when it came to God's plan and the workings of time itself, this mastery meant very little. He would call upon it when it could be best used, and then he would be an instrument of justice, even God's vengeance. Now, he was a man about to be loaded into a shipment container to infiltrate the Unclean headquarters facility.

Marya returned with two of the same cellophane-wrapped

bars Yaakov had given him when they'd first met on the streets of the city. She handed one to Lukas and the other to Aaron. "For the journey," she said.

"Is this any better than... porridge?" Aaron asked, eyeing the bar in his hand with an optimistic grin.

"Basically the same thing in a portable form," Lukas said, shaking the thing by its wrapper and unable to contain a wry smirk.

"But it sticks." Cephas approached them and shook both their hands. "God speed."

"Thank you," Lukas said.

Cephas and Aaron went to the front door, and then Marya finally stepped up to Lukas without trying to get him to eat or drink something.

She looked down at her clasped hands, then took another step toward him until she was so close, he could have reached out his arms and wrapped her entirely within them. When she lifted her head, her brown eyes glistened, but there were no tears. "There are so many things I wish were different," she said, studying his face. "And other things I wouldn't change for the world."

"I know." In any other circumstance, this would have seemed an inadequate response, but it was all he could say in the little time they had.

"Wherever your path leads you, Lukas, I'm glad you stepped into mine." Marya took one of his hands between her own and held it there, smiling.

Lukas covered their shared grasp with his other hand and nodded. "Me too." He wanted to add that he hoped their paths would cross again, but if he succeeded today, that would never happen. He meant to return the world to the way it was originally designed, and he doubted Marya would exist as herself in that timeline. If he failed, well, that would be the end; he couldn't imagine making it out of the headquarters facility alive without the use of the quantum orb. So he told her instead, "I want you to be safe."

She looked like she was about to laugh, but she didn't. "I am definitely safe. There's a lot I can do beyond making tea and firing a weapon. You've never heard me sing, have you?"

"Actually—"

"Lukas," Aaron said, turning from the front door to catch his eye. "We should go."

Lukas gave Marya's hands a gentle squeeze, then released her. There was nothing more to say, and they had a shuttle to catch.

———

Cephas had provided Aaron with a handheld device much like Marya's, loaded with directions to Cyrus's contact and the schematics of the Unclean shipment docks. They'd decided to eat the nutrition bars on their brisk walk through the lower level streets toward the man named Hayim, who had quickly and unceremoniously tucked them into two black plastic containers barely large enough to hold them. These were far too similar to the crate in which Ben's severed arm had been delivered, doing nothing to improve the prospect of being driven across the city disguised as new shipments.

Lukas hadn't had the opportunity to see the vehicle in which they were now being transported, but the back of it where their containers had been strapped down filled with a low whine. And now that he thought about it, he wasn't sure if eating the nutrition bar had worsened or improved the state of his stomach; the ride was fast and bumpy, veering around unseen corners with no warning as he bucked and thumped around inside the container. On particularly rough patches, he heard Aaron grunting in the container beside him and tried not to laugh.

Then the vehicle stopped. After listening to the rumble of

opening doors and the exchange of a few muffled words, he had to brace himself against the wall of the container as it was tilted on its side and carted down the ramp of the vehicle, presumably into the headquarters facility itself. Thankfully, he was tilted onto his feet and not his head, and he hoped Aaron enjoyed the same such luck. Then they were loaded onto some kind of wheeled carrier, and the long minutes of smooth movement punctuated by stops—during which he guessed the Unclean soldier entered security codes to bring them through door after door—drew on much longer than Lukas had expected. Perhaps it had something to do with lying on his side while the close walls of the black container pressed in on nearly every inch of him.

Finally, their journey seemed to have come to an end. They stopped moving, and Lukas heard the hydraulic hiss of some door's opening mechanism. Booted footsteps moved slowly away from him, and then the click of handles being unlatched filled the room, which was fairly large, judging by the echo. The footsteps retreated, the door hissed again, and nothing else made a sound.

Just to see, Lukas raised a hand against the lid of his container, but it didn't budge. Apparently, the soldier had only seen fit to unlock one of them, and by the sound of it, that had been Aaron's. Lukas heard the lid slide off before Aaron unfurled himself from the crate with a low groan. Then the lid on Lukas's container was unlatched and removed. Aaron peered down at him with a raised eyebrow, and Lukas pushed himself off the floor of the crate.

"I think this is my last volunteer mission," the veteran Enforcer said, and while Lukas knew it was given as a joke, the man sounded entirely serious.

They gave themselves a few more minutes to stretch out the kinks. The supply room, which was where they'd been told they were going first, was larger than the lab in which his cousins and the quantum orb were being held. This, though, was stacked with containers of dark plastic and steel in a huge range of sizes. There were two doors on every wall, all of them identically nondescript and unmarked. The crates the men had been smuggled in rested in the center of the room on what looked like a low pushcart, though Lukas saw it had no wheels and must have used some hovering technology he didn't recognize.

Aaron took out Cephas's handheld device and studied it, then turned about the darkened room and pointed. "Well, wasn't that nice of him," he said dryly. The door at the end of the massive supply room had been conveniently left open, perhaps to show them the way out in case they hadn't come prepared. Lukas was almost insulted.

They made their way to the open door, and Aaron stepped through it first. He nodded to Lukas that the short hallway ahead was clear, and then they pushed open another door that spit them out right in the middle of the wide, brightly lit hallway of the sub-level labs. There were no soldiers stationed anywhere along the wide corridor, no echo of approaching footsteps, no signal of alarm. Nothing. Lukas recognized where they were, recognized the illuminated symbol over the lab three doors down, though he still did not know what it meant. The Qumranians exchanged a skeptical glance, then Lukas nodded down the hall.

Still, nothing moved to stop them when they paused at the door, leaning back against the wall just in case they met with Unclean forces inside the lab. "This is a trap," Aaron muttered.

Lukas took a deep breath. "Definitely."

"Well, when the way is opened..."

Lukas swung around and burst through the laboratory doors, steeling himself for the barrage of fists or weapons fire or whatever other attack he'd expected from the Unclean. But there was none of it. The lab was entirely empty save for the supplies and the command consoles and the workstations. Not even the cages with Ben and Deborah remained, and Lukas's heart sank until his eyes fell on the counter at the far end of the lab.

There—it was still there. The quantum orb rested in its steel cradle, the circuitry stable and dormant within the swirling, liquid-like membrane and the fluctuating core. He didn't have time to think about why it had been left behind or what had happened to his cousins. Lukas lurched forward toward the other side of the lab, his heart pounding in his chest. All he wanted was to reach out and connect with the machine's circuitry, operate it from where he stood. It was all he *had* to do, so close to this final act he had made his only remaining purpose. He heard Aaron close on his heels, and then Lukas stood in front of the machine, reaching out as quickly as he could while still being cautious of the machine's fragility.

Someone cleared his throat behind them, but Lukas didn't turn to see who it was. He didn't have the luxury of time; he couldn't waste a single millisecond with curiosity or concern.

"You're very punctual."

He recognized the voice instantly as Damian's, the Unclean commander, but that didn't matter now. Everything would be put right. Lukas would finish this.

Just before his fingers made contact with the supple membrane of the quantum orb, a searing shock burst through every nerve in his body, far more agonizing than what the Pharasai had delivered with his rod. Lukas felt his consciousness being jerked away from his flesh, from the machine, from his redemption. He had failed.

28

His head had never throbbed this much in his life. Lukas opened his hand, then realized his fingers only twitched where they lay beside his head, so he tried again. This time, he managed it, feeling cool steel wiring beneath his palm and his cheek. He tried to sit up and flailed in sudden panic when he couldn't feel his legs. But then the pain overwhelmed that fear; the blood rushed back into his legs. They were crumpled awkwardly beneath him, and he realized he'd been tossed into a cage.

Slowly, his vision blurred, and he managed to push himself up and lean back against the tiny, cramped prison in which he'd been locked. It was cold and hard against the back of his head. The bright lights of the room swirled and spun around him like wheeling carrion birds. It took longer than he would have liked for the dizziness to subside. When he could see clearly, he clamped his eyes shut again in shame.

He had been thrown into a cage, yes. So had Aaron. And whatever they'd done with Deborah before this, she'd now been brought to join her fellow Qumranians, also still in her own low prison that left no room for anything more than sitting or curling up to lie down.

He'd come to free her and Ben, and to use the machine they'd created together to save the millions of other souls for whom he'd made himself responsible. The thought occurred to him that maybe he should have tried to find his cousins first; the Unclean would not have expected him to put two people over the importance and the power contained in that small, swirling orb. Their commanders had known its worth and had come for it first and foremost among all the things they could have and had pilfered from Qumran before destroying it. Why would he not do the same now? Judging by how quickly Damian had found him and how prepared they seemed to have been with extra cages, he realized he'd been doubly fooled—by the Unclean and by his own pride.

"Lukas." It was a hoarse whisper, barely loud enough to hear, but he knew it immediately as Deborah's voice. With a low, strained sigh, he leaned forward and turned his head, still seeing two or three of her at a time. "Lukas, can you hear me?" Her voice squeaked at the end.

"Yeah, Deb," he managed, blinking. "Are you okay?"

"I don't think so." She sounded like she was about to burst into sobs. "I don't know what's going to happen. I don't know what they're going to do..."

"Hey, it's okay," Lukas said, grunting as he tried to push himself further up into sitting. "It's okay. We'll be okay. I'm going to get us out of here." Just as soon as he could see straight again, he'd be better able to make good on that promise. "Where's Ben?"

She took in a sharp breath, followed by a terrified sob before she clamped her hands over her mouth. "This world is nothing like they told us, Lukas. Nothing like what I believed the Above had become. These people... these people are *not* the same as the ones we found when we were kids." She squeaked again, her swallow loud and audible amid the hurried breath bursting through her nose. "I thought I could change things. Make things better for everyone by going Above."

"Deb..."

"But there's nothing to be done. This world is so horrible, Lukas. These people are monsters. I'm so—" Another sob escaped her, and she sniffed repeatedly, on the verge of hyperventilating. "I'm so ashamed I doubted our Elders and the Law..."

"Deborah, stop it," Lukas said, hating to take this harsh tone with her but needing to get her attention. It would be a lot harder to get them out of here again if he had to shepherd a hysterical woman out of the facility. "Listen to me. I came here on purpose, okay? They didn't take me—" She let out a high whine, and he clenched his eyes shut against the relentless vertigo. "Deborah. Deborah, shh. Everything's going to be okay. I have a plan. Can you tell me where they took Ben?" Her sobbing moans rose again, and he wished he could wrap his arms around her and give her whatever little comfort she could take from that.

The last glimmer of his wavering vision settled and cleared, and he took a deep, steadying breath before finally being able to study his surroundings. They were in the same lab; he had a remarkably clear view of the quantum orb a few yards in front of him, resting untouched and undisturbed in its cradle on the counter. The fact that these cages had been removed for his and Aaron's arrival and then returned with them inside struck him as particularly odd—far more theatrical than for practicality's sake. What was the point of that?

On the other side of Deborah, he found a type of cream-colored privacy screen set in a portable steel frame on wheels. It reached nearly to the lab's ceiling, and while the plastic-looking screen seemed as if it should have been somewhat transparent, he could see nothing behind it. But he did find a trail of thick, insulated cords protruding from behind one side of the screen, snaking across the floor to where they'd been plugged into a massive black control panel that took up nearly the entire far wall. That didn't make any sense. If the Unclean wanted a viable power source for whatever lay behind that screen, they could have just plugged into the quantum orb.

In the other cage beside him, Aaron stirred, then sat up way too quickly before Lukas could advise him to move slowly. The man grabbed his head with a groan. "What *is* this?"

"Aaron?" Deborah's voice trembled, and she scrambled up against the side of her cage to get as close as she could to their old family friend.

"Deborah." The veteran Enforcer let out a long, shuddering sigh. "Sweet Deborah. I'm so sorry you've had to endure this. We'll make it through this. You'll see."

"You have no idea what they're capable of," she whispered harshly, her terrified eyes flickering between Aaron and Lukas above her straining grasp on the thin bars of her cage. "We tried to resist them, Lukas. You have to believe me. We would never willingly give them what they wanted. But they just..."

"Hey," Lukas said, trying to ignore the fact that she seemed to have lost her mind completely in this place. "Deb, hey. None of this is your fault—"

"No. It's yours."

Deborah cowered at the sound, whimpering into her hands, and Lukas whirled in his cage to see the woman commander standing on the other side of Aaron. Her armored black boots, glinting in the harsh white glare of the overhead lights, clicked slowly against the tiled floors. How had he not heard her enter?

"You have failed at so many things," Lucia said, "and yet you still cling so desperately to your hope. I would think such a brilliant scientist as yourself would have been more calculating, less capable of such foolishness. Or perhaps that brilliance has merely blinded you to it."

"What do you want?" Lukas spat, glaring up at her from his cage. Though his clenched fists rested upon his thighs, he didn't move. His first instinct was to shift into a defensive crouch, but he didn't want to give this woman the satisfaction of thinking she threatened him.

"I want to undo you, Hedge Master." She spat out his title like a bite of rotten fruit, the hiss in her words giving her a decidedly snakelike quality despite the sharp, cruel points of her spiked armor. "For the pure pleasure of watching you and your God fall." She moved with a surprisingly languid stride toward the center of the lab between the cages and the quantum orb, as much to give each of her prisoners a view of her as to gaze upon all of them herself. "I must say we are particularly grateful for the part you've already played in all of this."

"You're insane," Aaron hissed, slamming his palm against the front of his cage.

Lucia slowly turned her head just a little so she could peer directly at the Enforcer. She raised her eyebrows and merely hummed at him, as if the thought had never occurred to her before and she'd need time to give it the proper consideration. "Do your new friends know what you've done?" she asked, then slid her darkened gaze away from Aaron and back toward Lukas. "Did you tell your fellow Qumranian how you *changed the world?*" Her head shook in a mockery of ecstasy, and her lips curved up into a ravenous grin.

Lukas glanced at Aaron in the cage beside him, who merely frowned in wary curiosity. His friend had been there at Cephas's when Lukas remembered the time he'd lost—his mind pressed into oblivion and his body seized by the Angel of Darkness. Aaron had never questioned Lukas about his revelation or what he'd meant when Cephas and the others told him they'd already known, but now it seemed Lukas's sins were being stripped and laid bare in front of those he'd loved his whole life. He shook his head and had to look away from the old man.

"Perhaps your cousins may have benefited from an explanation," Lucia continued, "but it seems a little flippant to worry

about them now, don't you think?" Her black eyes slid toward
Deborah. As if the woman's glance were a cold, clawed hand,
Deborah flinched away and buried her trembling head in her
arms. The Unclean commander clicked her tongue. "Oh... none
of this was wasted, Hedge Master. I can promise you that. At
least, not on you. Your ingenious machine. Your clever design.
Your hand that pulled the trigger and slaughtered the infant
Messiah on a bed of straw..."

"Lukas, what in God's name is she talking about?" Aaron
whispered, though it was impossible not to be heard by the vile
woman.

Lukas shook his head again and swallowed. He'd already
relived the horror and the shame of that moment; he didn't need
this again—not when it dripped like poison from this witch's
tongue.

"My master is quite pleased with you," the woman said,
"despite all your attempts at defiance. This new world suits our
purposes far better than before, and my lord Ahriman wishes to
keep it this way. He reigns supreme in this world and every
other, but he does not overlook the deeds of those who serve his
omnipotence." Lucia kept moving across the lab until she
reached the dividing screen on wheels. Then she wrapped a
hand that could have been a talon around the cold steel bar of its
outer frame. "At one point, we thought to use your machine
again. Since you were so determined to run away and leave your
cousins behind, Hedge Master, we had to look elsewhere for the
key to operating it." She gave the dividing screen a swift shove,
and the clack of its wheels rolling quickly across the tile floors
jarred Lukas enough that he did not immediately see what it had
been pushed aside to reveal.

He heard Aaron pounding against his own cage again in
shock and rage. "What is that?" he shouted. "What did you do to
him? Ben? *Ben!*"

Lukas blinked, unable to fully process the image of his cousin strapped to an upright table, both arms pinned down by his sides though the left one ended in a bloody stump below the elbow. But he'd already known about Ben's arm, and that was not the worst of it. His cousin's head had been completely and roughly shorn, a few patches of hair remaining in scattered places amid deep gouges that had already bled and dried. And from his head protruded innumerable wires that, even from Lukas's distance, had clearly not been attached with electrodes or any humane measure of decency. Instead, they'd been inserted directly into Ben's skin and skull with what Lukas could only assume had been agonizingly sharp needles with force enough to somehow move through bone. He prayed to God his cousin hadn't been conscious when they'd done this to him, but the Unclean had already proven their lack of concern for their prisoners' physical comfort. Now, Ben's head lolled to the side against the standing table, the thin wires, tubes, and huge, thick cables spilling onto the floor to become the winding collection Lukas had previously noticed plugged into the wall-sized control panel.

"He would not willingly give us the information we wanted," Lucia continued, apparently satisfied with the reaction such an unveiling had produced. She walked around Ben in a slow circle, her hands clasped behind her back as though she were instructing a class on the matter. "So we took it from him. He was so weak, Hedge Master. A sharp mind, I agree. Sharp enough to have aided you in building your machine and designing its purpose, but nothing remotely close to your genius, I'm afraid. Still, we found what we were looking for, and he didn't even put up a fight." She slipped her hand below a section of the wires and let them fall through her fingers, as if stroking the long hair on a child's head. "We downloaded his entire memory—every cell, every firing neuron, every particle of molecular history. What you choose to call a soul, I believe. And this"—she gestured to Ben's body—"is nothing more than a used husk, useless and ready to be disposed of."

The woman's hand moved so quickly, Lukas didn't realize what she'd done until the crack of flesh on flesh echoed through the lab. She'd slapped Ben full across the face—not in anger but as a butcher slapped a slaughtered hog, beheaded, blooded, disemboweled, and ready for carving. Ben's head swung life-lessly to the other side, and the standing table rocked on its wheels, sending a wave of movement through the cables flowing onto the floor.

Deborah shrieked and burst into sobs again.

"How *dare* you!" Aaron's enraged shout echoed quickly behind the last of the ringing slap, and he shook the cage again.

Lucia ignored them both. "And then, of course, plans changed. As they sometimes do." She stepped away from Ben and came to stand just in front of the counter again, where all her prisoners could view her and the quantum orb behind her. Lukas swallowed thickly, lifting a prayer for his cousin's soul and at the same time cursing the vile woman who had taken Ben from this world in such a terribly cruel way. "But my lord Ahriman is not entirely without mercy," she continued. Another smile graced her lips, and if Lukas didn't already know she had no capacity for compassion, he would have called what he saw behind her eyes a form of sympathy. "He has decided to reward you. He wants to set you *free*." She held Lukas's gaze for a few more agonizing seconds, then reached her hand out toward the quantum orb.

He thought she was going to use it, immediately anticipating the swift, unfeeling death of the web field coursing over and through him to burn every trace of him out of existence. But then he just as quickly realized he was too far out of its range.

Lucia did not touch the orb; she merely reached a hand toward it. Then she pulled her gaze away from Lukas to consider the machine and flicked the air with her finger. The delicate membrane containing the product of all Lukas's scientific endeavors burst as if she'd bludgeoned it with a club. Some of the swirling nanotech within spilled forth with the force of released pressure, the rest of it oozing out of the machine to splatter the floor with glittering particles. The delicate tendrils of circuitry that had responded to Lukas's hand—something like a lover's touch or an infant's first grasp of his parent's finger— shuddered and sparked, then fell limp with a hiss. It all slid from the gaping hole in the membrane now, spilling over the side of the counter as dead, useless filaments and nothing more.

Lukas couldn't breathe, choking against the obliteration of what had been his last hope for redemption. He stared with wide, unblinking eyes at the remains of the quantum orb, the creation that had summoned the undoing of the world he'd known to cast the foundation of this age of darkness. And now he could never use it to correct his own mistakes—his own terrible, unforgivable sins. There was no going back. There was no hope. There was only this place now. Forever.

"Ah..." Lucia closed her eyes and took a deep breath, then tilted her head and looked at him. "Doesn't that feel *good*? The choice has been made for you, Hedge Master. Now you can unburden yourself from this ceaseless urge to change things. The responsibility is lifted from your shoulders. There is nothing you can do."

The inexplicable kindness in her voice brought a new rage flaring through him. He would kill Lucia, given the chance. Any chance she gave him, he would do it. Slowly, he raised his head and met her gaze with a renewed defiance. This wasn't the end. Gritting his teeth, he found himself breathing heavily through his nose, rocking on his knees and glaring his hatred up at this woman who was brazen enough to speak to him this way. He wanted to fight, to use his fists and the rage fueling him, but he had to wait.

"Yes, of course," the woman said, as naturally as if this were an actual conversation. "That is only half your reward." Her thin, dark brows drew together, and she raised her left hand before clamping it into a tight fist.

A low, droning buzz came from beside him, followed by a garbled choke. Lukas turned to see Aaron sitting rigid in his cage, his entire body trembling and his eyes rolled back into his head. The cage buzzed and sparked, and the Enforcer bucked against the high voltage being pumped through his body from all directions.

"No," Lukas gasped, scrambling to the side of his own cage. "No. Aaron—" His friend toppled onto his side, completely unreachable, thrashing now as the shock jerked and contracted his muscles in their last, desperate spasms. "What are you doing?" he shouted at the commander. "Stop it. Why can't you—"

When he looked at Lucia again, he saw she'd already raised her right arm now, and with a discerning tilt of her head, she pressed her thumb and index finger together, as if she'd caught an insect between them and meant now to crush it.

"Luk—"

Horrorstricken, he whirled around in his cage to see Deborah on the other side of him, her mouth opening and closing in silent panic. Her eyes were wide—so wide and so scared—as her fingers fumbled at her throat to release the grasp upon it that wasn't there. Her chest heaved, trying to pull air into her lungs, but she only managed a desperate click of her throat working in vain.

"No, no, no, no." Lukas launched himself to the other side of his cage, then threw his shoulder against it with as much force as he could muster in such a small space; the thing was bolted somehow to floor. But that didn't stop him. "Deb! Deb, hold on." He bashed himself against the cage again, and again, screaming now because he had to get to her. A tiny squeak stopped him, and he paused to look at his cousin. The blood vessels had burst around her bulging eyes, her face a horrifying shade of deep, reddish gray. She'd leaned her head against the side of her cage, her fingers hooked through the metal bars while she stared at him. Then she was gone, her face pressed ungraciously against the mesh while the rest of her body sagged under its own lifeless weight and her hand slid down to thump on the cage floor.

The next thing he knew, Lukas was on his knees, the thin bars of the cage below him pressing painfully into his forehead. His whole body shook, and he wondered for a moment if this was what Aaron had felt; he wondered why it didn't hurt more. Because surely, after all this, the Unclean commander meant to kill him too. Then he realized the grievous sobs echoing through the lab came from his own throat, that the hot sting on his face wasn't blood from a still unnoticed wound or the rush of pressure from suffocating; it was his own tears. As if from somewhere else, he watched them fall from his cheeks, through the bars beneath him, and onto the tile floor, where they pooled and glistened in the harsh light. All this—all this cruelty and devastation—and this was his response? Then the lights above him darkened in a slowly moving shadow, and he smelled some type of pungent incense mixed with sweat.

"Oh, Lukas. Lukas…"

The sound of his name on the woman's tongue, her voice so close now from just outside the cage, pulled him back inside his body to regain some semblance of control. He ushered the rest of his sobs into a low moan, sniffing and trying to catch his breath, then pushed himself up onto his hands. But that was all he could manage.

"Now you are free, Lukas. You no longer have anything to distract you. No futile mission. No ties to what once was. No one to protect and drag you down. You can stop fighting. You have nothing left."

Nothing. He had absolutely nothing—not even the opportunity to try. He'd been so foolish for thinking he could do anything, so selfish in his aim to use the machine and correct the past he himself had broken. Now that machine was gone. His cousins, Aaron, his family—all gone. All because of him. It wouldn't have surprised him if even God rejected him, writing him off as one of those souls who just could not be saved because he had failed so completely. Because he had destroyed what should have been the world's salvation.

Slowly, he raised his head, his arms quivering beneath the suddenly impossible weight of his own body. Lucia knelt on the ground before him, her face inches from the cage, studying him with those black eyes above a cruel grin of barbarous delight. He couldn't help himself. He lunged at her with a scream, banging against the cage.

Lucia's only reaction was to sit back on her heels and laugh. The sound of it was like glass shattering and the earth crumbling into oblivion—not merely her own voice but two, ten, a thousand. A dark form shimmered and expanded behind her, and then the laughter stopped. She raised a hand, and dozens of Unclean soldiers marched into the lab to gather behind her. It was far more than the twenty Lukas had been trained as a Hedge Master to subdue; nearly three times that many men in black uniforms with red stars on their hands surrounded his cage and their brutal commander.

"When you're finished," she said, speaking to the soldiers but staring at Lukas, "let him go. Our master wishes to bestow upon the last Qumranian a long, *long* life. So he may come to truly appreciate our lord Ahriman's mercy." With this, she rose from her knees in one fluid motion and moved swiftly through the gathered throng of her soldiers.

Lukas sat up, eyeing the enemy all around him and daring them to try. One of the soldiers activated the red star on the back of his hand, typed something into the row of glyphs and characters alighting on his arm, and the front of Lukas's cage jolted and swung open. That was all he needed.

The Hedge Master launched himself from the cage into the small army before him. He ducked the first soldier's punch and whirled to bring his elbow up into the throat of the next. But as much as he tried to center himself and summon the responses of all his training—the mastery of his body and mind that he'd worked so hard to obtain—he only saw Aaron writhing on the floor of his cage and Deborah's wide, terrified eyed speckled with red.

He moved as quickly as he could, ducking and lunging, spinning with flying fists and powerful kicks that might have gotten him out of this if he faced fewer men. But he did not. Something crashed against the back of his head and knocked him off balance, then a vicious right hook caught him just below the eye. He reeled back, but two more blows landed in his stomach, and the air in his lungs vanished. Another soldier shoved him down to his knees, and one after the other, they beat him without hesitation and without mercy.

It seemed he laid on the cold tiled floor of the Unclean laboratory for ages, suffering the kicks to his legs, back, and chest, thinking before the pain dragged him into oblivion that the only kindness he could pray for now was death.

29

His first gasp into consciousness was wet and garbled, rasping in his throat as if he'd just been pulled from a raging river. It might have been the physical pain that brought him back, but the realization that he was alive was far more agonizing.

Lukas drew his hand across the filthy ground from beside his head to push himself up. All he could manage was a weak roll until he lay on his back. That didn't feel any better than when he'd landed on the streets of the city's lower levels, face-first in the muck—right where he belonged. His eyes were so swollen, he could barely open them, but what little he could see was enough to remind him of his overwhelming worthlessness. The roiling sky was lit now by the morning sun, its once life-giving rays barely managing to pierce through the film of static, noxious clouds this world had shamelessly made of fresh air. He took another rattling breath and knew his body was broken, though where shattered bones and torn flesh could eventually mend, his forsaken soul could not.

This was his punishment. God's wrathful judgment and Ahriman's so-called mercy were one and the same, and Lukas had earned every inch of it with his pride and his weakness. He knew this in his core as surely as he knew his own name or that he remained to endure this life while Ben, Deborah, and Aaron...

A moan escaped him, and he did not try to move again, even when the tears spilled from his eyes to mix with the awful sludge forever coating the street beneath him. He had fallen, and the best thing now was to never get back up.

Slow, soft footsteps echoed through the alley in which he'd been tossed like garbage. He didn't care who was coming to see him in his despair and torment. Let them come. Let them judge him, too, because whatever atrocities of living these people suffered had been set upon them by his hand.

Shadows moved toward him, over him, blocking out the sickened light of the sun. A kind, round face loomed in his vision, wide eyes roaming from his head to his feet and back again. Then the woman he did not know knelt beside his head and placed soft, cool hands on either side of his face, brushing his hair aside.

"Everything's okay now," she said. "Don't be afraid. We can heal you."

More figures joined her, whispering things Lukas did not hear. The kindness in this woman's voice—the fact that she still thought him worthy of her aid—made him squeeze his swollen eyes shut despite the pain. His tears were unending, and he took in another gasping, shuddering breath.

"Oh, God," he whispered, rocking his head. "I'm so, so sorry."

"Hush, now," the woman said. "You're in good hands."

He felt himself lifted by countless hands and placed gently down again, then either the swaying motion of moving between these strangers or the pain or the knowledge that he did not deserve such grace dragged him back into darkness once more.

The sounds of a curious, excited crowd returned him to himself.
Lukas thought they were here for him—to see the man responsible for their horrible world pay for all his crimes and the sins he
had committed. But as he waited, no one came for him. Finally,
he opened his eyes and found himself in an unexpected place.

Some kind of tent was situated on the sidewalk against the
wall of a building; whether or not it had been erected for the
purpose of aiding him or had just been borrowed for such a use,
this was where the women had tended to him. Lukas fully
expected to be overwhelmed again by the agony of very likely
broken bones and pummeled flesh, but that had all but vanished.
His eyes were no longer swollen, and his head only retained a
minor ache, easily ignored. When he sat up on a type of
stretcher, what should have been the torment of battered ribs
was only a dull stiffness. He couldn't imagine that he'd been
lying in this tent long enough for the injuries he'd sustained from
the Unclean to heal naturally; this was not a hospital, his clothes
had not been changed, and there were no IVs attached to him.

Then he noticed a box on the sidewalk inside the tent, much
like the box Yaakov had retrieved from Cephas's room to
bandage Lukas three nights ago. Its lid lay propped open, and he
spotted the pen-like injections with the cartridge boxes attached,
some far larger than those Yaakov had used to treat him before.
While Lukas didn't by any means feel in perfect shape—probably not even enough to fight effectively at this point—he had to
admit the medical supplies available to those within the lower
levels of the city were remarkably advanced. Or perhaps they'd
been stolen.

A new wave of excited voices rose from the crowd gathered
close by, and Lukas slowly pushed himself up to standing. He
had to place a hand against the wall to gain his footing, then
ducked beneath the tent's low awning and stepped out into the
street. There were so many people, all pressing forward to see or
hear whatever transpired at the center of the throng, though they

all did so with a patient eagerness without struggling to overcome their neighbors.

One woman stood back from the crowd, and when she saw Lukas emerging from the tent, she jumped a little and hurried toward him with a smile.

"I'm so glad you're feeling better," she said.

Lukas swallowed and had to look away. He didn't know yet whether or not he was grateful for her help; he would have been content enough to lie in the street where the Unclean left him so he might meet the fate he deserved after all this. Staring vacantly across the street, he muttered, "You should have saved your medicine for someone who deserves it."

He felt warm hands take his own, and the woman gave them a gentle squeeze. "We are all deserving of kindness, no matter what we've done." The words forced him to meet her gaze, though he clenched his jaw and did not understand how anyone could ever say that of him. "My name is Jeza," the woman added, her eyes shimmering with hope and love and a gentle acceptance of the stranger standing before her.

Lukas remembered the name; Marya had given it when Cephas went with his healer friends. "You're a friend of Cephas's?"

"I am," Jeza replied. "And a student of Jesse. Don't worry. I don't blame you for the work I had to put into Cephas's arm." She winked and released Lukas's hands.

His heart nearly broke at the compassion behind her eyes and the truth of what she told him. Why, after all he'd done and everything he'd desecrated, did people here still treat him as if he were as free from sin as a child?

"Thank you," he said; it was all he could manage.

"Of course." Jeza turned her head quickly toward the crowd. "Jesse is speaking here." Her grin made her look so much younger. "Have you heard him yet?"

"A few times," Lukas replied.

"Come, then. Come with me. Every time listening to his teachings is like the first time all over again." She gripped Lukas's wrist and pulled him gently across the street.

Lukas wanted to wrest his arm from her grip and run down the street. Knowing his friends—the people who had helped him in every way they could despite his disastrous failings—so admired Jesse made him feel like an intruder among those gathered now to hear the man speak. He couldn't face the man who had told his students to wait for the stranger from Qumran, to aid him and give him everything he could possibly need—to risk their lives for him. Lukas knew now he had never been worthy of such gifts, and he could not bear to face the shame when Jesse realized it was Lukas himself who had changed the past, murdered a *family*, let the quantum orb slip through his fingers, and being entirely useless to save the lives of his loved ones. Surely Jesse would see how wrong he'd been to put any faith at all in Lukas. Surely he would cast Lukas out from the city, tell his students to abjure the Qumranian, rescind all the open invitations because Lukas was no longer worthy—had never been worthy.

When he and Jeza reached the gathering, slipping easily through those standing on the fringes of the crowd, he heard Jesse's voice. His shame filled him like bile, and he turned his head away despite his inability not to listen.

"Our Way is a life of giving," Jesse said. "We offer everything we have to those in need. Not only to our friends or those we know, but to strangers. To beggars. To the poor, the sick, the hungry. Give your clothes to the homeless man beside you, and you also clothe God. Feed the man dying of hunger, and so too is God fed by the love behind such an act. We do not want for anything by giving away what we have, even if it's very little. My Father sees every act, and he returns each in full to those who walk this Way in love."

Something in the man's voice roused a deep longing inside

Lukas. If only the world could be so simple; he wished he could redeem himself enough to find the Way of which Jesse spoke. The man sounded so certain, so happy to share his knowledge, as if it had been written down for centuries and only now rediscovered as the truth. Despite Lukas's willing readiness to turn himself over to the darkness of despair and the rightful judgment that awaited him there—the punishments he deserved—he found himself wanting to listen to Jesse speak just a little longer.

He did not notice there were Phar-asai in the crowd until one of them spoke. The man in the brown leather robes stood closest to Jesse, and he folded his hands within his long sleeves.

"Teacher," he said, his voice low with deference. "We know you impart only what is true. You do not favor any one man or class, and you hold no bias toward or against anyone. You teach the way of God in accordance with that truth, and yet, we still have questions. Is it right for the city's people to keep paying taxes to the Consortium? You know those syn-creds do not go back into helping the poor, destitute people of whom you speak. Obviously..." The man waved a hand around at the crowd.

Those closest to him did not look up to meet his gaze, fearing he might see how much they disapproved of his words. Those standing farther back in the crowd, however, mumbled their frustration and whispered to each other. Lukas had also thought, for a moment, that the Phar-asai spoke to Jesse with a genuine sense of curiosity and concern, that perhaps Jesse had begun to reach some of the Consortium's officials themselves with his teachings. But everyone realized rather quickly that the brown-robed man was merely another of those who took it upon himself to ridicule and goad Jesse into discrediting himself.

Jesse's thin eyebrows drew quickly together, then released again when he met the Phar-asai's gaze. "Who created the syn-cred?" he asked. "Who counts it and distributes it and has marked it with its own image?"

The Phar-asai tilted his head, as if he were insulted by such a question. "The Consortium. Why does that matter?"

Jesse's lips formed a gentle smile, though Lukas thought it was rather forced; the man seemed a bit irritated by the antagonistic line of questioning interrupting his teachings, but he answered with a steady, awe-inspiring patience. "I'm saying we should give to the government what belongs to the government. And then we should give to God what belongs to God."

With a snort, the Phar-asai dipped his head in mock agreement, though his scowl was discernible even from where Lukas stood. Jesse resumed speaking to his followers, and the man in brown robes slipped slowly away from the center of the crowd to stand along the outskirts, glaring at the man in its center.

"A new life is possible, my friends. God has not abandoned any of you, though I know sometimes it may be difficult to believe His love for us endures through all trials. You will see. A new door has been opened by His hand, and it beckons all of us to step through it with hope, loving kindness, the strength nurtured and reinforced by offering these things freely to our neighbors, our brothers and sisters, our loved ones and strangers. In my Father's house, there is enough for every one of you. More than enough. We just have to follow the Way. There is still God's power, even when we fall..."

Lukas swallowed. He felt as if Jesse were speaking directly to him, and though the words did not explicitly leave the man's mouth, Lukas heard him saying, "I forgive you." His breath left his lungs in one massive sigh, and while he sagged in the weightless release overwhelming him out of nowhere, he could not take his eyes away from Jesse still speaking to the crowd. Marya's words entered his mind. *The first time I spoke to him myself... I felt I'd been given a second chance.* It had sounded to Lukas like wishful thinking at the time, perhaps even infatuation on Marya's part. But that had been before he knew her as he did now and before he'd had the chance to hear Jesse's teachings and actually listen. Now, he thought he knew exactly what she'd meant by it.

Now, he did not think Jesse was merely a man stepping into the role of teacher. He was something else—something *more*—and Lukas thought he understood what that might be. He'd been told numerous times that the babe who'd died at his hands, despite the lack of his own conscious willingness in doing so, had been the first Messiah. The Unclean commander, vile woman though she was, had said so herself, and Lukas didn't think she had reason to lie to him, given all she'd done. If that child had in fact been the first, sent to bring salvation to the world and taken far before his time, perhaps God had found another way. As Yaakov had told him that morning, nothing lay outside God's plan. Marya had said explicitly that she believed Jesse to be the Messiah; the group had talked about it around the table the night before, and Lukas had thought them a bit too hopeful. But now... now he wasn't sure. What if Jesse really was God's Messiah sent again, in this time, to finish what had been started and so abruptly snuffed out by Lukas's unknowing actions?

"This is how we—" Jesse stopped speaking and turned his head toward where Lukas stood. The man's calm, patient eyes found Lukas's gaze and trapped him in their knowing intensity. "Yes," he said, answering the question Lukas had thought, but never asked. "I *am* the Open Door that cannot be closed. I *am* the Way that cannot be barred. Anyone who believes in me will live and never die."

It seemed Jesse stood directly in front of Lukas, speaking to him as if they were alone in a room and not separated by at least a dozen people. Lukas's breath caught in his throat, the things he saw in this man's eyes now entirely familiar and impossible and true, because Lukas remembered. The babe lying between his murdered parents in the hay had looked at him with those same eyes—all-knowing, all-powerful, full of love and life and forgiveness for everything Lukas had done and still had yet to do. In that moment, Lukas thought that if that child had been able to speak, he would have told Lukas that was not the end. He had known, even then, what would come. And now, Jesse's eyes—the Messiah's eyes—were telling him this was just the beginning.

The Qumranian gasped and fell to his knees right there on the street, surrounded by strangers, students of Jesse, and those curious enough to stay. A few of those closest to him stepped back a little, not in alarm but because they seemed to recognize his need for a little room—a little fresh air to soothe the power of such a mind-altering realization. A few more tears fell from Lukas's eyes, but these were no longer from despair and shame and a desire to end his torment. These tears came from the hope he'd never thought would bloom again within his heart.

30

For the rest of that day, which should have felt very long indeed
but seemed to pass in only a few hours, Lukas stayed to listen to
Jesse. The man's words filled him with hope and peace and a
longing for more of the same. He didn't know the people who
two times throughout the day passed him a cup of the hot, sweetened tea and a bar wrapped in cellophane to eat while he
attended Jesse's teachings. But he thanked them and stayed,
focused on the teacher's words and their meaning and how they
seemed so very much aimed toward everything Lukas had been
through, both in his previous life as a scientist and Hedge Master
of Qumran and now as the last of his people, broken and
deposed and yet given a second chance.

The gruesome sky darkened into the complete blackness of
night—or as black as it could ever be with all the flashing lights,
blinking screens, scrolling messages of glyphs and unknown
characters. Most of those who had surrounded Jesse, even those
who had appeared after Lukas, had mostly filtered away now to
go home and wrap up their days, sustaining themselves on the
words of their teacher. Even Jeza and the women who had lifted
him from the alley to heal him here had left, though their tent

remained. Only Lukas and maybe twenty other men had stayed, all of them now sitting around Jesse in a much more intimate gathering in the darkness. Lukas had not settled as near to Jesse as the others, choosing instead to sit apart, listening on his own. After many more hours, the twenty had dwindled down to a dozen, including Lukas, and the night seemed to be coming to an end.

Finally finished with all he had to share, Jesse stood. He nodded to those still sitting with him, though he did not look again at Lukas or seem to know the stranger remained among them. "You can come with me if you want," he told his friends, and they rose in silence to walk with him.

Lukas hadn't known Cephas was there until he noticed him at the rear of the group, walking slowly, as if some deep thought had struck him, his arm still wrapped snuggly against his chest. At first, Lukas wanted to call out and ask where they were going, but Cephas looked troubled. Maybe it wasn't the best idea to distract him from his thoughts right now, especially this late at night. So Lukas waited until all the men had rounded a corner between the buildings before he got up to follow them in silence.

Jesse led his friends on a winding path through the city, and none of them realized Lukas brought up the rear of their party. Or if they did, they didn't turn around or stop or acknowledge him in any way. Eventually, the tall rise of the Consortium's massive edifices filtered out into shorter, sparser buildings. Then they came to a high wall surrounding this part of the city, rising what seemed like miles into the sky. The flashing lights and the dizzying hum of the hovering, beetle-like crafts still existed this far on the outskirts, but they were muted, quiet, almost nonexistent in comparison.

Without preamble, Jesse pushed against a steel door at the base of the thick stone wall and stepped through it. His friends followed, filtering one at a time through the doorway, Cephas being the last of them. The bearded man left the door open behind him, revealing nothing but a thick darkness beyond. Lukas waited a few more seconds, then slowly approached the door and peered through it.

Desert—that was all. Rolling dunes for as far as he could see, punctuated by rising mounds of dull-red rock, dry and crumbled, their haphazard formations making it seem as if they were giant crumbs dropped from the sky and never cleaned up. One of these outcroppings sat just a few yards to the left, while Jesse and his students had turned right to walk along the city's outer wall. They didn't go far before Jesse stopped, and Lukas took the opportunity to dart from the open doorway within the wall and hide behind the rocks. He wanted to keep listening, to see what this man did among his friends when everyone else had gone. Maybe he'd even get the chance to speak to Jesse himself.

The teacher turned toward the open desert and folded his arms across his chest. It was so incredibly dark out here, the thoroughly charred sky blocking out what little light used to come from the moon and stars, whenever this version of the world had still been pure. But even then, the air around the man seemed lighter, less snuffed out, as though Jesse himself were a tiny, muted lantern. Lukas blinked and thought maybe he'd had too little sleep in the last three days.

"So many people think the desert is a barren, desolate place," Jesse said as his friends stood around him. "But it's not. Never has been."

As if it had been told to do so, a small, brown and red spotted gecko skittered through the sand, leaving a tiny furrow in its wake. It stopped in front of Lukas's hiding spot, seemed to eye him with a wary acceptance, then darted beneath the rock formation and disappeared.

Jesse turned from the wide, sprawling desert to face his students. "Thank you for coming with me," he told them. "Your friendship gives me peace when I feel I need it most."

The men with him accepted his words and smiled, though

the shadow of fatigue bloomed beneath their eyes and in the way they swayed on their feet. Then the man turned to Cephas and nodded. He did the same with two other men, and Lukas immediately recognized Yaakov and Yohanan, though he had not realized they'd also come. As if their teacher had spoken their names aloud, the three men stepped forward to join him in a bit more privacy, though Lukas realized that, if he could hear them, so could Jesse's other students.

"I've seen so many things," Jesse told them. "I know what's to come soon, and I... I can't help but wish things were different. Will you stay with me and keep watch?"

"Anything for you," Cephas replied, his brows drawn together in concern and confusion.

Jesse bowed his head with closed eyes, then looked back up at Cephas and placed his hand on the man's shoulder. "I know what's in your heart, Cephas. I know it will always be there. I also know that you'll smother it with lies three times today. And when three votes are cast, you'll remember this."

"Votes?" Cephas shook his head. "I don't know what that means. But I would never lie about you."

The teacher held his gaze a little longer, then might have tried to smile but didn't quite succeed. He removed his hand from Cephas's shoulder with a deep sigh, then acknowledged Yaakov and Yohanan. "I'm going to pray. Stay with me?"

His students nodded, and then Jesse turned and stepped away from them, closer to Lukas's hiding place. The Qumranian withdrew further behind the rocks, not yet wanting to be discovered secretly watching this man's desert vigil.

Jesse sank to his knees and dipped his head all the way down until his forehead pressed into the fine sand. "Father," he said, his voice quivering. Plumes of sand sprayed up from where he breathed. "I don't want to have to make this choice. But if you will it, I will do it." His long sigh trembled in the sand, then he pushed himself to his feet.

Lukas had focused so intently on the man praying on the ground that he'd paid no attention to what Cephas, Yaakov, Yohanan, and the other students were doing with themselves out here. When he saw Jesse's frown of disappointment, Lukas followed the man's gaze to find most of Jesse's students sitting against the city's outer wall, their heads bowed or tipped back against the rough brick as they slept. Cephas and the brothers had not returned to the wall, but they too sat in the sand, drifting off into hazy sleep.

"Wake up," Jesse said. It was gentle enough, but it roused his students from their drowsing. Their teacher huffed out a sigh of resignation. "Just another hour. That's all. I only need you all for one more hour. Please, stay with me."

"We're here, Teacher," Yaakov said, getting to his knees so he could sit back on his heels.

Jesse nodded at him; the man looked so sad, and Lukas thought he saw fear there, too. From such a man who had bravely spoken amid crowds and to the Phar-asai themselves, what seemed like wavering doubt was so odd.

Then the man turned away from his friends and took his same position on the desert sand, splaying his fingers out along the fine grains as he lowered his head. "Father, it's almost time for me to choose. Give me the strength to do as you will." He drew in an agonized breath, then rose to his knees and turned back toward his friends. "This is weighing heavy on—" When Jesse saw that his students had not been able to stay awake with him for even such a short time, he closed his eyes and sat perfectly still, as if trying hard to keep from yelling at them in anger or weeping over whatever was pressing on him so hard.

In that moment, Lukas wanted nothing more than to streak across the desert and kneel beside Jesse, to offer him some comfort. The Hedge Master felt wide awake, eager, ready to play a bigger part. But something kept him in his hiding place, and he only watched.

Jesse turned toward the desert again and bowed. "The time is here, Father. I know this is your will. I know this is your plan. I will do what you've asked of me."

The man spent such a long time prostrate in the sand that Lukas wondered if the teacher himself had fallen asleep this time. But then slowly, so very slowly, Jesse finally stood and turned. When he saw the men fallen into exhausted sleep again, he marched toward them.

"You couldn't stay up with me?"

Cephas jumped, and the others pushed and prodded each other back into wakefulness.

"Forgive us," one man said; Lukas didn't recognize him.

Jesse's brows drew together, and he worked his jaw before exhaling a loud sigh. "The choice has been made." He took a moment to look into each of his students' eyes, opening his mouth but pausing, as if he didn't want to say the words. "It's time. And the man who hands me over is here."

Those words filled Lukas with an inexplicable dread. He knew Jesse had spoken the truth when he'd said he could see things, that God spoke to him about what was to come. And this was the first time this teacher of the Way had revealed such knowledge with anything other than patient joy in the fact. While Jesse had looked troubled and heavy hearted, now all that was wiped away by a wave of acceptance and resolve.

Lukas couldn't see what the others saw when Jesse's students rose from against the wall and stood to face the newcomer; he thought it even more important now that he remain hidden, so he stayed where he was and watched what he could. It didn't sound like only one man approaching now but many, their footsteps whispering through the desert sand. Lukas couldn't have been more surprised when Cyrus stepped into his line of sight from where he crouched behind the rocks to approach Jesse. The man's cane burrowed into the sand beside his bad foot, letting it rest there as to free up both of his hands, and he gazed up at Jesse with his brows drawn together. Then Cyrus opened his arms, offering an embrace that would seem normal between close friends.

Jesse did not resist his student as Cyrus leaned in to hug his teacher. The minute this warm greeting was exchanged, the desert around them exploded with movement, the rustle of many footsteps and the clink of something metal echoing toward Lukas from the city's high outer wall. Then he saw them from his hiding place—three Phar-asai with half a dozen Janiss-arai in tow. He'd come to believe the Phar-asai were nothing more than a nuisance bent on troubling Jesse while he spoke. They did not carry the same terrifying authority in his mind as he knew they did for most of the city's people. But the hooded, unseen figures in the black leather robes, their faces masked by darkness itself, were something else entirely.

Here, in the darkest part of night before dawn and amid the vastness of the sprawling desert, the inky pool that surrounded the Janiss-arai like a cloud of despair grew even more concrete. The sky was almost bright compared to the blackness they brought with them, and what small glow Lukas had thought he'd seen around Jesse vanished when the black-robed figures surrounded the teacher. One of them nudged Jesse forward with a gloved hand.

"Jesse, son of Hezro," one of the Phar-asai boomed, "by the power of the Consortium and the authority of the Phar-asai, you are hereby under arrest on charges of conspiracy and sedition against the city. You will be held in custody until the charges are reviewed by the city's judges and its people, where you will then be convicted under public opinion." The second Phar-asai produced his electric rod and held it at the ready, as if he actually thought Jesse capable of physical violence. The third removed a set of steel manacles that glinted even under the awful night sky and stepped forward to place these around Jesse's wrists. Though Jesse even extended his arms to make the

Phar-asai's job easier, the man in the brown robes fumbled with
the manacles, shaking visibly, until after the third try, he finally
clamped them down around his prisoner's flesh. All the while,
Jesse gazed at Cyrus, calm and what Lukas would have called
impassive if he had not already known and experienced for
himself the depth of this man's emotions.

Cyrus blinked furiously, then tore his gaze from Jesse's and
shuffled uneasily backward, as if he'd just slapped his teacher
across the face and now awaited reproach. But none came. The
Janiss-arai closed in behind Jesse and ushered him forward
behind the Phar-asai. When another black gloved hand reached
out to push Jesse forward, the cellophane-wrapped bar fell from
the prisoner's hands onto the sand with a soft thud.

Jesse's students protested, shouting for Jesse to fight back,
that the Phar-asai couldn't do this, that the Consortium had no
right. The man in brown robes who had announced the charges
stopped in his march toward the city's outer wall and glared at
the eleven men calling out for their teacher. Then he removed
his own rod from within the folds of his leather garment, and
instantly the students fell silent. Cephas tugged at his beard,
glancing uneasily between the threatening rod and his teacher,
now stopped behind the Phar-asai. Yohanan put a reassuring
hand on Yaakov's back, while his brother gritted his teeth and
flushed enough to be seen even in the near darkness. But none of
them said another word. Then the Phar-asai jerked his head
back and strode dutifully once more toward the open door at the
base of the city's wall, followed by his peers and the Janiss-arai
surrounding Jesse.

When they passed Lukas's hiding place, none of the Consortium's emissaries seemed to notice his presence. But Jesse turned
his head ever so slightly as he walked and caught the Hedge
Master's gaze, as if he'd known all the while that Lukas had
joined them and witnessed everything. Lukas wanted to shrink
back against the rough, chiseled rock but found himself immobi-

lized by what he saw yet again in the man's eyes and this time
understood. God stared back at him from behind Jesse's eyes,
full of infinite knowledge and righteousness and the full power
of love so rarely glimpsed in this place and in this time. That
glance pierced through to Lukas's very soul, and then Jesse was
gone.

Everything was still outside the wall, the air as thick with
horror, anger, and debilitating sorrow as if the Janiss-arai had
executed Jesse right there on the sand. One of the man's students
took off running through the doorway without another word to
his friends, then disappeared. Another followed, and soon each
man hurried after their teacher, or away from him, or to tell the
others in the city what had happened so they might know to
watch for the Consortium's judgment. Yaakov seemed frozen
where he stood, and it took both his brother and Cephas to coax
him into leaving the open space of the desert for the suffocating
decrepitude that was their home inside the wall. These three
brought up the rear of Jesse's students re-entering the city, and
Cyrus limped toward them, his cane thumping desperately in
the sand.

"Yaakov," the man called, blinking still against what Lukas
could only guess were the tears of shame glistening in his eyes. "I
didn't—"

Yohanan stopped to fix the man with a silencing glare. Lukas
hadn't expected the normally silent, compassionate man to be
capable of such a furious glare, let alone the emotion itself. But
the sight of it now made even Lukas wince where he stood
hidden behind the rocks. Cyrus said nothing more, his mouth
opening and closing in a silent plea before Cephas and the
brothers resumed their tedious journey back into the city.

When they'd disappeared through the doorway, Cyrus
gasped, and a strangled sob broke free from his throat. His hand
lost its grip on the cane, making him stumble on his bad leg
before he fell to his knees beside it in the sand. Another louder

groan rose within him, and then he snatched up his metal rod and scrambled desperately back toward the wall. Then he too was gone, and Lukas was alone.

The Hedge Master swallowed thickly, unable to entirely acknowledge what it was he'd just seen. Cyrus—the man who had twice helped him into the Unclean headquarters at the peril of his own life, at the very least—had brought the Phar-asai to arrest his teacher. And Jesse had *known*. He'd said it: *"And the man who hands me over is here."* A week before, even two days before, Lukas would have marveled at such a revelation, would have wondered how it was even possible and maybe suspected someone had warned Jesse of such a betrayal. But now, knowing what he knew, it was not strange at all—only devastating.

No one returned through the open doorway to call out for him or beckon him to return, and Lukas knew only Jesse had seen him there behind the rocks. With the heavy weight of sorrow in his chest, he slowly stepped around the rising structure and made his own way back to the wall; he could do nothing else. With his head slumped, his eyes fell upon the fine sand and an overwhelming emptiness hit him as he pondered the fact that this would be the location of Jesse's last vigil—the open desert and very likely the last place on the Earth untouched by the vestiges of the Consortium's dominion and ravaging of the natural world.

If Lukas had any remaining doubts of Jesse's divinity, there, in the hopelessly desolate desert, green shoots had sprouted from every place Jesse had stepped as he was marched away. Out from the deceptive grains of sand, shoots with fragile leaves shuddered in the breeze blowing east across the desert. Lukas closed his eyes. *"There is God's power even when we fall."* Jesse had said the words just that morning, when Lukas had all but given into shame and despair and hopelessness. The man knew all these things, he walked the Way of the Open Door, and submitted himself to God's will.

The Hedge Master rose then, surprised by the prayer he offered for the long life of this new, green growth amid the desert sand. When he looked up at the doorway in the city's wall, he found the door slowly closing. Acting quickly, he leaped across the loose sand and slipped through just before the metal door shut with a thick click and a resounding boom. Something told him that once that door closed, there was no opening it again from the outside.

31

The city's lower streets seemed so calm against Lukas's pounding heart, so ignorant to the devastating reality of what Jesse now faced. This simple observation filled him with a rage he could not pin down. Why did no one fight for this man? Had all the world been reduced to cowards and traitors?

A woman carrying a huge bundle of reeking cloth bumped into him as he rounded a corner, and he nearly growled at her in frustration and disgust. She stared at him with wide eyes and offered pleading apologies, but he ignored her. His mind had room for one image only—what he'd seen in Jesse's eyes. Cyrus had been so unfathomably selfish. What had he gained from such a perverse deception? Like Lukas, Cyrus had been given a second chance, an opportunity for forgiveness as a discharged soldier from the Unclean forces. What base instinct drove him to turn against Jesse? Lukas imagined all the things he'd do to Cyrus if he ever saw the ex-soldier again—horrible things, but righteous in Cyrus's deserving of them.

He wandered aimlessly through the streets, fueled by his rage and his grief and the anxiety of not knowing Jesse's fate. Not like the man seemed to know himself. That truth, apparently, he had not shared with his students. Lukas had no idea where he was going, but in that moment, it didn't truly matter. He was lost, restless, drifting again just moments after he'd found refuge in a world so devoid of hope. Briefly, he considered storming after Jesse and summoning his Hedge Master's training, using centuries of study and knowledge filtered down into the memory of his own muscles and the quiet of his mind to break free the man who had saved his soul. But that would only bring the Unclean down upon him again, and it was not bravery and devotion but idiocy that drove a man to repeat the same failure a third time. Even if he had a chance against the Unclean and the Consortium's Janiss-arai forces, he had no idea where the Phar-asai had led them.

Once, as the mid-morning sun burned down through the atmosphere and the charred, roiling sky, he thought he was hungry. His hand went on its own to the food bar stowed in his pocket, and then all the memories of what he'd seen in the desert before sunrise came flooding back. Then his anger flared anew and chased away whatever semblance of hunger he'd had.

Finally, after what seemed like a lifetime of wandering, he stumbled out of a smaller street and into a much wider avenue, where the holographic screens on all the largest surfaces of the rising buildings were lit with the same images. These circulated one right after the other, showing a man from all different angles now stripped down to nothing more than a set of thin, loose shorts, standing erect with his head raised and his hands shackled in front of him. In every image, the man's face was skewed, as if all his features had been blurred by the same invisible shroud Lukas had seen in previously displayed images. But he knew it was Jesse.

Apparently, the others gathered in the street knew as well. A group of men huddled together in front of a display screen over a storefront, jostling each other and shouting obscenities at the images of Jesse.

"How is your new Way going to help you out of this?!" one of them jeered. He threw something at the holographic projection, and the projectile smashed against the storefront to spatter a dark yellow sludge across the wall. His friends laughed.

Three women walked past Lukas, all of them sniffling. One of them pointed up at another display showing a different image of Jesse and sobbed something he couldn't understand. The others tried to comfort her ensuing wails, but they were obviously almost as distraught as their companion.

Other small gatherings displayed nearly everything across this spectrum of reactions to Jesse's arrest, and a heated fight broke out just down the street when friends quite clearly disagreed with one another. Lukas crossed the wide street to avoid being swept up in the frenzy there, but the dispute was temporarily settled. Everywhere, the holographic displays flashed a revolving set of images, all with Jesse's face obscured.

"There's obviously nothing wrong with the remo-cams," a low voice boomed from unseen speakers. The high volume made Lukas's head pound. *"They've been tested three times since the man was brought in for questioning. All systems have been verified."*

"And, of course," a second voice declared, rattling between the buildings lining the streets, *"there's no possibility of Jesse harboring a personal EMP device to morph his own image. The man's in his underwear, for crying out loud."* A mixed chorus of jeering shouts and devastated wails rose from the different crowds at that remark.

"Right," the first voice replied. *"The remo-cam technicians are still looking into it, so as soon as we hear from them about what seems to be the problem with the man's face, besides the obvious, we'll be sure to let all of you know."*

Lukas clenched his fists and forced himself to look at the image now projected—Jesse now walking inside a hall with white, sterile walls, a hooded Janiss-arai prodding him with an outstretched hand gloved in black leather. Then he had to look away.

When he did, his gaze fell directly upon Cephas, who glanced up at the images with tears in his eyes before backing into a wide tent. The bearded man searched the streets furtively, as if he feared the Phar-asai would come for him too. A few yards away behind a stack of metal crates, he found Yaakov and Yohanan as well. Yaakov sat on the filthy sidewalk, staring down at his hands, and his brother stood behind him, glaring at the groups of onlookers who'd decided Jesse's arrest warranted their harsh abuse.

At first, Lukas's initial reaction was to join the men he recognized, to offer what little comfort he could amid such a devastating turn of events. But though Cephas and the brothers had been overly generous and kind to Lukas since they'd found him alone and naked on the streets of this horrid city, they'd also been friends with Cyrus. They'd named him a fellow student of Jesse and had entrusted their lives and Lukas's by going to the ex-soldier for help in infiltrating the Unclean headquarters. Lukas had grown fond of these men, yes. He didn't see any sign of Cyrus now, but he couldn't ward off his growing suspicion of this place, including a wariness of his new friends. Really, he hardly knew them, and he couldn't be sure that they too hadn't had some part to play in Jesse's arrest and subjection to this vile debasement in such a public way.

"Looks like it's time to begin," the announcer called. Lukas hated thinking of these disembodied voices that way, but what else was he supposed to call them? *"We're switching over to the live feeds now."* All the huge, unignorable projected screens flashed together, and then the holographic images moved with a swiftness that made Lukas dizzy at first.

There was Jesse, standing in a room made of glass with two Phar-asai in front of him flanked by two Janiss-arai in black robes. His shackles had been removed, but he stood there in his undergarments and nothing more, his hands at his sides, and calmly faced those who meant to tear him down.

"Those remo-cam techs really need to step up their work," the second announcer called.

"Sorry, folks. Looks like you won't be seeing the man's face any time soon."

"He's probably crying, anyways."

Lukas shut his eyes against the blatant disrespect, but that did nothing to drown out the voices. He looked back up at the screens.

A small, static whir filled the street, followed by a pop, and then the audio must have been switched on to capture what was said inside that glass room.

"I charge you under oath," the first Phar-asai said, drawing out the words as if they themselves were Jesse's sentence, "by the Consortium and the Law it upholds, as a fraud and a charlatan. You claim to be the Messiah. The son of God. Is this true?"

The street fell silent as those watching strained to hear Jesse's answer, though it would have been impossible not to hear it with the resounding volume of such a display.

"It is as you say."

Shouts and hisses exploded from the crowd, punctuated by rising screams of sorrow. More refuse was hurled at the holographic projections to shatter against the walls behind them.

"When the time comes," Jesse continued, and the outcries died only a little, "and it will come soon, you will see me sitting at the right hand of God with dominion over all the stars of the heavens."

A deep pride flared within Lukas's chest to see that this man who was more than a man was also not so easily broken. Even still, debased and ridiculed as he was, Jesse did not turn from the truth. But Lukas had expected this interrogation by the Phar-asai to be much like those he'd seen of Jesse in the streets—questions, answers, and a bitter denial from the men in brown leather robes. He did not expect what happened next.

Almost too quick for the live feed to capture, a Janiss-arai stepped forward and swung his gloved fist into Jesse's face. The sick thud filled every pocket of sound in the street, and Jesse stumbled under the force of such a blow. Lukas choked on his own breath to see it, but steeled himself, because he would not turn away from this man—not now, not ever.

The crowd responded in kind, erupting again into their own angry, vilified, tortured, or flaring reactions to what the figure hooded in black had just done. Finally, when Jesse righted himself and stood to face his inquisitors once more, things settled only a little.

"You say you have seen God's visions of the future," the second Phar-asai began. "That you rival the mystics in your knowledge, who are all dead and buried and took their wisdom with them. Do you deny it?"

The blurred outline of Jesse's head bobbed on the screen, and his voice was muffled but firm. "I cannot deny the truth or God's will with it."

The shouts now turned to screams, hurled obscenities, vengeful hatred aimed at the man who had wanted nothing more than to show these people a new Way to live, an Open Door straight into the arms of God through faith. The second Janiss-arai moved just as quickly as the first, but this one did not strike Jesse in the face. Instead, the hooded figure brought his fist upward into Jesse's stomach with enough force to send the man flying backward against the wall of glass. It shouldn't have been possible, but the force shattered the glass; huge, jagged shards fell from the ceiling and the frames of the wall.

Lukas watched in mute horror, the projected images slowing down before him as if time itself wanted to forestall the inevitable. Mixed with the dismay of seeing Jesse treated like this was an overwhelming dread of what he'd seen the Janiss-arai perform; perhaps the figure had stricken Jesse so forcefully because the teacher was merely too weak to resist the blow, but Lukas thought differently. What he saw was something so startingly like a strike delivered using the fundamentals of the Hedge that Lukas thought he might lose himself entirely in the rage brought on by such a violation. No one else was supposed to know how to summon that kind of power, especially not one of those unseen monsters hiding behind the black robes.

The second Phar-asai glanced at the Janiss-arai who had just delivered the blow and gave a slight nod. The black-hooded figure took two steps toward Jesse, who struggled now to rise amid the broken glass, and delivered another swift punch to his jaw. The blow spun Jesse nearly all the way around, and his hands reached out in reflex to catch himself from falling on his face. He succeeded in this, but his hands did not find safe purchase; instead, they slammed onto the rising, glistening shards of broken glass still protruding from the wall's frame. The sound of ripping flesh made Lukas's head spin, heralding what the rem-cams picked up as the image of Jesse's palms impaled through their centers by the wicked sharpness of two shards of thick, jagged glass. Jesse's gasp of pain filled the silence. A cry of horror rose from the crowd, those set so intently against Jesse momentarily forgetting their hatred for the man amid the shock of such a brutal misfortune.

The rem-cams caught the glance of surprise shared between the two Phar-asai in the glass room, then one of them signaled toward a black-robed Janiss-arai. The dark figure stomped across the broken glass, his boots impervious to their cutting edges, and grasped Jesse's forearms before jerking them mercilessly upward and off the shards that had sliced him through. Their prisoner gasped again but made little noise otherwise, and Lukas's eyes filled with tears.

The Janiss-arai returned to his place beside his apparent

master in the brown leather robes, who muttered, "Turn around."

Slowly, trembling a little, Jesse did as he was commanded. Even the patter of his blood as it dripped from his skewered palms to fall onto the glass-strewn floor was loud enough to sound as if it was all happening right there in front of them instead of within some room elsewhere in the city.

"You have one more chance to recant your lies and atone for your sins, false mystic," the first Phar-asai hissed. "Tell us the truth. Life ends in death and nothing more. For everyone. Say it!" The man looked wildly hysterical now, desperate to break his prisoner in any way he could.

No one could see Jesse's face, but no one had to; though his voice trembled now, the conviction in it could not be ignored. "Life never ends," he said slowly. "And in my Father's house, it is everlasting. Anyone who listens to me and believes in me will never find death. Only the Open Door..." Whatever else Jesse had meant to say, it faded now as he swayed barefoot upon the broken glass, the blood spilling out of his hands in a constant stream.

"This man's insane," the second Phar-asai shouted, spit flying from his lips. "Only poisonous lies and blasphemy come out of his mouth, and even now he chooses that over his own life. Everywhere he goes, unrest and rebellion follow. We don't need anything else." The man whirled around and moved briskly to the glass door of the glass room.

His counterpart motioned to the Janiss-arai, one of whom stepped behind Jesse and shoved him forward again. Their prisoner lurched forward, and his bare feet scraped against the broken shards all over the floor. Jesse tried to steady himself, then stumbled, and more glass crunched beneath him before he let out a muffled cry. A pool of crimson bloomed beneath one of his feet, and the Janiss-arai behind him shoved him forward again. Jesse fell to his knees, and when the hooded figures in black seized him by the arms and jerked him to his feet, the fallen teacher actually did scream this time, throwing his head back and nearly collapsing. But his unknown jailors merely hooked their elbows under his arms and dragged him from the room. Jesse's head hung low against his chest, and his passing left a thick, bloody trail across the room's white tiled floor with the last, horrendous image of crunched glass protruding from the soles of both his feet.

The holographic screens all around them flickered, darkened, and then a new image appeared. Three men in gray robes, all looking rather disinterested given what had just happened, glanced up into the rem-cams from where they'd been studying something on the table in front of them.

"Board of Judges, cast your votes," the second announcer called, his voice distinguishable by its high-pitched drone. A low buzz of anticipation filled the street now, the people apparently awaiting what the men who called themselves judges meant to say about the situation. Lukas clenched his fists. How could something like this become dependent on a *vote*, of all things? Did no one else see what was happening?

"Hey." A young woman's voice rose from just down the street, and Lukas peered around the people beside him to see who had spoken. She stood in front of Cephas, two plastic crates stacked in her arms. "Aren't you one of his students? That man? Jesse?" She jerked her head toward the huge screen behind her.

"Execution," the first judge decreed, waving his hand in the air as if he had much more important things to do.

Cephas's gaze flicked from the hologram to the young woman's face. "Don't be ridiculous," he muttered, then frowned and shook his head at her. She gave him an odd look but continued on her way, apparently unaffected by the goings on. Cephas swallowed and glanced around the street, then looked back up at the screen and pulled at his beard.

The second judge seemed to take a little longer in his ruse of consideration. "The most extreme sentences are rarely necessary." He sounded as if he were discussing a mathematical formula and not the fate of a man's life. "I'd consider this to be one of those rare cases. Execution." Then he sat back in his chair and folded his arms with a scowl.

More shouts and raucous jeers rose among the crowds, but they were more subdued now, the certainty of Jesse's death seeming to sink in before it had been officially ruled. Two men beside Lukas whispered Jesse's name and spat on the ground, neither of them looking remotely ashamed.

"Don't you know that man?" An old woman had stepped up beside Cephas, her clawed hand shaking as she extended it toward the huge projections on the walls.

"Never seen him before," Cephas replied, then cleared his throat. The man seemed unwilling to look her in the eye, and Lukas found himself swimming in regret. He'd thought Cephas had been so devoted to Jesse, so ready to deliver his message and live by his Way. Now, it seemed even the deepest loyalty had its limits in this place.

"Yeah, I've seen you with him," another man added, his face riddled with open sores. "You tried to get me to come listen to him speak once—"

"I said I don't know him!" Cephas screamed into the man's face, shaking with either fear or anger or both. Then, as if he wished to prove himself further, the bearded man lowered his head and spat onto the already filthy sidewalk.

"This is a waste of all our time," the third judge muttered on the projections overhead. "Execution."

"*That's it, citizens,*" the first announcer boomed, as if they were to kick off some ribald celebration. "*The Master Judges have cast their three votes. Coming soon, prisoner roulette!*"

As if his own name had been called, Cephas whirled from his unintended target to stare with impossibly wide eyes at the holographic screens. His mouth worked soundlessly, and he backed up against the wall, stricken with a grief so terrible, Lukas recognized it immediately. And he knew why.

He'd heard Jesse's words to Cephas himself, when he'd hidden behind the rise of crumbled stone in the desert. *"I know what's in your heart, Cephas. I also know that you'll smother it with lies three times today. And when three votes are cast, you'll remember this."* And it had been true—all of it.

Now, without a doubt, Lukas knew Cephas had recognized the same thing, and the man's eyes glistened before he closed them. Tears poured down his cheeks to stain his beard, and he thumped his head back against the wall.

"Cephas?" Yohanan asked, looking at his friend with curious concern.

Cephas's eyes flew open, and he could only manage a brief glance at the brothers before he pushed himself from against the wall and stormed off down the street.

"Cephas, wait," Yohanan called after him, but the bearded man had already disappeared through the milling crowd.

Lukas's heart went out to his gracious host—the man who had done so much for him and given so much of himself; the man who had brought him to Jesse the very first time with an eagerness Lukas thought he'd never understand. He also never expected to sympathize with the terrible shame he'd seen in Cephas's glistening eyes. No, the man's betrayal here in the lower levels could never compare to what Cyrus had done, but Lukas imagined quite easily that Cephas now felt as if he'd driven that glass through Jesse's palms himself.

32

"*This program,* By Popular Vote, *is brought to you by your corporate sponsors at Zanaquil.*"

The screens lighting up on every surface across the city flashed in a twenty-second ad for some pharmaceutical product guaranteed to "make you satisfied with the life you never knew you wanted." It made Lukas sick. This entire travesty had somehow been made into a form of entertainment, designed to falsely empower the masses and subdue them long enough for the Consortium to get away with murder. And no one seemed to think it strange.

He couldn't help but wonder how many alleged criminals had perished in this way, how many more would be falsely accused, imprisoned, charged, and executed. He knew now that was what these monstrous people intended to do with Jesse, no matter what anyone else in the city said they wanted. After what he'd seen in the crowds gathered along the street, stopped between their bartering and trading and conversations with friends to watch the holographic projections, he suspected the city's people thought this was exactly what they wanted—to feel better about their own empty lives by watching someone else's end in agonizing shame and torment. Lukas wanted to scream at them all to listen to themselves, to think about what they were doing, but that would have been just as effective now as trying to break Jesse out of the Consortium's custody.

The projections now showed a still image of Jesse's blurred features and below it some type of listed information Lukas still couldn't read but wished otherwise. Then a new voice boomed over the city's audio systems. *"Citizens of this great city. This is Governor Zeev calling to you from the citadel. I ask you now, who shall I release to you? Your options are as follows. This prisoner who refers to himself as 'The Gift', arrested and charged with three counts of murder two months ago."* A new image of a man with shorn hair and wide, terrified eyes popped up on the screens beside the blurred picture of Jesse. *"Or this man, Jesse, who claims to be the Messiah of his and all people."* Jesse's marred visage blinked at the words. *"Key in the appropriate code right now for real-time vote tabulation."*

Lukas felt as if he were dreaming. Everywhere he looked, the people in the street pulled out handheld devices, some of them incredibly large and sleek, others as small as the handheld Marya had given him. Almost all business and trade stopped entirely so the citizens could respond to such a call to action, standing beside one another and simultaneously flipping through their devices to do what had been asked of them. Of course, Lukas understood none of the flashing, scrolling characters across the screens in people's hands and the same reflected in the projected images all around him. This made him feel even more helpless, even more an isolated stranger in this place where no one seemed to understand the simple and very real difference between right and wrong.

Glyphs flashed repeatedly, and the so-called governor's voice returned. *"What a remarkable response. The votes are coming in almost as fast as our systems can count them. And it... it looks like an overwhelming number of you wish this murderer to go free..."*

The man sounded surprised by such a reply from the citizens, as if this governor had never expected these people to favor a murderer loose among them above a peaceful man merely wishing to spread his knowledge. *"This Jesse, then, will face execution as the judges have voted. Remember, citizens, vote now and vote often. We aim to give you want you want, so tell us."*

A few more minutes passed, and Lukas heard the shouts rising, first from one or two throats but soon growing to many.

"Drain him!"

"Empty the liar. Make him bleed!"

"Execution!"

The accusations and calls for death pummeled Lukas from every direction, and though they were not aimed at him but the man he now knew to be the Messiah come again, he felt each jeering stab as if these people wanted him dead, too. He whirled around, fists clenched, just waiting for the excitement to carry some ignorant degenerate his way. He wanted someone to confront him, to ask why he hadn't voted or seemed so rigidly against the whole process; it would be just the excuse he longed for to lash out and release all his furious dismay. But no one seemed to notice him at all.

The scrolling characters blinked in overwhelmingly bright colors, shifting and changing now too quickly for him to follow. And then a dinging chime sounded, as if the people of the city had won some type of prize.

"Look at that," the governor's voice boomed. *"Well, would you just... look at that. You seem to all have very much the same thing in mind. Are you certain this—"* The audio cut out briefly, as if someone had turned off the program for a moment of private conversation. *"The... the people have spoken. Jesse will be emptied and recycled as a resource. That is... well, that is your decision."*

The characters at the very top of the screen's listed options grew nearly ten times in size, flashing across the holographic surfaces to take up almost the entire width of them. *"This is amazing,"* the first announcer shouted, the governor obviously having stepped down from his brief role. *"The highest ratings and citizen interaction we've had since the Cavorous Uprising seven years ago..."*

Lukas had to turn away from the screens, had to get away from all these people screaming and stamping their feet and hissing for the death of a man they should be begging their government to release. This was wrong. All of this was so very wrong.

The lull in excitement only intensified his anxiety as the screen projections boasted what felt like hours of short, blaringly pushy ads for this drug, that food, countless trivial personal amenities. And no one seemed even remotely aware of how immune they were to such repetitive displays and at the same time susceptible to its propaganda. They seemed to have forgotten Jesse and his fate entirely until the screens burst back to life with a little jingle that made Lukas want to bash his head against the wall.

"And here we are, citizens. The final moment of your prisoner's sentencing. Jesse, son of Hezro, has been taken to the executioner's block in the Consortium's Chambers of Supreme Justice. Coming to you live now from the city's finest in rem-cam technology, the execution you've all been waiting for."

The holograms blinked again into an image of a long, narrow hallway with walls of glinting steel. Here, the recording of Jesse split again to show different angles—from above, his head bowed as he shuffled across the floor; from ahead of him, capturing the two looming figures in black robes who prodded him forward; from behind the Janiss-arai, where the view narrowed toward the floor to show the smears of blood and glass trailing along behind the prisoner. They had done nothing about Jesse's previous wounds, and Lukas could only imagine the agony the man now endured in being forced to march to his own death with shards of broken glass slicing through his flesh with every step.

Jesse faltered in his path, and one Janiss-arai produced a massive whip, all steel and coiled cables, the tip split into many ends like dangling vines. The figure pulled back the thick, gleaming handle and brought the whip down across Jesse's back with a hissing crackle of electricity and the slapping rip of flesh. The screens flashed bright white, then dimmed as rem-cams adjusted to the visual. Jesse had fallen to the floor of the hallway, slipping in his own blood. The Janiss-arai's whip had flayed open half a dozen long lines in his back, smoke rising from where the hot tips of the flail had cauterized the wounds. Blood oozed from these charred furrows, and Lukas swallowed, thinking he could smell the stench of burning skin and muscle.

Jesse tried to stand and cried out at the agony of doing so. The whip came down again, flashing brilliantly amid new tendrils of smoke and the crackle of its searing contact. The crowd around Lukas screamed in ecstasy, as if this man had personally wronged them and their families—as if they'd never been more delighted by the sight of such a horrid thing.

The second Janiss-arai gripped their prisoner firmly by the upper arm and hoisted Jesse to his feet. There he stood, swaying, his agony not fully captured by the rem-cams that could never seem to correct the skewed image of his face. The hooded figure with the whip raised it again and brought it down a final time but from the side, almost as an afterthought. The blazing, white-hot tips ripped the flesh of Jesse's ribs and lower back, glancing up across the base of his neck, and the man cried out. Blood splattered the reflective steel walls, smoke curled up from the wounds, and the last flicker of the whip's many flails skittered against the second Janiss-arai who held their prisoner upright for more punishment.

Lukas couldn't believe it. The Janiss-arai should have recoiled from the glancing blow of the searing whip, should have at least jerked away in surprise or reflex. Only a quick flare of impossible darkness bloomed from the second Janiss-arai's shoulder where the flail would have torn the robes and left a smear of blood and smoke on any mortal man. Those were not mortal men; the Consortium had something else in their employ, hidden behind the black cowls.

The Hedge Master strained against such a revelation, fighting it off with every ounce of will he still possessed. That made this even worse—the thought that those hooded demons, whatever they were, were not of man and most definitely not of God. Lukas thought of his shameful submission to Ahriman, Angel of Darkness, though he'd not known it then and could never have possibly hoped to resist it. The Janiss-arai could very well have been retainers of Ahriman, just like the Unclean and that godawful woman commander. And no one here would ever know.

Perhaps they did. Perhaps these people knew full well what hid beneath the black leather of the Janiss-arai hoods—no doubt the Consortium had employed the dark figures because of it— and these lost souls had willingly delivered Jesse into their hands. More than willingly—they'd *chosen* it.

He'd been standing too long; that had to be the reason for his shaking legs and the fact that he almost couldn't feel them anymore. Lukas backed up against the building, between a tent marked with something that looked like ocean waves. There sat a group of three homeless men in rags, their hands uplifted toward any passersby who found themselves generous enough amid such an exciting development today to offer a little more good-will than usual. Lukas ignored them, unable to see their need from behind his own despair, and slid slowly to the ground. Looking up at the screens everywhere, he watched the procession of Jesse being half pushed, half shoved down the rest of the blood-spattered hallway toward what he hoped was the end to such a farce of justice. This had to end.

But it did not. The rem-cams followed Jesse and his jailors toward a door at the end of the hall, where they then entered a room similarly walled with garishly bright steel, no windows or other doors in sight. A man in gray robes stood there waiting for them, his eyes glinting behind the spectacles placed securely on the bridge of his nose. In the center of this cold, sterile room was a large round table, pristine and startling in its white purity and contrast to the lifeless silver steel all around. Jesse was prodded toward the table, forced roughly upon it by the Janiss-arai, and jerked across it to lie in its center. The squeak of flesh across the clean surface came with surprising clarity over the speakers, and Lukas could only imagine how excruciating it must have been for the cauterized lashes across Jesse's back to have been forced roughly open again by the act.

Jesse lay on the white table, quite still and entirely silent as the man in the gray robe moved slowly, stretching Jesse's arms out to the edge of the table before clamping his prisoner's wrists in tight manacles as white as the table itself. He did the same with Jesse's ankles, though these were pinned together in one larger shackle. Then another man in white robes entered, his face hidden entirely behind a white, mesh-like screen across the opening of his hood. He pushed a large steel cart in front of him, and on it rested three steel buckets and an assortment of clear plastic tubes coiled neatly on the top tray.

The man in the gray robes, who obviously thought of this task as his alone in his own domain, retrieved one of the tubes and brought it toward Jesse. One rem-cam zeroed in on this seemingly innocuous tool to show its true purpose; at the end of the tube stretched a long, thick bar of steel the width of a man's finger and ending in a wickedly sharp point. He stood beside Jesse's left arm and did not once look up to consider the man before him. As if he'd performed this procedure countless times —quite likely, given the state of this ungodly place—he bent over and pressed the tip of the massive needle against the inside of

Jesse's wrist. With a brusque, curt shove, he jammed the huge point into the man's flesh and up inside his arm. Jesse gasped and choked with the agony of it, and the crowds in the streets erupted into more screams of delight and shouts of "Empty him!" and "Drain it all!"

The horrid, open slice where the broken glass had skewered Jesse's palm burst again in a rain of blood onto the white table. The man with the spectacles slowly stepped away, as if this were nothing more than a surprising consequence of his duty. Then he continued, taking another giant needle and connected tube to Jesse's other wrist, where he performed the same barbaric maneuver, all to the great elation and raucous jeering of those gathered outside to watch. The third tube ended in a split section, two needles protruding from its end, and these the gray-robed man shoved up into Jesse's calves from the base of his ankles.

Every cry and groan of pain pummeled Lukas where he sat against the wall, unable to look away from the grotesquely large projections of such torture. Would he have managed such a thing if Jesse's face had not been so misshapen and hidden by whatever interference it seemed to have with the broadcasted images? The memory of Jesse's eyes flashed before him then— wide, endless, glistening with hope and love and forgiveness and the knowledge of everything that ever was. Lukas briefly closed his eyes, thinking it did not matter if the broadcast did not show Jesse's face. Lukas had seen it himself, and that was enough.

After each inserted needle by the gray-robed man, his apparent acolyte in white behind the mask of white mesh followed, placing a bucket on the floor and reaching up to lift the connected tube toward a hook that hung almost two feet down from the ceiling. Through these he strung each clear tube, so the image of Jesse lying there, speared and gasping, made Lukas think of Ben in the Unclean laboratory, the ropes of wires and thick cables spilling from his head and across the floor. But Ben had, he hoped, not lived long enough to experience much of that agony. For Jesse, this looked as if it was going to last quite some time.

Finally, the bucket in front of Jesse's skewered calves was placed on the cart itself so the tube traveled up and into it from the table. With everything apparently settled just the way he wanted, the spectacled man stepped back, pressed a panel on the steel wall beside the door, and surveyed his handiwork. The round table jolted with a hydraulic hiss and rose as its stand elongated from the floor. Then it tilted further until it no longer looked like a table but a giant, solid white wheel, suspended in the center of the room with Jesse strapped to it only by the bright white manacles now digging into the flesh of his wrists and ankles. The horrific needles didn't budge from where they were embedded in his flesh, and from the new height of the table, their tubes dangled through the hooks in the ceiling into the waiting buckets below.

It almost looked like Jesse wielded great whips of clear plastic, suspended in time before he drove them onto those who meant to end him this way. Lukas wished that were so. Part of him wanted Jesse to fight back, to call on God's wrath and use it now for divine retribution. In no way did he doubt the Messiah could do this thing. And yet, even with all that supreme power at his command, Jesse accepted his fate, as if it proved everything he'd said and everything he'd wished to show those who would listen. Lukas clenched his teeth. This only proved that Jesse could die, just like any man. The Hedge Master regretted not having told Jesse he believed.

There were no machines or technology needed now to do what gravity and time alone managed perfectly well. Blood dripped from the open wounds in Jesse's palms and from the mangled patches of shredded flesh that had once been the soles of his feet. It ran down the white table behind him, the cauterized wounds of his lashes obviously not completely sealed and still opened again by this treatment. And the needles feeding into the plastic tubes did what they were designed to do. The hooks from which the tubes hung were leveled at the exact height of Jesse's outstretched arms and the needles within them. This, of course, cruelly ensured he would not bleed out in minutes. Instead, this treatment forced his own heart to do all the work; as it pumped and tried to sustain him, a crimson trickle filtered along the bottom of the tube at an agonizingly slow crawl. Then it reached the bend in the clear plastic and dripped almost weightlessly down, filling the streets with the tinny patter of drops pinging into the metal bucket below.

It had taken what Lukas assumed was close to an hour, if not more, for those first drops to fall. The crowds had waited with abnormal patience, as if they knew their time for satisfaction was close and they only had to carry on with their lives before it greeted them. But the city was remarkably quiet for what it was, bristling with energy, subdued beneath the weight of expectation and not, as Lukas wished it was, the horror of what they'd done. When the sound of bodily fluids falling into the metal buckets echoed along every building and down each winding, labyrinthine alleyway, the city sprang to sudden life again. One might have thought the sound was a mighty battle cry, a call to defense, a celebratory toll to signal some ruthless enemy conquered. And all for a man's last few hours and the echo of his blood dripping ceaselessly from his body with no one there to comfort him or to stop it.

Angry tears stung Lukas's eyes, but he could no more move from his place on the unimaginably filthy sidewalk than Jesse could free himself from the fate to which he'd willingly been shackled.

33

The City – Inside the Worldveil

High above the Earth, in a place unseen by mortal eyes but perhaps echoing in some of their hearts, the stars themselves shuddered. Beyond the constructs of time and space but still inexorably linked to them, the worldveil wavered and shook, bulging with the force behind it. Then it ripped open to reveal a vast armada of glittering, crystalline ships, their forms spiraling in both mathematical perfection and the natural, curving beauty of life itself. Thousands of them, tens of thousands, all hovering there in tense, eager anticipation on the pinnacle of this day—the nexus of all that ever was and all that ever would be.

Glimmering Protectors and armed Warriors flared to existence along the streets of the city, above the cold peaks of metal and glass aiming to pierce the noxious sky. They waited in the air, suspended over alleyways, standing beside children, lingering in doorways of homes and businesses and empty rooms. Their etched forms penetrated the darkness of the worldveil with so much light, unseen in this place where time itself had stopped to allow them their preparations for this day. For the end and the beginning.

From above what had once been the Dead Sea and the breath of life to so many creatures came a tumbling roar of thunder, fear, and rage. The worldveil quivered, and a new force joined the moment of waiting. Dark, lifeless bulges emerged from the tears in space, ripping through the sky with an echoing groan of approach. Huge black ships glided forward, their shapes undulating with hungry tendrils as one desperate mass. Smaller ships and individual figures burst from the larger hosts like maggots from a corpse, swarming toward the city.

The visages of sparkling light ready to engage their enemies of darkness, poised with sharply honed swords, deadly spears, blazing arrows of truth and fire, wisdom and essence forged into weapons with one purpose only—to be victorious. Their dark adversaries approached just as confident with swift readiness and armed with swords and daggers and firing bolts ablaze with black fire and dripping the weight of their need to engage.

All remained still, tense, waiting. The time was nigh, but not yet...

34

The world still moved, he knew. It had to; time did not stop for one man, one people, one city in the middle of the desert. But for Lukas, everything stood still despite the slow drift of movement through the streets. So many people passed him as he waited, numb, watching the agonizing process of Jesse's undoing projected shamelessly everywhere he looked.

Most people looked away from the screens now. They shook their heads, tending to their own tasks as if they could not fathom how a man could let such a thing happen to himself. A mother walked by, wrapped in the same fraying rags as her two toddlers and steered them down a particularly unsavory-looking alley just to spare them the sight they could most likely not escape anyway. A man and his wife spat on the ground at Lukas's feet, not at him but at the huge image of Jesse, splayed on the upturned table, projected on the building behind the Qumranian. Lukas drew his knees up toward his chest and away from the thick phlegm added to the slime coating the sidewalk.

But there were others like him as well who seemed to know what all this really meant. He spotted the woman Jeza who had healed him. She ushered three other women down the street, one of them wailing incomprehensible things in her sorrow as her friends gently implored her not to draw too much attention. The woman who had spoken to Lukas just before they'd carted his broken body away and just after he'd awakened—healed and resentful of it—turned her face up to the largest screen broadcast against the tallest building in this part of the city. For only a few seconds, she watched Jesse's agony, then she hurried her friends onward, tears streaming silently down her cheeks. One man he recognized from those who had followed their teacher into the desert early that morning; his startlingly blue eyes were red-rimmed beneath heavy lids, and he took longer than the vendor had patience for in purchasing something from his stand. He kept fumbling with whatever handheld device Lukas thought they used to exchange syn-creds, sniffling and blinking rapidly while never meeting the vendor's gaze.

Now that the uproarious energy of the crowds had abated—that mindless force that had boiled within the city like water about to spill over a pot on the stove—more people who had either called themselves Jesse's students or had listened to and been moved by his words stepped out of the alleys and walkways. They emerged from where they'd hidden in isolated mourning to watch what became of the man they all loved in their own way. There were far fewer of them than the confused, angry citizens who had called so vehemently for this to be done to Jesse, but their numbers were larger than Lukas would have guessed. There did not seem enough space for them to truly grieve such a barbaric thing; their voices were hushed, their tears repressed, their sobs and wails muted by fear. But they were there.

Yaakov and Yohanan had been just as affected as Lukas himself; they hadn't moved from where Yaakov sat beside the stacked crates and his brother leaned heavily against the wall behind him. Now, though, Yohanan had chosen to sit as well, and not once did they look at Lukas to share with him their grief.

He didn't think they'd noticed him there amid the show of brutality, but he still wondered if they would have joined him had they known. He preferred to be left on his own, anyway. He neither saw nor heard mention of Cephas.

The sun had already reached its highest point above the city in the desert, baking down through the thick film of spoiled, poisoned sky. It had begun its descent toward the western horizon, yes, but that did not account for or explain what happened next.

A shadow moved across the world. Not a cloud, not a storm, not even an eclipse of the sun still so natural and predictable even in this timeline. This was a darkness that, despite the desert heat and the cloying humidity of the slick, crowded city streets, made Lukas shiver all the way to his bones. It felt like some massive, dark power loomed over all of them, seizing the opportunity to remind the people what they had decided and the fate they had all taken part in sealing for this man—Jesse, the first and second Messiah, the son of God.

Everywhere, the citizens paused in their usual dealings—as usual as they could be for a day like today—and craned their necks toward the sky to see what had cast such a sudden gloom over their lives. There was nothing there, no evidence to explain the sullen phenomenon. The shadow made Lukas feel as if he sat on the precipice of some sheer cliff, immobilized by an unseen presence and waiting for the hand that would either pull him away from the drop to safety or push him over the edge. And he could do nothing.

Despite the anticipatory dread brought on by the change in the sky or the air around them or whatever it was that had darkened, Lukas found himself finally feeling as if the pain and the horror of Jesse's end was being recognized for what it really was. The Messiah's life was seeping out of his veins through plastic tubes, leaving him alone and forsaken for everyone to see, but the world seemed to know what that meant for them, and the world was crying out.

For three more hours at least, by Lukas's guess, the world turned in this new darkness. The people came and went—did their chores, ran their errands, called to their friends, delivered their curses or their tears to the image of the man hanging before them on every crisply detailed screen. By now, Jesse's flesh had lost the pink vitality of life, and the steady drip of his blood falling into the buckets had slowed to a punctuated echo every few minutes. The only thing to show the city that their condemned man still lived was the rise and fall of his chest and the steady, rattling hush of his breath coming through the speakers. No detail was spared for the citizens owing the Consortium their allegiance; Lukas knew that if Jesse's face had not remained so indiscernible on every hologram, the rem-cams would have zeroed in on the man's terrified eyes, the tears glistening on his cheeks, his quivering lips. Or perhaps Jesse merely hung there with his head bowed, fighting for every breath but with a resilience that was silent, tolerant, yielding.

Lukas wanted to imagine Jesse this way, just as he'd seen the man in the desert while he prayed to his Father with obedient acceptance despite being so obviously troubled, something like anxiety moving behind his eyes. That was how he wished to remember him, though he could still hear the blood dripping into the partially full bucket and the slow, weak, labored breathing moving in and out like gentle waves along a calm and steady ocean shore. An ocean of madness, Lukas thought. This was all madness.

When a new sound moved through the speakers and jolted him from his reverie, he didn't at first understand what it was. Then it came again, and he realized Jesse was gasping, his voice rising in a low moan as if he were about to finally break down and sob. Then he took a massive breath, and the image of his blurred face lifted toward what was the ceiling of his prison but looked like the very darkened heavens above the city itself.

"Father," he cried, his voicing rattling between the buildings and pausing all movement for a moment. He took another sharp, gasping breath. "Forgive them. Forgive them *all*."

Lukas's heart dropped into his gut. He fought to catch his own breath when the sadness and the agony in Jesse's voice pressed him down and down, further into the dark hole of which he'd thought he'd already seen the bottom. People turned to look up at the unexpected sound, the first thing Jesse had said since his trial had ended and his sentence began. A few of them laughed, but it was nervous and hollow. To Lukas, the laughter sounded like shame. A loud pop and a hiss blasted through the audio, and the onlookers flinched in surprise.

The condemned man drew one last gasping, grievous breath, the air whistling through his throat as it fought its way inside with seemingly nowhere left to go he let out his last exhale, and whispered, *"Finished."* Jesse's upturned face, hidden in the jumbled projection, fell forward against his chest, and he was gone.

A woman's shriek pierced the silence, and then the world groaned. Lukas thought it was his own sorrow for a moment until he saw the man walking in front of him stumble and veer sideways, thrown off balance by the quaking ground beneath him. A vendor's stacked crates toppled over onto the floor, spilling whatever cheap, plastic wares they contained all over the sidewalk. Friends clung to each other amid the rocking shudder of the earth. Lukas remained sitting against the wall, though he drew his head forward so it wouldn't crack against the building. He'd grown up with tremors in Qumran, where even miles below the surface, the earth moved. This was different. Some of the great screens projecting Jesse's death crashed to the ground, people screamed, running for shelter. The sky that had grown dark now seemed angry and roared with thunder, releasing lightning that destroyed whatever it hit. The people that scorned and mocked Jesse or passively went about their business as the world's Messiah died now were forced to take notice and wonder, maybe this man was who he claimed to be... the Messiah... the son of God.

Lukas knew this quake would end, though the deepest part of him wished it would not. If this was the end, he would accept it gladly. Death was far better than a world that had been robbed of its Savior... twice.

Another hiss came through the speakers, morphing into an electrical buzz. Then the thousands of remaining holographic display screens flashed simultaneously amid the earthquake, and the entire city went black.

35

The clash within the worldveil sent a rippling shatter through every stone of the earth, every vein of power and energy beneath the surface, every pocket of silent darkness. Otherworldly screams of eager rage and shouts for glory and life filled the infinite space of this realm in one long, cacophonous battle cry. The glittering forces of Protectors and Warriors moved with the speed of their own light to meet the dark, roiling, lifeless masses of Ahriman's eternal army above the city.

They clashed with tremendous might, unseen figures darting around shimmering forms, spinning, turning, attacking, destroying. The battle for time and life itself raged above the city, close enough for the people below them to see if they had indeed ever possessed the means with which to see this place. Soldiers of both masters fell, erupting into glittering shards of light or consumed by the black fire fueling them.

This was the moment for which they all had waited, called into this realm for this very purpose, a vicious encounter that held billions upon billions of lives on the balance of its unbearably thin edge. Protectors and Warriors and the hard-edged, glistening battalions behind them had never been needed as they were needed now. They'd waited, watched, stepped in when they were commanded because it was their duty and what they were created for; they had always been ready for this. With their fury and their righteousness unleashed, they were formidable, terrible, glorious. They had to hold their ground, the dark warriors could not be allowed to cross over.

The forces answering only to the Angel of Darkness had schemed and plotted, entering the physical boundaries of this world and manipulating events from the worldveil, their time of waiting had ended. Ahriman had delivered when he secreted himself into the world taking possession of Lukas's body and time itself to do what had to be done to secure victory. Finally, it was time for Ahriman's dark creatures to cross over and seize for themselves and their master, and claim dominion of the last citadel that in the past seemed far beyond their reach. But now, having killed God's Messiah twice, nothing was impossible for them. They meant to breach Heaven itself and destroy the light, and it was becoming more apparent the Protectors were going to be unable to stop them and Ahriman hadn't even joined the fight yet.

From every place within the worldveil, every particle that did and did not exist, deep, thunderous laughter cracked against the foundations of reality, as Ahriman watched knowing his final victory was at hand.

36

After a time, the worst of the quakes subsided. Most of the damage had been done to the city's outer wall itself, according to the informative voice crackling back to life some hours later when the projections came back up and the city returned to its loud, beeping, flashing, chaotic former self.

The brief announcement that all remained well and the technological issues had been rectified was replaced almost immediately by the view of the execution room and table. But strapped to it was not the same man; the Jesse who had lived was gone.

The rem-cams captured the gray-robed man with the spectacles pushing a steel, high-lipped tub on wheels across the floor. Then he pressed the panel on the wall, and the round white table lowered on its retractable center and tilted down a few inches. The man returned to Jesse's body, pulled a scalpel from his robes, and sliced it across the abdomen of the now-dead man with as much emotion as if he were checking his watch for the time. Blood and water seeped from the incision, but there was hardly any left within the body, and this seemed to satisfy the man. He unceremoniously yanked the enormous needles from Jesse's wrists, then his calves, and left the tubes to dangle there and drip what remained in them into the buckets below.

Then he set to unlocking the glaringly white manacles from around his charge's wrists and ankles, and with a squeak of flesh across a dry surface, he heaved Jesse's body by the shoulders and off the table. The man hid his awe as he noticed the huge crack in the seemingly unbreakable white surface. He briefly pondered what great force could do this and why. Who was this man? Remembering he had a job to do, he focused his attention back on the body and to any observer he was coldly and calculatingly going about his business, but internally he was shook. Maintaining his standard demeanor, he treated the corpse just as indelicately as it had been when it still drew breath, letting it tumble into the steel tub with a clang. He had heard that sound a thousand times, but this time it hurt his heart, and as every second passed, he didn't know why, but he became more and more convinced that this man was the Messiah...the son of God. The man, hiding his small sobs, got behind the tub and pushed it back out of the room again, Jesse's bloody, lifeless hand spilling over the side.

Lukas found himself caught by the image of what now remained in that room. Where Jesse had been bound, the blood from his pierced hands and his flayed back and the shredded soles of his feet had dried upon the starkness of the round white table, forming a crimson T studded with dried, crusted droplets.

Every display throughout the city cut off then, but Lukas thought he'd have the image of that bloody T on the white table embedded behind his eyes for the rest of his life, however much of it he still had left. His survival seemed more precarious now without a teacher to spread the word of the Open Door and the new Way. Peace, love, humility, kindness—they all seemed impossible now after this horrible day. The devastation of Jesse's torturous passing was as real and all-consuming as it had been when Lukas watched Qumran fall before his very eyes. This time, though, after all he'd lost and discovered and come to accept, the wings of hope had stopped beating within his breast. That, too, had died.

"*Another execution sentenced and delivered,*" the announcer called, fracturing the moment of near-complete silence. "*That was a particularly long one, I'll give him that. But now it's over and done with. You all should commend yourselves, citizens of the city, for upholding the Supreme Law of the Consortium.*"

This was no law, Lukas seethed. Not like the Law he'd spent his life protecting and training to uphold. Qumran would never have stood for any of this.

"*Let's turn now to some of the weather reports coming in to the Information Center. Lots of strange things happening today. Huge amounts of seismic activity. We all felt that. A massive tidal-wave surge on the Eastern Sea, and those living within the projected range have been ordered to evacuate. There's another storm brewing over the desert and coming our way, though no one had predicted it and still can't pin down exactly what its pattern is. And... yes, just now, we've gotten word from Consortium astronomists that they just analyzed their results of what is the largest solar flare ever recorded in human history. What a day, citizens. And yet here you are, safe and sound in your homes, shel- tered by the Consortium's omniscient hand...*"

The man went on and on and on, and finally, Lukas no longer had a reason to pay attention. It didn't matter to him at all that the world seemed to be turning on its side, that even nature itself—or what was left of it—rebelled against the death of this one man. Jesse was gone. Lukas thought very few things still mattered, and he didn't know what those might be.

He expected to be in far more pain when he stood, bracing

himself against the wall after sitting there in one place for so long. Not even aching muscles and stiff joints could break through the haze of sorrow overwhelming him. The thin sandals he'd borrowed from Cephas seemed too heavy, his head a lead weight resting precariously upon his shoulders. He shuffled down the street, wanting to get away from the screens everywhere and the noise, wanting to finally be alone. But he had no idea where he was, his head swimming with everything and nothing and making it impossible to even try orient himself. Even more, he had no idea what he would do in true solitude, away from the public streets, away from anyone who could offer comfort, stability, hope, a reason not to give in completely to the darkness suffocating the city and strangling his heart.

"Lukas!"

His eyebrows twitched; it felt like years since he'd heard that voice. He just kept moving.

"Lukas." Marya jogged toward him, her skirts lifted in one hand until she dropped them to throw her arms around his neck. The impact made him sway a little in her embrace, but he found his own arms unwilling to obey his command of hugging her back. "Oh, thank God you're okay," she said, her breath tickling the hairs on the back of his neck. Then she seemed to remember herself and pulled away, her hands lingering on his shoulders before she released him.

"I'm not, Marya," he replied, his voice echoing in his head from somewhere far away. Lukas swallowed. "I don't think I ever will be."

Marya ducked to catch his gaze, but his eyes slid away from hers to fall back onto the grimy sidewalk. "But you're alive," she said.

"It doesn't matter."

"It matters very much. To me." She straightened, then glanced up and down the street. "Come on. You've spent enough time out here, I think." With a nod, she took his hand and gently drew him down the street, toward wherever she wanted him to be. Lukas didn't have it in him to pull his hand away.

37

They had lost so many of their own to the darkness, they would have lost hope if such a thing existed in them. Unwilling or unable, they would not admit defeat; instead they fought with everything they had—everything they were created to be—struggling desperately to hold the line.

The mortal world of men would have marked this passage of time as two days and two nights, just before the glistening sun rose into the despoiled sky of this world. But within the world-veil, time was nothing more than a whisper. The Protectors and the Warriors fought for centuries, eons, and mere seconds all at once; they had always battled this enemy, and yet this time it seemed different.

The balance had shifted against them. They were losing, but bravely fought the oncoming darkness churning and splintering the air with black fire and the piercing wails of victorious expectation. Ahriman's woeful legions had already destroyed so much, snuffed out so many sparks of glittering, sharp-edged light, they tasted the sweetness of this final triumph on their always bitter tongues.

As if to lend credence to the anxious, trembling energy of

anticipation, the sky of the worldveil split open again behind the skittering, swarming forces of darkness, and an ebony fortress loomed from the other side of reality. As large as this Earth's highest mountain peak, it moved at once with swift urgency and an agonizing slowness, settling over the city on the other side of the worldveil with a groan of bedrock crumbling to rubble like bones broken and ground down to dust. Filaments of dripping black flame curled and retracted along the firmaments, hissing at the fortress's arrival, whispering of the terrible presence yet unleashed upon the worldveil and the ignorant peoples beyond this realm.

Ahriman, Angel of Darkness, had come.

His awful form bristled through the fortress and out into the open expanse of time and space, fluctuating, undulating, like a mass of constantly writhing bodies held together by a mold of disproportionate terror. The dark, fiery forces battling the light screamed in both ecstasy and dread at his coming, fueled by the power he had gained and the throne he meant to seize.

The Warriors and Protectors, now small in numbers, remained silent, patient, unmoved by the approaching horrors because they too were fueled—by righteous light and Truth. They had but to hold.

With a crack like breaking thunder, Ahriman moved forward to join his legions. Outstretched arms, clad in wickedly curving armor that glistened in this lightless place like the thick black shell of some monstrous insect, opened to the sky and the earth and all that lay between.

"*I am everything*," the Angel of Darkness screamed. The earth trembled, the sky quaked, the oceans rocked in their watery beds as if stirred by nightmares. "*The Messiah is mine at the bottom of the Lake of Shadow. I have unmade the Word and broken Time. God has abandoned him and you, and I am all there ever was. All there ever will be!*"

The blurring, stuttering swarms of his dark legions cried out again, keening and wailing in both mourning and celebration, for they knew the rage of the black fire and the depth of the darkness; they abhorred it and craved it and could not fathom the world with or without it.

The Protectors and the Warriors, the glistening armada of ships made of light and swift, cutting edges, facing defeat, did not stir. They would not lower their weapons or fall to their knees even under such vast and terrifying power pressing upon them. Ahriman was a force more awesome and terrible than any this world had seen—than this realm had seen. But he was not theirs to worship.

His presence raged forward, surges of his host spilling beyond him toward the final stand against the light. And then everything stopped. Everything.

Ahriman reached forward, but even his own might could not break the shackles of timelessness binding him in his final moment. Fury rose in him, but still he could not move. The black fire froze, tongues half-lapping at its intended prey. The roiling masses of insect-like demons and wrathful forms studded the expanse of the worldveil without so much as a flicker of motion. The very glinting shine on the Protectors' righteous blades and the Warriors' vengeful speartips flared in piercing brilliance and never winked out. All was still. All was silent. All existence was submissive to the moment. Whether by choice or by force, nothing moved.

An immense opening of brilliant light drew across the reality of the worldveil. The light forcefully filled every particle, eliminated every shadow, blistered every darkness and took root in every thing, filling it with light. Nothing could escape it; nothing was without it. From outside of time and space itself, where it always was and always would be in every conception both imagined and realized, the light bowed and laid low as if making way for its master and creator. Majestically stepping forth from the light, on the light, and yet somehow the provider of the light was

Jesse, the Messiah, the King of Kings and Lord of Lords. The brilliance of the Messiah's glory hid even himself and the hungry, wrathful, monstrous glares of His enemies turned to fear, and out of self preservation they averted their eyes. Even the Warriors and Protectors, the righteous host, the battalions heralding the battle for Truth could not gaze upon Him wholly. But in His eyes glistened the end of Ahriman's dominion. In His eyes existed worlds upon worlds, time unending, love and light and God.

The breach in time was lifted. As if they'd never had a chance and had always known it, the dark forces scattered with shrieks that rocked the worldveil amid their retreat, desperately trying to escape the glory of His divinity. Conversely, the host of light remained silent; they had no need to voice their exaltation. The Messiah had no rival, no equal, and had never known defeat, and would not know it now or ever. Ahriman was right, Jesse had been at the bottom of the Lake of Shadow, but he wasn't sentenced there as Ahriman thought, he chose to go there to free all of its captives. And now rising victorious from it, over it, the Messiah passed through this realm on His way to another victory for him and for all people from all times, and for all time.

Before his abandoned fortress, the Angel of Darkness pulsed in surprise and rage, and yet he had no more sway over what happened next than a leaf upon the highest branch could choose when it fell to the ground.

38

Marya had taken Lukas back to Cephas's apartment after Jesse's body had been carted away without ceremony and without being released to his students. What the Consortium planned to do with the man's body, Lukas did not know, though the announcer's voice echoed the sentencing in his head—*recycled and used as a resource.*

That night, he'd fallen asleep before he reached the top of the narrow staircase, before he turned the handle on the door to his bedroom here, before he sank onto the pallet on the floor and finally let himself weep. He only saw Cephas again the following day when, still asleep, Lukas had moved slowly back down the stairs because he'd been summoned; when he sat on the pillows and stared at the fake grain of the plastic table; when Marya had offered him a steaming cup of sweetened tea that tasted only like the tears he'd already shed.

On that second day, the apartment was silent. Yaakov and Yohanan joined them, though now both brothers remained deathly silent. Yaakov, once so talkative, had fallen into an inability to interact with the world in much the same way his brother had accepted and embraced such a wordless existence.

One other man joined them—the man with the blue eyes Lukas had seen fumbling with the vendor's handheld the day before. This man had also been a student of Jesse, had stepped with the others beyond the city wall and into the desert, and he said his name was Stephon. Marya had had to introduce Lukas for him; the Hedge Master could not find his tongue, or his appetite, or his thirst, or his sense of time.

And Cephas no longer smiled. He did not gaze at Lukas with gracious willingness to serve. He did not speak in light-hearted jesting. He did not offer anything to anyone, though the silent extension of his hospitality remained with so many others gathered in his home.

Marya seemed the only one who could say or do anything, not because she didn't mourn Jesse's death but because she did so in a different way. She cooked them the acrid sludge, of which Lukas could only take a few bites and nothing more. She brought them tea and canteens of horridly bitter water, washed their dishes, handled whatever needed to be accomplished when she left the apartment so the five men within it could grieve together in a way that only perpetuated itself.

Through the entirety of the day, Lukas had wanted nothing more than to remain asleep, to hide away in his room, alone, unconscious, without the unbearable, suffocating weight of what they'd lost bearing down on him every second. The only thing that stopped him from doing so was the knowledge that these men had known Jesse far more intimately and for far longer than the mere three days since Lukas had first heard their teacher speak. He didn't think it right to act as if his pain ran deeper than theirs while they sat here together. So he'd stayed, silent, sullen, reeling within himself because now there was nothing left at all. He was lost entirely; the man who had pulled him back from the brink of his own destruction had been brutally seized from this world, and now all of them were truly alone.

By mid-morning on the third day, nothing had changed.

Lukas never expected it would. This day was one more notch on what would be a long, useless, unending sprawl of them, stretching across the emptiness of his life's future until whatever end met him. He faced that end now like one faced the numbness of biting cold or the baking heat of a summer day; he could no more deliver himself from his apathy than he could summon the weather as he wished it to be.

The telling knock didn't even come this time before the door to Cephas's apartment flew open and Marya burst inside. "He's alive," she panted, her face lit with a joy Lukas no longer knew how to feel.

The men turned from where they'd churned in their individual silences to gaze at her standing there, hands raised and spread in excitement.

"Who?" Cephas asked.

"Jesse." She let out a wondrous laugh that fell flat on its audience. "I saw him. Just now."

Lukas stared at the table, and the others looked away from Marya in silent disapproval. This kind of hope was dangerous; sometimes, it was too much.

"Marya," Cephas said gently, as if he were speaking to a child who thought she had a mythical creature hidden in her room. "I wish that were true just as much as you do. We all do. Jesse's dead. The Consortium has him..." He waved his hand hopelessly, as if to say nothing was within their power anymore.

"No they don't." With a little jump, Marya came to kneel on the pillows between Cephas and Yaakov, her skirts billowing behind her. "Jesse is *alive*. I saw him with my own eyes, Cephas. I spoke to him. I touched him." She stared into her friend's eyes, seemingly unaffected by how clearly he doubted everything she said. "He's coming to see you. Right now, he's coming. He'll be here soon."

"I want to believe you," Yaakov said, his voice low and weak, as if he hadn't used it for years. "So desperately, I want to believe he's alive. But I can't, Marya. Whatever you saw—"

"I know what I saw," she replied, and though she'd cut him off, it was gentle and unassuming. Then she turned to Lukas. "Lukas." She almost whispered his name, her eyes dancing with expectation and wonder. "Lukas, he's coming."

He couldn't tell her that was impossible, and yet in the few seconds of meeting her gaze, he thought he'd never seen the woman this certain about anything.

"Sons, daughter."

Grinning, Marya spun around, and the others slowly turned their heads to view the newcomer. Cephas shouted in surprise, and Stephon lurched backward from the table.

"It's all right," Jesse said, somehow standing in the room with them even though he did not come through the front door. With his hands raised in a gesture of peace, he said, "Don't be afraid."

No one said a word. Lukas thought his heart had stopped at the sight of the man in loose, undyed clothing, alive and well and almost glowing with life. Cephas let out a trembling breath, as though the vision would shatter and disappear if he made a sound any louder than that.

"Jesse!" Marya practically shouted when no one else could even speak.

Smiling, Jesse entered Cephas's apartment and then joined them at the table. He lowered himself to his knees and sat back on his heels between Marya and Cephas. Cephas leaned away, if only to get a better look at the man who should never have been able to enter his home and sit beside him.

Jesse looked at everyone sitting around him and smiled, clearly amused by the situation. "Why do all of you look so surprised? Marya brought you the truth, and so have I." He placed his hands on the table and turned them over so they could all see his palms—sliced through but whole, marked by the same scars that also covered the backs of his hands. "I'm not a projection. I'm not a ghost. None of you have lost your minds. I'm here." He blinked and gave a single, slow nod. "Go ahead. Touch me. It's all real." One of his hands stretched toward Cephas, the other reaching past Marya; as the only one in the room who'd believed this impossible thing from the start, she nodded at Yaakov.

Cephas trembled before he touched his teacher's hand, then grabbed it in both of his own, eyes wide as he studied the scars that would never have healed this much on anyone else in just three days. Yaakov did the same and bowed his head to press the back of Jesse's hand to his forehead. Yohanan moved across the pillows to sit behind his brother, bowing beside Jesse before his teacher placed a hand on the man's head, bringing tears to Yohanan's eyes. Stephon stood abruptly, staring down at all of them.

Jesse peered up at him and grinned. "Really."

The student of Jesse's with blue eyes, whom Lukas hardly knew, leaped around the table and fell to his knees before Jesse, bowing so low his head, chest, and arms touched the floor.

"My Lord and my God," he gasped.

"Get up." Jesse gently lifted his student by the shoulder. Stephon's eyes glistened, his nose already red when he rose and stared at the man come back to life—flesh and blood in front of them all. "Marya saw me before anyone, but this was the first place I wanted to be." Marya beamed, and the man's brows drew together in a small frown bordering on confusion. "Does anyone have something to eat?"

Lukas watched as Marya got up to get Jesse some food, but then caught sight of Cephas's elation at seeing Jesse alive. Cephas suddenly buried his face in his hands, but then Jesse touched his arm and the bearded man burst into explosive joy and laughter.

Curious about this moment, Lukas would later ask Cephas about it, and this is what he told him.

"I was so happy to see Jesse, but then I was overcome with shame. I had betrayed Jesse three times, just as he said I would. I felt like I needed to confess and seek his forgiveness, but how would I tell him? How would I tell you, Marya, and all our friends that I betrayed Jesse, and all of you? Jesse knew what was in my heart, and without saying a word, I heard Jesse's voice in my head, but even more in my heart. He said, 'I forgive you.' Tears filled my eyes. The words came again, 'I forgive you.' Doing my best to fight back my sobs, they came one more time, 'I forgive you.' Three pardons to match my three denials. My sadness and shame became gratitude and redemption, and somehow I knew that moment would serve as a foundation for the grace and salvation I was to share with others in Jesse's name."

His friends joined in the laughter, unaware of what had just transpired. Marya's eyes met Lukas's, her joy infectious.

Lukas wasn't sure quite what to think. This was indeed the same man he had come to understand was more than anything he could possibly fathom; the same man he'd realized as the first Messiah, the second Messiah, the true Messiah; the same man he'd spent an entire day watching before death came for Jesse and spirited him away.

Jesse fixed his calm, loving gaze upon the Qumranian, then extended both hands beckoning Lukas to place his hands in Jesse's. Then he gently squeezed. "Thank you, Lukas."

That was all Lukas needed to convince him of the miraculous. He'd known Jesse was the Messiah and had been before his death, and now he knew the same Messiah had returned once more to life, risen with the power of God humming through his fingertips. He'd never given this man his name—never spoken with him in person or exchanged so much as a single word—and now he felt as if he'd known Jesse all his life. This was the holy day every Qumranian had been raised and trained to anticipate, and Lukas was the last of them—the only one to see it arrive in this world. His heart soared, his flesh electrified with elation and wonder and hope. There were no words to express any of it, and he only smiled before Jesse released his hand.

The Messiah now acknowledged the food they had placed in front of him and picked it up. He took a few bites, chewing slowly, then set the unfinished food upon the table and looked at his students and friends, all gathered closely around him like children expecting a marvelous tale from their favorite storyteller.

"When I was with you," he said, "I told you that all of this would happen. Everything that's been written about me in the true Law, the histories of the mystics, and the very songs themselves must be and will be fulfilled. I came here because I AM the *Way*, the *Truth*, and the *Life* and everyone is invited to come to the Father through faith in me. Listen, and you will know more." Jesse closed his eyes, and those gathered with him fell silent.

Then Lukas's entire being was filled with the most brilliant light and warmth, unseen but felt—understood. He was taken from the small, crowded living room of Cephas's apartment to a place beyond his comprehension, as if Jesse had gently grabbed his hand and whisked him away. He entered the vastness of time and existence, part of it all yet still somehow himself, seeing through his teacher's eyes the Word and the Truth—all that was and ever had been and still remained ahead. He saw what he had to do. He saw who he had to become.

39

Ahriman bellowed in rage as his roiling fortress within the worldveil shattered with unbearable, seething brilliance simply because Jesse, the Messiah, the King, paused in the worldveil on his way to his rising from the dead. Whatever forces under Ahriman's command that had not fled when Jesse appeared before them had dissipated with the shock of such an igniting force simply emanating from the Messiah's presence. They did not return to Ahriman's domain of black fire and consuming shadow. They did not escape the blaze of the Messiah's glory, but merely blinked out of existence, no trace of themselves left behind.

With the Messiah now returned to life, the legions of Protectors and Warriors were the only ones left to witness Ahriman's imminent banishment, but ever defiant, he roared at them, *"I will always return!"*

A new light flared, and in its place appeared two immense white figures on either side of the Angel of Darkness, glistening with the radiance of the light and impossible to fully recognize. Between them stretched a massive chain, forged in the glory of Heaven, and with this they bound their fallen enemy, wrapped the searing links around his flickering, scattering form that recoiled under such sanctified weight.

The master over so much impotent darkness laughed at his imprisonment, not daring to struggle within his bonds; once chained, they were never meant to be broken. *"This will not hold me forever,"* he spat, then released another deep, echoing chuckle. *"I am omnipotent. I am forever. I—"*

The blazing figures that had made themselves his jailors opened their hands, and their white wings stretched wide from behind their backs with a deafening crack of the lifeless air within the worldveil. *"This will be forever,"* one of them said. *"Laugh all you like."*

With another sweep of their dazzling hands, the winged beings summoned one more opening in the fabric of reality. A dark, whorling hole blistered into being ahead of them, the silence of it louder than any rising cry of ten thousand tortured voices. Their wings shuddered, and Ahriman's laughter shook the earth once more. Together, his jailors seized him within the chains and hoisted him forward, through the gaping maw of eternity churning before them, then released their hold.

The appetite of that place beyond could never be sated, and it swallowed the Angel of Darkness like nothing more than a scattered morsel, drawing him further into time unending and nothing else. His laughter echoed with his receding visage, and then the open portal blinked closed like a snapping jaw, never to be reopened in this way again.

The immense creatures spread their arms wide and submitted to the blazing light. It took them and the crystalline legions with it when it vanished from the worldveil to send them home, their glorious purpose fulfilled.

"His absolute reign is finally begun." Lucia broke the seal on one of their last two bottles of Metaxa Aen, confiscated with immense pleasure from conquered Grecian forces during the Fourth World War—back when Greece had still existed. She did not usually drink, as it dulled her senses and slowed the flow of her master's power more than she liked. But after the last three days of overseeing their Unclean forces—who'd swept the city and culled its filthy masses of those most likely to rebel against the man Jesse's death—she rather thought she deserved it. And her brother had suggested such an act of celebration. "This world is rife with ignorant fools."

"I'd call them a plague," Damian replied, holding his goblet out for her to fill with the pungently smooth, amber spirit-wine.

Lucia smirked. "They will learn soon enough, when they see for themselves their hope is vanquished and there is nothing left but to obey and serve." She filled her own glass, watching the drink slosh into the crystal goblet. "Our master will be pleased with what we—" A searing heat cut through what once had been the woman's heart, severing her bond with Ahriman himself as if it had never been. Pain and a deafening stillness raged through her, devoid now of the humming power she'd been fed by the Angel of Darkness for centuries, like a leech was fed by the host whose blood it drained. Her fingers jerked open, and the goblet fell from her delicate grasp. It shattered on the floor of her brother's quarters, and she hardly heard the echoing peal.

Damian reared back and stumbled against the ancient bookcase behind him. A few dusty volumes clattered onto their sides, and he drew in a long, rasping breath. "Master..."

"No!" She looked up to meet her brother's shocked, desperate gaze and found the fury behind them mirroring her own.

"Now do you see the folly in letting your pathetic little pets live?" he spat. "You should have—"

"This is *not* my doing." Lucia's boots crunched across the broken crystal until she stood before her brother and slammed her palm into his chest, crushing him against the bookcase. "Do *not* blame me."

Damian scowled at her beneath his darkened brow, studying her black eyes and breathing heavily. She knew he wished to fight her, as he always had, but her brother had never managed to become as much as she. Instead, he slowly raised the goblet in his hand and set it on the bookshelf behind him with a muffled clink—the only act of defiance he could still give without evoking her wrath.

Lucia removed her hand from his studded breastplate and let it ball into a fist at her side. "I know where they are."

She whirled away from Damian and stalked toward the massive desk against the wall. Her hawkish helm glistened in the low lighting of the room, and she seized it with a swift fury to pull it viciously down over her head. When she jerked open the door, she didn't turn around to tell him, "You will join me."

40

After he showed them all the impossible things that were in fact the truth and the world to come, Jesse left them. No one thought it cruel or abrupt, because he'd left them with so much more than any of them could have dared hope to receive. There were no tears of farewell—no regrets or mourning. They'd spent that already over the last three days, and now they only had room in their hearts and their thoughts for the expanse of infinite knowledge Jesse had shared. It was his final gift to them, at least until the *Paraclete*, the Spirit of Fire would come.

Those gathered in Cephas's house had sat in silence with each other, with their shared experience, with the brilliance of Jesse's revelation burning within them. They knew what they had to do, as it had been written before they'd been born and revealed to them on this day. Still, they gave themselves some time to be with their newfound hope among friends.

Lukas was pleased to find that so much of the Law he'd fought to protect as a Hedge Master was now being fulfilled. Of course, never in his wildest dreams had he expected it to come about in this way, in this version of the world. But now he felt he had a new opportunity to perpetuate the knowledge that had once bloomed through Qumran and the sacrifices his people had made. Without them, this day would never have come. They'd prepared and studied and trained and waited for the Messiah to appear among them, their entire existence dedicated to that single event, which some days had seemed a faraway promise. No longer.

Over the next few hours, three more men joined them in Cephas's home, and Lukas recognized each of them from Jesse's last journey into the desert before his execution. Tobias came straight from the Vendor's Quarter, wide-eyed and grinning, bringing news of at least a dozen Phar-asai having fallen under some incomprehensible attack on their persons and succumbing to death. The news projections—if it could even be called news in this place—wrote these off as heart attacks suffered by old men after the vicious earthquakes two days before. A number of Janiss-arai, he'd told them, had simply disappeared.

"I saw it yesterday. Three Janiss-arai around a man screaming for justice. Then two of them vanished. I don't mean ran away or used some other devilry to disguise themselves. Those black robes fell to the street with nothing inside them. And the third actually fled."

Palti arrived with news of the droves of Unclean soldiers finally having cleared from the streets after three days of patrols so rarely seen within the city at large. The man's beard was a flaming red, and he spoke with a victorious eagerness, as if he'd driven off these forces himself.

The last man to appear was named Malachai, and he boasted two large, fresh slashes across his cheek above a purpling bruise beneath his eye. He'd lived in an apartment complex not far from the Unclean headquarters facility, and he'd been on his way home when the research facility itself was struck by one of the vicious bolts of lightning on the day Jesse died, causing the facility to erupt in a massive explosion, shattering the huge building and leaving a wake of devastation spanning a few more blocks in every direction. Luckily, the man had been far enough away from his home that he'd survived, but he hadn't escaped a few shards of flying glass—or metal; he didn't know—that had been thrown from the blast to slice his cheeks and pummel his body with debris. But even this close call wasn't enough to dampen the man's spirits.

All three of them had been visited by Jesse before they came to Cephas's apartment, impossible though it seemed, and he'd revealed to them the same visions he'd offered Lukas and the others. They'd each faced some trying peril or devastating news on their way here, yet they'd arrived with smiles and kind words, eyes alight with renewed hope and purpose.

"I think we're all that's left of his students in the city," Palti said. "The rest were chased off, or they fled, or—" He winced and clenched his eyes shut, as if he'd meant not to broach the subject and too late realized his mistake.

"What?" Marya asked, frowning for the first time since she'd burst into the apartment that morning.

Palti opened his eyes and looked up at Cephas. "Cyrus." Their host blinked rapidly in surprise and what Lukas thought was an attempt to hide his own shame around what the ex-soldier had done. Palti took a deep breath. "He took his own life. His business partner found him on the streets before Jesse—" He shook his head. "Before that string of horrors was broadcast all over the city. They're having a ceremony for him at the club tomorrow, and I think Cabraius will take over running the place now." Cephas stared at the man who'd delivered such a brutal message, his brows drawn together in anguish and regret. "I'm sorry, Cephas."

"Thank you for telling me," Cephas replied, then bowed his head for a moment.

Lukas heard Marya sniff beside him and turned to see tears shimmering at the corners of her eyes. But she did not wail or cry out, and no one else said a word on the subject. Cyrus had, in fact, been the one to turn Jesse over to the Phar-asai and his eventual sentencing and execution. He'd betrayed their teacher —betrayed all of them—and they'd treated him as such. And yet, without events unfolding as they had, Jesse would never have returned to them as he was; they would never have been given the glimpses of all the sanctified knowledge of the Law and the Word that only Jesse's death and return to life could bring them. Lukas himself had considered Cyrus a friend, if only for the fact that the man had done so much to help him not once but twice in infiltrating the Unclean headquarters. The Hedge Master's attempts at redemption—both with the quantum orb and in protecting his cousins—had failed, but everything that could have been done had been done. Despite all this, the news of Cyrus's death was just one more hard truth for them to face.

The overcrowded living room fell remarkably silent, and then Yohanan raised his head. "I think we should leave." They all looked up at him. "The city is falling apart. It's not safe for any of us here anymore. But beyond that, Jesse gave us such a gift. We can't stay here and risk his word being swallowed by what this place will become." This veritable speech for how seldom and with few words Yohanan ever spoke surprised Lukas, and the rest of those gathered seemed to share the sentiment.

Yaakov studied his brother, then placed his hands steadily on the table. "There are other great cities on the other side of the desert. And across the oceans. They're far enough away from the Consortium's immediate reach that they're bound to be more sympathetic to our people and our cause. We should go to them. Tell them what happened here and what we know of the things to come."

The others considered this, then murmured their agreement, the unknown of such a prospect quickly becoming a reality as they realized this was part of what they were now meant to do.

Lukas looked at Marya, who beamed at him with encouragement and pride. They were really going to do this.

Without warning, the lights went out completely—not a flicker, not a buzz or electric pop of some circuit over-firing. Everything just went dark. "The city *is* falling apart, Yohanan," Cephas said, slowly pushing himself up from the table. "I'll take care of it."

A loud groan filled the apartment, something like a huge tree bending in the wind but entirely unnatural. Lukas felt the room tremble and not tremble at the same time, and the shadows deepened.

"Cephas..." he called in warning, knowing this wasn't a blackout of the city's electricity mainframe but something else altogether. Something he almost recognized.

From the back of the room, where the darkness was thickest just beside the staircase, two figures emerged. The wickedly curved spikes of their pauldrons glinted as they stepped forward, the shapes of their meticulously crafted leather and black metal armor rising from the shadows like smoke from a fire.

"So nice of you all to gather together in one place," Lucia crooned. Her teeth flashed in a grin. "That makes this easier."

"For us," Damian hissed.

Cephas whirled around to face the intruders, and Lukas leaped to his feet. The others moved with far less speed, and he did not know if any of them knew how to fight. But as he prepared himself to defend these people here, the vile woman's fingers moved in a complicated gesture and everything stopped. Lukas found himself frozen, his hands halfway toward his lower back and the position that would have signaled his body to employ its knowledge of the Hedge. Malachai was paralyzed in a half-crouch on his way to standing, and Stephon leaned impossibly forward on one leg, the other suspended in a partially completed step. No one moved. No one made a sound. No one could.

Lucia gave that insultingly false smile of sympathy and tilted her head. "My brother and I can't let you leave, now, can we? Scattering to the winds like seeds to plant your hope stained with lies in new soil. This ends here. You end here. Forever."

"Your souls will never return once we've bound them," her brother added.

In unison, the Unclean commanders clapped their hands together, and when they drew apart their palms, a thick, churning darkness coalesced between their clawed hands. Words in a language seldom spoken by human tongues fell from their lips, rising in a chanting cadence unlike anything Lukas had ever heard. From the darkness between their hands slithered black tendrils of some awful force, flickering and straining in rhythm with their incantation. They moved steadily outward like consuming fire, like wagging tongues, like hungry snakes, reaching toward the commanders' frozen victims.

Lukas strained with everything he had against the force rendering him immobile. Whatever it was, he had no knowledge of how to break its hold, despite his muscles quivering with tension and the sweat beading on his brow at such an attempt. A low grunt came from Cephas, and someone else wheezed with their own struggle to break free, perhaps even to attempt to speak. No one moved against their entrapment, and the terrifying vines of darkness inched closer still from the creatures who commanded the Unclean.

He did find, however, that he still possessed the freedom to look about, and his eyes flicked desperately toward Marya beside him. A single, writhing black tendril inched toward her face, and she eyed it with a wary assurance that seemed impossible when facing such a thing. Her lips parted only slightly, as if she'd fully relaxed herself, and a sigh escaped her. The darkness that had almost touched her cheek flinched, drawing back in what looked like hesitation.

The dark, writhing fingers had reached Lukas now, crawling

across his skin in a cold, wet trail to wrap themselves around his throat, across his chest. They squeezed with incomprehensible force, and he gasped for breath, unable even to lift his hands in an attempt to pull away the icy grip. A choking wheeze sounded from behind him, quickly followed by many more. This seemed like the end for all of them, and still Lukas fought. He couldn't give in now, not to these monstrous things dressed in human skins, nor could he resist them.

A straining squeak fell from Marya's mouth, and another. Then, with her next deep breath, she managed a single, humming note. The darkness that had reached for her withdrew immediately, veering away to focus on its other victims, and Marya's hum became a lilting melody, hauntingly pure and growing in volume with every note. The black snakes of unholy power shuddered and withdrew from around Lukas's neck and throat, sending a shiver down his spine before he drew in a gasping breath. He heard the others behind him responding similarly, and they watched the tendrils twitch and writhe, retracting back toward the armored commanders who had summoned them.

Even the forceful chanting of the Unclean rulers seemed an echo of itself beneath the immaculate virtue of Marya's song. "A song?" Lucia spat as her brother continued the incantation. "I know your gifts, foolish child. They will not save you."

Her voice rejoined Damian's, and he lifted his head, as if to reassure himself that they remained in control. "Ours comes from the Lake of Shadow," he growled. "From the Abyss of Cold Space itself, plucked from the screams of a billion dying stars. You are nothing against this power."

His chant rejoined Lucia's, and together, they nearly screamed the ancient, unknown words. The darkness between their hands flared into greater being this time, and the unnatural groan filled the room once more. The dark tendrils undulated furiously now like so many whipping flags blown by a stormy gale, but still, Marya sang.

Now her mouth formed words, still unknown to Lukas and seemingly from a different time—a different age of the world entirely. He recognized it as the song he'd heard her sing his first night in the city, when he'd all but collapsed on the sidewalk and watched the beautiful woman he'd never expected to meet projected on the screen of the building before him. Then it was simply a beautiful song, but now he recognized the power woven into every note, every word. The power of it was more familiar than the melody, it was the same power he felt when Jesse took hold of his hands.

Her voice rang out within Cephas's apartment, growing in strength and terrible beauty and hope. Lukas felt himself relax, though he still could not move; a relieving warmth spread through him like a loving caress, a reassurance that this would soon be over and he had nothing to fear.

Marya spread her arms, her song a triumphant battle cry. The flapping tendrils of darkness slowed, paused, and stopped completely where they were, extended from the trembling hands of the Unseen commanders. Then the snaking vines of their weakening chant stiffened, solidified, crackling from their tips all the way back to the source. The cruel beings in spiked armor chanted faster, the cadence of it desperate now, their eyes wide with wonder and horror and defeat. The darkness between their hands took on solid form, binding them together, and with another groan that did not this time come from their dark power, their Unclean armor shifted, extended, grew to encompass both bodies before the siblings were joined together as one mass. Their words cut short, their forms disappeared, and they became the base of the new, wondrous thing rising now from where they stood.

The last extended note of Marya's song quivered in the air, Jesse's name uplifted with such righteous purity that tears sprang to Lukas's eyes, even as he stumbled forward when the invisible thing holding him vanished. The lights flared back on in Cephas's apartment, and he heard the deep breaths of relief and then awe from the others behind them as they too were freed to gaze upon what Marya had done.

The Unclean commanders and their vine-like weapons of darkness had become a huge tree in Cephas's living room, bursting with life. The branches rose even through the ceiling, as if it were not solid at all but a mere illusion, making Lukas wonder how far the glory of it truly stretched above them. Every twig sprouted with thick green leaves, and before their eyes, white buds grew with impossible speed along the branches. They bloomed and opened, shedding stark petals to the floor with a scent more tantalizing than anything Lukas had ever expected to smell again; the others in this room had most likely never even seen a living tree, let alone experienced the glory of fully opened blossoms. Fruit swelled from within the branches, glistening and ripening until full, gorgeously red apples dangled there right in front of them, exquisite in their natural perfection. Birds twittered in seeming joy, hidden within the lush branches, and an actual bee hovered lazily around Lukas's head before returning to the sweetness of the nectar in which it had been created to enjoy such pleasure.

Within the span of a few rapid heartbeats, their torment had become the most heart-wrenching beauty. Life and hope bloomed again within a place almost completely abandoned to the lack of it.

Marya finally lowered her arms and turned to face her friends and the students of Jesse within Cephas's home. A knowing smile graced her lips, tinged with only a little tiredness, as if she'd just awakened from a pleasant dream.

"This is meant to be shared with the world, starting with the people in the city, who need it most," she said. "Jesse's Song is the Tree of Life. It always bears fruit for those who would listen and sing it fully in their hearts."

Heavy, awed breath rose from every chest at the sight of what she had done here. She turned, stepped toward the tree, and plucked an apple from its lowest branch. There she stood, cradling it in her hands as if it were the most precious gem. Without hesitating—without even thinking but following what his heart told him to do—Lukas joined her. The apple he chose felt almost warm in his hand, as if the sun had been holding it to keep it ready just for him. Its red skin glinted in the light, smooth and perfect. He turned to Marya with nothing but the fullest adoration, and she held his gaze in kind while the students of Jesse each approached the tree to accept the gifts of His promise in a song.

This is what is written.

The Messiah will suffer and rise from the dead on the third day.

Forgiveness and grace, the Word and the Way, will be spread in His name to all nations and even unto the stars, beginning in the city.

You are all witnesses to these events.

Go.

Bear fruit and plant the seeds in your hearts.

41

Three months later...

Lukas stepped toward the crackling fire within the hearth. The warm glow illuminated the face of his wife, Marya, as she sat in the low chair, staring into the flames. Her eyes glittered with the light, and when he knelt beside her, she turned slowly to look at him. He reached up to cup her cheeks with both hands and drew her toward him for a long, deep kiss. When he pulled away, she grinned.

"I think I'll start tonight," he told her.

She took his hands in her own and gave them a gentle squeeze. "Good."

He looked back for another glimpse of her smiling in perfect contentment before he left the room and moved into his study. The large desk in the center of the room held two thin display screens, angled delicately toward the chair where he had spent so much time studying the content held within them.

Slowly, Lukas lowered himself into the chair, comforted by the familiar creak of its wooden seat, and glanced briefly at the screens again before sliding them to the far side of the desk. Then he opened the middle drawer and produced a sheaf of loose paper, so precious here, and a pen. The paper hushed thickly when he smoothed his hand across it, taking comfort in the blank canvas that would soon become his testament. Truly, it belonged to all of them, yet he could no longer bide his time in waiting to begin. The words poured from him with a delicate urgency, guided by a will not his own, the pen moving across the clean, blank pages without pause while he filled them.

Dear Brothers and Sisters loved by God,

Many have undertaken to draw up an account of the things that have been fulfilled among us, just as they were handed down to us by those who from the first were eyewitnesses and servants of the Word and the Way, the Open Door and the Tree of Life. Therefore, since I myself have carefully investigated everything from the beginning, it seemed the best thing for me to also write an orderly account for you, so you may know the certainty of the things you have been told. I would love to just play a video for you, but no one could ever capture the image of his face, and as I remember the words he told us, I know why.

"Blessed are you, because you have seen and believe, but more blessed are those who have not seen and yet still believe."

ACKNOWLEDGMENTS

I would like to acknowledge so many people because this was a lifetime dream made possible by God working through amazing friends and family. Thank you to my beautiful wife Lisa and my children Joey, Jade, and Jake for all your love and support. Thank you to all my family and friends for your prayers and support and specifically to those of you on my text thread and prayer group on social media. Thank you! Special thanks to those who contributed to this project: Matthew Thrush, Graeme Udd, Doug and Teresa Nichele, Rebecca Thomas, Nicole Sudhoff, Kathleen Kegel, and Scott Kegel.

I appreciate all of you and I thank God that I have you in my life.

ABOUT THE AUTHOR

Joe Basile, the host of HISTORY Channel's "The Jesus Strand: A Search for DNA" started simply as an Italian guy growing up in Chicago as the youngest of ten siblings. Much of his life was shaped by the death of his mom at a young age. He dropped out of high school and became a local rap artist.

As that evolved, his Christian friends' love and fearless sharing of the gospel, with confidence and no judgment, gravitated him to Christ. After he gave his life to Christ, he shifted to rapping about Jesus, but eventually felt called into ministry and currently serves as a pastor.

Over his life, he's had the privilege to experience the fullness of loss and the revival that comes through the generous love of others. He lives in Clovis, CA, with his beautiful wife and their three precious children.

facebook.com/JoeBasileAuthor

twitter.com/jesustattoos

instagram.com/pastorjoebasile